KATHERINE OF HARBORHAVEN

KATHERINE OF HARBORHAVEN

a New Beginning

GWENDOLYN HARMON

Learning Ladyhood Press

To Mr. Dutton, the reason this story has pirates.

Contents

I

Harborhaven

This was her last option.

Katherine straightened the folds of her "interview skirt" and tugged at the hem of her slightly uncomfortable but businesslike blue jacket. Her heart fluttered anxiously as she stood on the sidewalk looking up at the entrance to the Harborhaven Historical Society. She set down the small, old-fashioned suitcase she had been holding and flexed her stiff fingers.

She stood there for a long while, till her aching feet felt almost rooted to the pavement. Finally, she took a deep breath and climbed the steps. Her hand grasped the ornate door handle, only to find the door locked. Stepping back, she peered at a notice taped onto one of the tall narrow windows next to the door:

Harborhaven Historical Society Offices and Museums: open the first Saturday of the month, or by appointment.

A light breeze blowing in off the harbor played with the ends of her long dark hair as she leaned closer to read a smaller notice, one she had half-expected, but half-dreaded to find there.

Volunteers needed

Katherine sighed deeply as she turned and walked slowly down the steps to the sidewalk. She looked down the street, out of ideas. She had started the day full of hope and expectations, and now all of that had disappeared like the mist the sun dispelled from the harbor waters as it rose higher in the summer sky.

Across the street, she could see the owner of the ice cream shop watching her narrowly from the window. When she walked into the shop that morning, she had expected to find there the jolly old man with twinkling eyes who had been so kind to her as a child. He would certainly have given her a job, or else helped her to find one. Instead, she had encountered a surly new owner who was not at all kindly, questioned her suspiciously, and responded to her inquiry about job openings with a sneer and a tone of utter contempt.

As she began to follow the sidewalk through downtown Harborhaven, her blue eyes blurred with tears of disappointment. She blinked them back and looked up at the two towering rows of ornate Victorian façades. How stern they seemed, frowning and suspicious, like the owner of the ice cream shop.

Harborhaven had been her home once, years before; and in the happy dimness of her childhood memories all had been bright and welcoming. But now—Katherine kicked a stone back into the bed of pebbles in front of a shop window and sighed again. She walked on, bewildered and friendless.

When she neared the end of the downtown blocks, she suddenly noticed the most delicious smell wafting towards her from a nearby building. As she approached the building, she looked up. It was tall and narrow, with large, lace-curtained windows. The Victorian brick had been painted white, so it stood out from its surroundings; yet somehow, Katherine thought it still seemed to belong there, different though it was from the massive red hulk of the old warehouse next to it.

The windows and door were framed in bright yellow trim, and a small sign hung in the window of the shop's door. As she neared the door, she read the words inscribed on the sign in elegant script:

"*Do come in*"

Katherine scanned through her childhood memories but couldn't remember having seen this shop before. Glancing above the door, she read:

Miss Harriet's Tea Shop.

The delicious smells and the cheerfulness of the place seemed to call to her, and Katherine decided to go in, just for a while. After all, she did need to eat. She pushed open the door and was struck by the brightness and elegance of the place.

A willowy, middle-aged lady stepped out from behind the dark wood counter, holding a plate of baked goods she had just finished filling from several tiered trays on top of the counter.

"Welcome!" she said warmly in a British accent. She gestured to a small table by a lace-enshrouded window at the side of the room. "That table's open, if it suits you."

"Thank you." Katherine said, smiling for the first time since she had arrived in Harborhaven that morning. There was something in the gentle way this tall, graceful woman spoke to her that made her feel as if things were not so bleak, after all.

Weaving her way between the small groups of people seated throughout the room, Katherine set her suitcase down near the window and looked across at the daintily written chalkboard menu behind the counter. She was relieved to find the prices affordable.

Still, she thought, *it's probably best just to order something simple.* She wasn't sure how long her savings would last, and the morning's efforts proved that it would be much more difficult to find a job than she had expected.

She tried to push aside the aching mix of old memories and present troubles that welled up inside her, but to no avail. Her mind raced restlessly from one to the other until, lost in thought, she felt a gentle touch on her arm. She hadn't noticed the tall woman standing near her table.

"Hello, again." The woman said cheerfully, leaning down to catch Katherine's gaze.

Katherine looked up quickly with an embarrassed blush. "Hello."

"My apologies for not seating you personally when you came in." The woman said graciously, setting a small silver tray on the table. Taking a dainty china teacup and saucer from the tray, she set it in front of Katherine, explaining, "Friday noon is always a rush, you see." She smiled. "Tea?"

Katherine nodded. "And a scone, please," she added as the woman deftly poured out a cup of amber liquid from the small teapot on the tray.

"Coming right up. I'm Miss Harriet, by the way."

"I'm Katherine. And I wasn't offended." Katherine smiled in spite of the emotional turmoil from which she had just surfaced. "Is this your shop?"

"Yes, it is. It's my pride and joy... and my livelihood."

"Sounds like a pretty good deal."

"It is. I consider myself very blessed indeed. Now, what brings you to our lovely little harbor hamlet today?"

"I grew up here, actually." Katherine replied, trying to sound cheerful. "We moved away when I was nine, but no-where else ever seemed quite like home. When I graduated from college yesterday, it seemed right to come back here." She shifted in her chair, a little embarrassed. She hadn't meant to spill out her life's story before a stranger like that, but something about Miss Harriet invited confidence.

"Well, congratulations! And welcome home," Miss Harriet said heartily.

"Thanks."

"So then, you've finished school and are looking for a new beginning?"

Katherine smiled ruefully at how cliché her plan sounded when boiled down to its essentials. "Yes, something like that. I grew up here, and came back expecting, well... expecting a lot of things to be the same, that have evidently changed."

Katherine's deep disappointment clouded her face as she spoke. "I thought the owner of the ice cream shop might remember me and be able to find a job for me there, but I guess he sold the shop to someone else after the mill closed and the new owner made it *very* clear they weren't hiring."

A strange look passed over Miss Harriet's face when Katherine mentioned the ice cream shop, as if she were pondering something. But as she opened her lips to speak, a boisterous woman in a large hat called Miss Harriet's name from across the room and she had to excuse herself to see what the woman needed.

Katherine watched Miss Harriet glide gracefully away, then took a sip of her tea. She had never really tried tea before. Her parents and friends had always been coffee drinkers. She noticed it had layers of flavor. It tasted delicate and light, but strong at the same time, if just a bit bitter. She decided there was something comforting about this tea, calming, even. Taking another sip, she looked around her. As Miss Harriet had pointed out, it was lunch time, and customers filled nearly every seat in the place.

Seeing Miss Harriet fly about from table to table, darting gracefully in and out of the kitchen, Katherine suddenly felt a curious sort of longing and wished, rather than hoped, to one day have the sort of peaceful joy which radiated from this elegant middle-aged lady.

She noticed how everything about Miss Harriet seemed graceful and orderly, from her straight blonde hair, pulled smoothly into a French roll, to the light floral skirt that flowed respectably around her as she walked, to the neat little pastel blue flats and the precise way she had rolled up the cuffs of her spotless collared shirt over the sleeves of her light pink cardigan. This was a lady who personified grace, elegance, and meticulous attention to detail.

Miss Harriet disappeared behind a curtained doorway, and Katherine let her gaze drift over the other occupants of the room. She noticed a mother and daughter sitting at a table nearby. The little girl was probably around six, and from the looks of it, had decked herself in every piece of costume jewelry she owned. The two seemed to be enjoying themselves immensely.

Katherine thought of the imaginary tea parties she'd had with her mother as a child, and soon her mind was flitting back through the years she had spent at her home in Harborhaven. A wave of loss swept over her as the happy memories all tumbled over each other, rushing headlong into the shock of that last Christmas at home, when everything changed and the life and home she knew and loved had been so abruptly jerked out from under her.

Somehow, coming back to the little town where she had been so happy before only served to solidify the nagging, painful truth that those days were gone forever. She now was a stranger to the town she loved. She had no friends or family there to bolster the rush of courage that had at first driven her to return. She could feel it fading faster as the day wore on. Letting her shoulders slump, she stared into her teacup, overwhelmed by loneliness, and utterly daunted by the excruciating struggle of deciding what to do next.

After a while, Miss Harriet returned with a small plate of hot scones. Laying a hand lightly on the chair across from Katherine, she asked, "May I?"

Katherine nodded, and Miss Harriet took a seat.

"Katherine, I have something I wondered if you might help me with?"

"What is it?" Katherine asked, intrigued.

"Well, you can see how full the shop is today, and I'm the sole waitress, cook, and dishwasher. Would you mind helping out, just for the day? Of course, I would pay you."

Katherine's face lit up as she exclaimed, "Oh, yes. I would *love* to!"

Miss Harriet smiled broadly and said, "When you're finished with your tea and scones, come to the kitchen and we'll get you an apron."

Katherine found she enjoyed the work immensely. She spent most of the day bussing tables and delivering food, but Miss Harriet watched her closely and by the end of the day had allowed her to begin welcoming customers and taking orders.

As closing time approached, however, Katherine was again gripped by the need to decide what to do next. She realized that, although she had found work for that day, she now had no place to spend the night.

With a heavy weight in the pit of her stomach, she acknowledged to herself that she taken the job in hopes that something would turn up before the end of the workday, so she would be spared the awkward and bewildering task of looking for a place to stay. *What have I gotten myself into?* she wondered silently.

She had to find somewhere to sleep. There was the old Grand Hotel down the street, but she knew one night there would be sure to empty her bank account, even if she added in her day's earnings. Without a car, she would have to walk somewhere... or else... maybe she could get a bus to the next town. But something seemed to be compelling her to stay in Harborhaven. Maybe there was some other option.

She hated to impose upon the woman who had been so kind to her already, but she didn't know where else to turn. So she walked hesitatingly over to where Miss Harriet stood vigorously polishing the counter.

Before she could say a word, Miss Harriet, still polishing, said in a cheerful tone: "Well, then. You'll need a place to stay for the night, now, won't you?"

Katherine let out the breath she had been holding. "Yes. In fact, I was just coming over to ask you if you could recommend a cheap hotel nearby?"

"Oh, I can do better than that. There's a rather dreary little flat above the shop I keep up in case of company. You can stay there tonight, free of charge."

Astonished by the older woman's generosity, Katherine stuttered out her thanks. Miss Harriet laughed a sweet, bubbly, infectious laugh, then held out her hand.

"Give me your apron, Dearie, and I'll show you up." Katherine looked at Miss Harriet's warm and genuine smile and felt—just for a moment—that everything was going to be all right.

* * * *

Once settled in for the night, Katherine lay down, wide-eyed and not a bit sleepy, though physically and emotionally exhausted.

Just yesterday, she had walked across a platform in front of a crowd of people to receive her diploma. That was supposed to have been her new beginning, the start of a new life, a happily ever after. But when the ceremony ended, her parents drove her to their house, and all the old feelings of hurt and emptiness filled her afresh.

All the way there, she had stared out the window, knowing there was only one place she wanted to go: *home*. So that night, she bought a plane ticket and gathered a few things from the boxes in her parents' garage before throwing a few extra pillows on the old sofa. Curling up in a blanket, she had tossed and turned until daylight.

It wasn't as if she and her parents had fought. Everything had been fine on the surface, as it always seemed to be. They just never could manage to get any deeper than that superficial "fine"-ness anymore, and Katherine felt uneasy and out of place in their home.

As she packed her luggage into the taxi early that morning, she had felt convinced that leaving was the only option. Her parents waved at her from the porch as she left, smiling and calling out their goodbyes as if she were off to a grand adventure. She secretly wondered if they were actually just glad to be rid of her.

Finally aboard her plane, Katherine watched the miles melt away beneath her. Her heart beat faster as the plane banked and turned, preparing to land. Soon she would be there. Soon she would be home.

When the plane landed, Katherine hurriedly collected her one suitcase and caught a bus to Harborhaven. The thrill of expectation gripped her as she began to see familiar land-marks race past the windows: she was almost home!

Katherine closed her eyes, reliving the bus trip. She knew she had been running. She *meant* to run: away from her parents, away from the reminder of that catastrophic last Christmas together and the misery that followed, away from the rift which had formed that moment when everything changed, away from their new life—the life she didn't belong in anymore—and toward the one place she'd been dreaming of returning to ever since.

Katherine shifted her head on the pillow. All she had wanted was to be home; *home* in Harborhaven. Now, here she was, in that very place, and what did she have to show for it? No job, nowhere to live, no one to care what happened to her. It was bad enough to have a rift between her and her parents, but now it seemed there was a rift between her and the whole world.

Sitting up in bed, Katherine cradled her head in her hands. She had to figure out what to do. Trying to slow her thoughts down, she forced herself to focus on the problem at hand. She couldn't go back to her parents—there was really no place for her there if she did go, unless she wanted to live out of a suitcase and sleep on the couch.

She *wanted* to stay in Harborhaven. Her heart had been whispering inside her all day, pleading to stay, but what could she do? Her brand-new history degree was of little enough use in a large city; but in a small harbor town where the historical society manned its offices and museum with volunteers, she couldn't possibly hope for a paid position. She could try for a waitressing job somewhere, but the ice cream shop had been her best chance for that.

Miss Harriet had been kind, and Katherine would have asked her for a job, but it seemed obvious that Miss Harriet was perfectly capable of running the shop by herself. Katherine suspected her day's work had only been the result of the soft-hearted woman's compassion. No, the only option she could see was to move on.

Perhaps she could find a job in the next town up the coast. Then she could at least come to Harborhaven on her days off. In spite of all the disappointments she had experienced that day, she still felt a tie to the old town. She felt that she could make a life here, a *new* life in this place that held so many dear memories of the old one. She would have to move on, but she hoped it would not be too far.

* * * *

The next day, Katherine went down to the tea shop as soon as she heard Miss Harriet arrive, meaning to thank her for her kindness and then be on her way, wherever that might be.

Miss Harriet came out of the kitchen with a cheery "Good morning! Did you sleep well?"

"Yes, thank you."

"That's good! I want to talk to you about something, and it's always better to chat when one is well rested."

She motioned for Katherine to sit at one of the tables, then took a seat across from her. Katherine rubbed her hands together nervously under the table, not sure what to expect.

"Now, Katherine, I've been thinking. It was so nice to have

your help yesterday, I'd like to hire you on." Katherine's eyes grew wide as the older lady continued. "If you are willing, I can offer you three days a week with good pay, opening to closing, with the flat upstairs thrown in, if you'd like. I only ask that you agree to stay at least one month. What do you think?"

Katherine stared, speechless. This would meet her needs exactly, and she certainly had enjoyed her work the day before. Having waitressed her way through college, she knew exactly what she was taking on—and a place to stay thrown in! It all seemed too good, too easy to be true.

"Yes... Yes, I would like that *very* much!" she finally managed to say, almost giddy with relief.

Miss Harriet smiled a satisfied smile and said, "Good! Now, let's get you some breakfast before you begin work. I've just pulled some scones out of the oven. Will that do?"

Katherine nodded, speechless, and still struggling to believe it was possible that she had *really* been offered a job in Harborhaven. Despite this seeming miracle of provision, she still couldn't quite surrender to the hopeful thought that began to tug at her heart: that this just might be the beginning of the new life for which she had longed.

2

Miss Harriet's

The more time Katherine spent around Miss Harriet's shop, the more she enjoyed it. The place was like a microcosm of the town, which Katherine found fascinating. She marveled at how, even though many of the people she had known in her childhood had been replaced by strangers over the years, the town as a whole still seemed just the same as when she left. She observed the shop's customers with interest, wondering if certain types of people were drawn to Harborhaven, or if the town itself changed them. She never could decide.

Miss Harriet's way of making everyone feel special and important had a profound effect on Katherine. She watched the older woman eagerly, trying to catch the trick of it, but never could quite succeed. As she served her customers, Miss Harriet seemed always to know just what to say or do to put a smile on the face of each one.

Katherine knew good customer service when she saw it,

but this was something more. Watching Miss Harriet talk to her customers was like watching tightly-closed buds unfurl their petals. The customers seemed to become better versions of themselves after talking to her. It all seemed so effortless—except when Katherine tried it. Still, she kept watching and learning, hoping someday to live up to the gracious woman's example.

Soon the month ended, and Katherine hardly noticed its passing, for she had become fully absorbed in her work. She liked the bustle of always having something to do, and on her days off, she would often volunteer to help Miss Harriet set the tables and get the shop ready for the day. Then she would go to the library and check out books, and, coming home with a small stack, would take them up to the little "dreary" apartment, which Katherine did not think dreary at all. Miss Harriet had fixed it up quite nicely, intending to live there herself; but it did not have enough windows to suit her.

"Lamplight just isn't the same," she had explained.

The apartment had one large window, which overlooked the street, and another window in the bedroom: a small, round window which looked out towards the cliffs behind downtown Harborhaven. In the street-view window, Miss Harriet had put in a deep window seat, filled with cushions.

A basket full of soft, warm blankets stood nearby, and Katherine felt as if the cozy little nook had been made just for her. She would curl up with her library books and a plate of fresh-baked scones carried up from the kitchen. Once cozily settled in, she would sit and read for hours.

She had always been a bookworm, but now she clung to reading more than ever, as a welcome distraction from the turmoil within her heart. Returning to Harborhaven had not erased the pain. She still ached over the past, still longed for relief. She tried to hide it, but was sure Miss Harriet knew somehow that there was something hidden behind her new employee's almost-convincing smiles.

Miss Harriet shared Katherine's love for reading, and the two would often discuss their current reads while they washed the dishes each night. That summer, Katherine revisited the classic novels of Jane Austen, and the two enjoyed lively and animated discussions over the nightly dishpans.

Katherine looked forward to this ritual of dishwashing and conversation. It was the one time she felt at ease. She enjoyed interacting with the customers, but when she and Miss Harriet retired to the kitchen at the end of the day, she felt she could finally be herself. Through their literary discussion, she found Miss Harriet to be a keen observer, whose insights into the characters made Katherine think about both them and the stories in new ways.

In addition to the fictional characters Katherine was reading about, the two also occasionally discussed the town and its inhabitants. So much had changed between the time Katherine had left for college and the time Miss Harriet had arrived, they had plenty to talk over. From some of these conversations, and from what Katherine overheard from the gossipy group of old ladies who called themselves "the Luncheon Society," she soon learned that another tea shop of sorts existed in the little town. And though no competition actually existed between the two establishments, relations between them had not been exactly friendly.

"You know, it's a good thing you got settled in *here*. Imagine if she'd tried to ask for a job over at the Harborside!" Rosie, the leader of the Luncheon Society, had exclaimed the day Katherine introduced herself to the group.

"Oh, my, yes, she would have regretted that for sure!" piped up another, and the whole group fell into nods and agreements.

Katherine was intrigued. "What's the Harborside?" she asked.

The table erupted into an affected wave of shock and surprise. "Just the town's *only* shop that carries tea. It's been around so long, the grocery store doesn't even bother to stock any, out of respect." Rosie's voice carried a well-practiced note of disdain.

"—and out of fear of public outcry if they ever did!" interjected the lady next to her. After a short burst of laughter and shouts of, "Can you imagine!", the little group's conversation jumped off into another subject, and Katherine, left to her curiosity, went to the kitchen to start their tea brewing.

After closing time that day, Katherine had asked Miss Harriet about the Harborside. Miss Harriet seemed surprised, saying, "I wonder you didn't remember it from your growing up years. It's in one of the old Victorian blocks at the other end of downtown. In fact, that's where we buy all the tea for the shop."

"So why did the ladies say I would have regretted asking for a job there?"

"Well…" Miss Harriet paused, as if considering carefully what to say. "I suppose it's because the owner isn't very nice sometimes—or at least, he has a rough manner about him that makes people *think* he's not nice." Miss Harriet seemed to be trying very hard to be gracious.

She went on to explain that she herself had found it difficult to get along with the Harborside's owner. "We fell out over tea, actually," she said, "and our disagreement has become a sort of feud between the two shops. Though for my part, I think I have *tried* to be reasonable, and really don't wish the Harborside any ill." A mischievous smile tugged at the corners of her mouth as she added, "But then, it's just so easy to provoke the man about his silly prejudices, I feel I simply can't resist."

Katherine frowned. "Prejudices? Over *tea*?"

"Yes. The Harborside has long been a bastion of the 'tea elite', you see, and it is in no hurry to change to accommodate a customer with more *common* tastes, let alone one who per-petuates such tastes by serving 'inferior' tea to others!" Miss Harriet rinsed a teapot and plunged it into the soapy water before continuing.

"They are so *serious* about their tea over there. Who has time to be so deeply passionate about such trivial matters like 'subtle nuances of flavor' and 'slight variations in processing methods?' I don't, now that's for sure. Just give me some good, plain, English tea and I'll be set for life."

This knowledge of the Harborside's disapproval did not faze Miss Harriet—nothing ever did seem to faze Miss Har-riet. She would laugh off the owner's snubs and order her "plain old British tea" from the Harborside week after week, almost delighting in the prospect of making the grumpy old man order the very same "inferior" teas he so despised and railed against. But this appeared to be the extent of her participation in the feud.

Still, it was enough to cause great consternation and irritation at the Harborside when the weekly order was filled. Katherine couldn't imagine anyone being rude to such a kind and good-natured lady as Miss Harriet. She thought the Harborside's owner must thoroughly deserve the derogatory comments she had heard about him from the luncheon society gossips. But then, she hadn't actually seen the Harborside or its owner yet.

3

The Harborside

As different as Miss Harriet's and the Harborside were from each other, their two owners seemed even more so. Elegant, gentle, and cheerful, Miss Harriet seemed to glide from table to table, her mild, smiling manner and sweet temperament charming her guests.

From what Katherine had heard, Miss Harriet's counterpart at the Harborside hid in his office most of each day, almost dreading a ring of the bell over the door that would force him to interact with a customer. Rough, blustery, and quick-tempered, he had apparently succeeded in driving off many of his customers.

"It's a pity," Miss Harriet had said one day to Katherine. "He really is quite knowledgeable, and I think if he would only smile a little, his customers would have a chance to see *that*, instead of the wall he throws up as soon as they walk in."

He was called Captain Jeremiah Braddock, though hardly

a person alive would have dared to call him by his first name. Most just called him "Captain Braddock", but Rosie from the Luncheon Society preferred to refer to him as "that horrible man at the old tea shop".

As a retired sea captain, he seemed the least likely sort of man to run a shop that sold tea. However, he had grown up helping in the shop and took fierce pride in the Harborside and its heritage, as well as in belonging to the Braddock family. The Braddocks had inhabited the town of Harborhaven for so many generations, their name had become as much a fixture in the little town as their shop. Over its many years, the Harborside came to be as much a symbol of the family's identity as a castle or manor house might be to an old European family, and anyone who ventured inside could tell that the place was steeped in history.

The Harborside Tea Shop had been founded in the long past days of the clipper ship, when the burgeoning tea trade was still a new and exciting venture, and had been passed from generation to generation of Braddock sons and daughters.

As children, each new set of Braddock offspring were put to work in the shop, where they were given an education in the art of matching each customer with the variety of tea he or she would enjoy best. This seemed to their customers to be an almost magical ability, though in reality it was more of a science. It used to be that people would visit from across the country just to find their "perfect tea" at the Harborside and marvel at the "Braddock gift."

The Captain himself had received the same education and still helped the few brave customers who dared to enter his domain discover just the right tea, but he practiced the art so grudgingly, many did not feel it to be worth coming back for more. They found the drive up the coast to the next town's grocery store much more inviting.

As a youth, Captain Braddock had chosen to follow in the footsteps of a long line of seafaring Braddocks. He had gone to sea as soon as he could, and earned his way up the chain of command until at last he found himself captain of a large cargo ship.

It had been a bulky thing, modern in every way, yet Captain Braddock's love of the wooden sailing ship—a natural result of growing up at the Harborside—had become so much a part of him that it was nearly impossible to imagine him as captain of anything else. When anyone met Captain Braddock, they naturally pictured him at the wheel of a tall ship, with towering masts and billowing sails.

Grey-haired and weather-worn, with a long scar down one cheek and a distinct limp when he walked, Captain Braddock looked the very model of an old sea-captain, right down to his heavy frown and his crusty manner. Though an unlikely sort of tea seller, he nevertheless seemed perfectly in his element in the Harborside. Perhaps this could have been because the little shop seemed out of another era, just as the captain did.

Despite the fact that each generation had left some kind of mark on the shop or the business, everything in the Harborside was old-fashioned in some way. It all had an air of antiquity about it, from the broad, high mahogany counter to the ornate shelves of dark oak which filled the opposite wall, to the antique cash register, tucked back into a recess in the shelves behind the counter, as if it were somehow too new to be given a place out front.

An old-fashioned wood stove stood next to the old-fashioned armchair, and an old-fashioned mirror hung on the wall behind the counter. Even the cedar-planked walls of the shop dated from the town's frontier days.

Captain Braddock could look around the shop and trace his family's history back through the generations to the first Harborside Braddocks, who had founded it, almost before the little harbor hamlet had even become a town.

Those were the days before shipping had been relegated to the uninteresting, unromantic freight barges of modern times. Inside the Harborside, however, those days seemed alive again, for all around the shop had been placed paintings and models of the ships which had served such a vital purpose in the Harborside's earlier days. These relics of the past gave the shop a museum-like quality: each had its own store of tales to tell, its own stock of memories to evoke.

The staircase, which had been tightly-spiraled into a corner, looked as though it had belonged on one of those old-fashioned sailing ships. Built of the same dark mahogany as the counter, it had a small but substantial door at the top which the Captain always kept locked.

The staircase was a thing of great beauty and fine crafts-manship, but it blended so well into its surroundings that most customers didn't even notice it, or if they did, they had not the courage to ask about it.

* * * *

Katherine would never forget the first time she had been sent to the Harborside to pick up Miss Harriet's tea order.

She had walked down the street with Miss Harriet's shopping list in her hand and a stubborn trepidation in her heart, which she could not get rid of as she wondered what she would encounter when she got there.

It hadn't helped that Rosie had taken it upon herself that very afternoon to inform Katherine of the mystery surrounding Captain Braddock's return to the Harborside.

"Oh, yes, there was quite a scandal about it. You see, his sister used to run the shop. Her name was *Serena* Braddock. Anyway, they both grew up there, but the Captain had gone away when still quite young, and hadn't come to visit as long as I've been here.

"Well, *she* was very nice, and everyone simply adored her, but then a year or so ago, or maybe two—I don't quite remember how long... Anyway, whenever it happened to be, Serena suddenly disappeared. Gone! Left without a word, so it appeared, and the shop stayed closed on a weekday for the first time in who knows how long. For the first time in living memory, I suppose. But then," Rosie leaned in and dropped her voice dramatically, "all of a sudden, the Harborside reopened, and instead of Serena, there was that horrid man! So different from his sister—quite a shock to all of us!

"And you know, his sister did *so* mysteriously disappear... you can't help but wonder if he had something to do with it. You never know about people. I mean, I read about a man once who..." and then Rosie dove off onto a lurid tale she had heard of some gory homicide. Apart from scandal, murder was Rosie's favorite topic of conversation.

Katherine knew better than to take Rosie's morbid

speculations seriously. But it did seem strange that no one, not even Miss Harriet, knew what had happened to Serena Braddock. Miss Harriet always looked sad and became strangely quiet whenever anyone mentioned Serena.

Katherine gripped the list of teas tighter and quickened her pace. She reminded herself that Miss Harriet seemed to be a very good judge of character, and certainly wouldn't have sent Katherine over to pick up the tea order by herself if she had thought Captain Braddock unscrupulous in any way.

She crossed the street and spotted the faded sign swinging above a dark green door. Through the large window to the right of the door, she saw shelves full of jars. As she opened the door, a silvery jingle rang out from a little bell overhead, and Katherine stepped into the Harborside for the first time.

The rich, perfumed air felt refreshingly cool after the heat of the sunny June afternoon. Katherine carefully pushed the door closed behind her. A man stood up from a desk in the next room and walked hurriedly towards Katherine, limping as he went. His brows were knit in what seemed to be a frown of habit, rather than emotion, so Katherine put on a cheerful smile.

"You must be Captain Braddock. I'm Katherine. Miss Harriet sent me for her order."

At this, the habitual frown grew into a real one, and the captain roughly took the list of teas Katherine held out to him and looked it over, still frowning. He grunted disapprovingly. "I can see yer' employer's tastes haven't improved since last Friday."

Katherine, unsure of how to answer such a comment, held

her peace. She had already determined she would be just as calm and cheerful towards this grumpy man as she felt sure Miss Harriet would have been in her place.

The Captain walked over to a large old sea chest standing against the wall and opened the lid. He began taking boxes of tea out of the chest and loading them into a sturdy paper bag, lecturing sternly about the "inferiority" of the teabag. With his back turned to Katherine, he continued to rant until he had finished packing the order.

She tried to listen politely, but as she gazed around the shop, she was soon lost in wonder, drinking in its every detail with sheer delight, feeling as if she had entered into another world, as if the pages of history had been turned back and she had been permitted to step into their midst.

She surveyed the dark wooden shelves with their glass jars and models of ships; she drank in the fragrance which filled the air and the way that one shabby chair stood so invitingly in a corner by an old cast-iron stove; her eye traced the spirals of the beautiful wooden staircase and filled with curiosity when she saw the door at the top with the heavy old lock hanging so mysteriously upon its latch. In short, she took in the Harborside at a glance, a glance which struck wonder to the very depths of her being.

That moment, Katherine fell in love with the Harborside. And at that moment, the Captain startled her by setting the bag down on the counter with a thud.

She looked around quickly, and he caught her gaze, returning her look of wonder with an almost imperceptible softening of his frown and the slightest twinkle in his eye as he asked, "Is this yer' first time in a *real* tea shop?"

Katherine laughed in spite of herself, and so began her unlikely friendship with the cantankerous Captain Braddock.

4

Katherine at the Harborside

After that first visit to the Harborside, Katherine volunteered to fetch the tea order every week. The time it took to fetch the orders grew longer and longer with each visit, and Miss Harriet gave Katherine an odd little smile whenever she betrayed her eagerness to run any errand near there. Katherine couldn't conceal how much she enjoyed visiting the old shop, for she had been smitten with its dusty charm the moment she laid eyes on it.

"It's an odd thing that you never stepped foot inside the Harborside before that day I sent you over, since you grew up here in town." Miss Harriet said as they were cleaning after hours one day.

"I know, it *is* strange." Katherine replied. "But I lived up on top of the cliffs, not far from the park. We came downtown sometimes—my parents and I liked to go to the ice cream shop when I was little, and then we moved away when I was nine."

Katherine shrugged and continued loading dishes and silverware from the tables onto a small cart. It was the first time she had spoken of her childhood since that first day at Miss Harriet's, and the memories brought back even by those few sentences reawakened the longing in her heart she had been trying so hard to suppress.

Miss Harriet opened her mouth to ask another question but, catching a glimpse of the tears which had begun to gather in Katherine's eyes, went instead to clear the tables on the other side of the room. After a while, she brought her stacks of dishes over and set them on the cart.

Katherine looked up. "Miss Harriet," she said in a thoughtful tone, setting another cup on the cart. "Did you know that the Harborside is the oldest shop in the town?"

"Yes, I think I did know that. Did you learn it from the Captain today?"

Katherine smiled shyly. "Yes. He told me that people used to come from all over the country to buy tea there, but the shop never seems at all busy when I go in. In fact, I've never seen a single customer in there. Most people just walk past without even glancing in. Why do you think that is?"

"Well, I'd imagine it might be because of how the Captain behaved when he first came."

"What do you mean?"

"Well, when he got here and opened up the shop again, the townspeople were naturally quite curious what had happened, but he was so startlingly abrupt with anyone who asked, it got to where people didn't like to go into the shop anymore. His manners made people uncomfortable, as did his persistence in refusing to tell anyone anything about his sister, or even himself. I honestly think he felt it simply wasn't anyone's business but his own, but it lost him much of the town's support." Chuckling, she added, "It didn't help that Rosie took it into her head that he had some sinister hand in his sister's disappearance."

Katherine's eyes lit up with curiosity. "What do *you* think happened to her?"

"I don't know. It was quite a shock to everyone, but I'm certain it was at least as much a shock to Captain Braddock. Otherwise, I think he would have handled things better and not run his customers off like that. Now he's got a reputation for rudeness, and you know a small town like this naturally has a habit of viewing outsiders with suspicion from the out-set. Treating people the way he did only made it worse."

"Did they think you suspicious when you first came?"

"I think they did, at least a bit. But I kept to myself until the renovations were finished and the shop ready to open. People seemed to like the shop, and I think that helped them accept me as part of the town. They certainly haven't made me feel unwelcome."

The two began to push the full cart to the kitchen when Katherine stopped mid-step and turned to look searchingly into her friend's face. "Do they think *me* suspicious?"

Miss Harriet laughed her silvery laugh and replied, "Of course not. You're a local—even if our downtown locals *didn't* know you back then. In fact, you're more of a local than they are, because you lived here before they did. Besides," she said with a wink, "I wouldn't have hired anyone suspicious!"

Katherine grinned, then took her end of the cart and carefully pulled it into the kitchen. Miss Harriet filled the sink while Katherine got out a fresh dish towel.

"It was different when his sister was there." Miss Harriet said with a sigh. "Serena Braddock was so gentle and kind, but smart and witty, and could give back as good as she got, I'm sure. It was remarkable to watch her when a customer would come into the shop: she'd cock her head on one side, rest her chin on her hand, and study them for a moment. Then a little smile would spread across her face, and she'd say in that quaint little way of hers, 'follow me, if you please', then lead them over to the jars.

"People instinctively trusted her recommendations, and I never heard even the faintest rumor of a disgruntled customer. —Not that I've necessarily heard of any with a specific grievance since the Captain sailed into port, but I can't help but think it's due more to lack of customers than anything else." Then Miss Harriet sighed again, and plunged a plate into the hot soapy water.

****

Captain Braddock sat at his desk in the small "office" room in the back of the Harborside looking over a stack of papers. Things were lean, to be sure. The captain's rough manners, along with the wild rumors which spread soon after his arrival, had indeed pushed the customers away to a worrying extent. There were the regular orders, like Miss Harriet's, which kept the shop afloat for now.

Besides, he reminded himself, *the Harborside's weathered leaner times than this in the past and come through all right.*

No, what really worried the Captain was the fact that without his capable and competent sister Serena to manage the shop, he found it difficult to keep things running. He would never have breathed a hint of it to anyone, but he found himself unable to juggle the many daily tasks necessary to keep the Harborside afloat.

With a heavy sigh, he stood and strode into the storefront. Turning the lock on the door and pulling the dark green shades over the windows, he turned and surveyed the shop.

"I suppose I'll have to hire on a first mate if I'm to keep things running." His deep voice echoed slightly in the empty shop. He had known for a while that he would need to hire an assistant; but saying it aloud made it final, somehow.

He had known since the first day Katherine entered the Harborside that she was the one he wanted to hire. In her eyes, he had read her heart and found her eager, joyful, thirsting to know all the shop's secrets, but too respectful to attempt to pry any of them out of him. That was just what he needed.

After all, he chuckled to himself later, *she's never even asked about my sister.*

All the locals who came into the shop inquired about Serena. In fact, they usually only ever came in for that express purpose. They never succeeded, however, for the Captain would only reply, "she's doin' just fine where she's at, thank ye." with even more gruffness than usual in his voice and an overexaggerated sailor's accent (the authenticity of which no one could *quite* determine).

This quelled all but the most curious inquirers, and those few presumptuous gossips determined to have the details and impertinent enough to pursue them were met with even more gruffness. But all this mystery made it so that few felt at ease in the shop, and even fewer enjoyed their visits.

Captain Braddock sat down at his desk with a sigh, pushed the papers into a stack, and pulled out an old ledger book. He looked over the month's sales. Most of the Harborside's business came from the few consistent weekly orders now: the old hotel, a handful of restaurants up and down the coast, a small bed and breakfast outside of town—and Miss Harriet's.

He sighed. Ironically, Miss Harriet's represented the largest and most lucrative of his ongoing orders, which was why he had submitted (albeit grudgingly) to the degradation of supplying her with the much-despised *bagged* teas. That, and because it gave him a supply for tourists who came in looking for the familiar and caring nothing about quality or the shop's heritage. The bagged teas had boosted sales considerably, but didn't attract the kind of customers who appreciated the Harborside for what it truly had to offer.

Captain Braddock walked over to the old sea chest full of the boxes of bagged teas, ruefully wondering if that would be his only mark on the Harborside.

If so, he shuddered, *whatever will the next generation bring in?*

It had never occurred to him before what a strange thought that was to think. He knew that there were no prospects of a "next generation" to whom the Harborside could be handed down. There must be some distant relatives somewhere, of course; but he knew of none that bore the Braddock name, which was a vital qualification in the captain's eyes.

He and his sister had been the very last of the Braddock line, so far as he knew; and neither had fulfilled their father's hopes for a Harborside heir by bringing forth children of their own.

If only one of us had.

He sighed again and looked around him, remembering the days of his boyhood when three generations of Braddocks bustled about the shop. None of them would have imagined that in a few short decades, one lone Braddock would be standing there, wondering how he was going to keep the Harborside running for a generation of Braddocks that didn't even exist.

Yet somehow, Captain Braddock felt sure that the Harborside would continue on, and that it would indeed be passed to some sort of a "next generation." Who that might be, he did not know; but he could not conceive of the idea of the venerable shop closing or dying away, or passing out of the family after so many years.

Belief in the Harborside's past, present, and future had been ingrained into his very being from childhood, and he could not imagine any different. He just had to keep the shop afloat until the time came to pass it on.

5

The "Dailies"

As Katherine settled into her work at *Miss Harriet's*, she soon noticed that some customers came with almost clockwork regularity. Miss Harriet lovingly referred to these guests as "the Dailies," for they came every day without fail. These faithful customers were greeted by name, their preferred seats reserved, and their usual orders made ready for their appointed time.

Each had such steady habits that if ever one of them failed to appear, it caused great concern. Miss Harriet would call, just to make sure they were all right, and had even been known to deliver their regular order to their homes, on occasion, if any of them were under the weather.

"Of course, I couldn't go during business hours before now," she explained one day, "because I had no one to mind the shop. But with you here, Katherine, it will be so much easier!"

Katherine loved Miss Harriet's maternal care for each of her guests. She had never known anyone who took such great delight in serving others.

The first customer of the day was always Mr. Harold James. He was a middle-aged man with black hair, and a mischievous twinkle that flickered every now and then in his dark eyes. He always wore a tweed sportscoat and collared shirt, and topped them off with a smart tweed cap, which he removed immediately upon stepping through the door. He looked quite professional and carried a brown leather briefcase, which coordinated with his neatly-polished leather shoes.

"Quite a gentleman." Miss Harriet had said, "Always so polite and well-dressed."

Each morning, he arrived punctually, a few minutes after opening, with a polite "Good morning, ladies." Then he would walk to his usual table, situated in the front corner of the shop, with his back to the wall and the window to his right.

"He prefers that seat," Miss Harriet had quietly informed Katherine in the kitchen her first morning, "because he likes to watch downtown Harborhaven wake up and start to go about its daily business. But it's quite a legitimate interest, you see, because Mr. James writes for the city's newspaper."

Katherine had peeked through the kitchen door with interest. "He seems distinguished enough. Do you get many journalists in the shop?"

"Just Mr. James." Miss Harriet replied, then said with a wink "But he's more distinguished than you might think. He's the only one of his kind in Harborhaven."

"You mean he's the town's only journalist?"

"Yes. The newspaper's staff consists only of Mr. James, an editor, a secretary, and the man who runs the presses."

"Oh. Well, I suppose it makes sense that a small town would have a small paper."

"Yes, but Mr. James takes his job very seriously, nonetheless. He is, after all, a very serious man, though not without a sense of humor. And he's very industrious. You'll notice that his breakfast here each morning is always a *working* breakfast."

Katherine watched Mr. James in the mornings to come, and soon she knew his routine as well as Miss Harriet did. He would seat himself by the window and move the floral arrangement out of the way. Then he would take from his leather briefcase the tools of his trade: his laptop, a fountain pen, and the small legal pad on which he took notes for his articles. Some days, books replaced the laptop, and Mr. James would pore diligently over their pages, making careful and copious notes on the legal pad.

Other days, he would take out only the pen and notepad, leaving the flowers where they were. This alerted Miss Harriet that Mr. James would be conducting an interview that morning, and she would have Katherine lay another place setting at his table and hold his order until his guest had arrived. Mr. James often stayed at the little table in the corner for much of the morning, working diligently while he sipped his English Breakfast tea and ate his cheddar scone.

Curious to know what Mr. James found to write about in such a quiet town, Katherine began reading the daily paper; a thing she would never have thought to do otherwise. She discovered that Mr. James was, in fact, a talented writer.

He could pull his readers into any story, even something as mundane as the changing of bulbs in a streetlight, which he had managed to turn into an entertaining two-page spread. This was a valuable quality in the *Harborhaven Gazette's* only journalist, since little of any import ever happened in Harborhaven. Without his expertise, the paper would certainly not have maintained its widespread popularity.

"Has Mr. James ever written about Miss Harriet's?" Katherine asked her employer one day.

"No, Dearie, and I don't suppose he could be expected to," Miss Harriet replied casually.

Katherine frowned. "Why not?"

"For the simple reason that it would put him in a very awkward position."

"It would?"

"Yes, it would. You see, if he were to write something favorable, he might be accused of bias, because he comes here so much. If he wrote something unfavorable, he would be sure to feel badly about it, and would be so bothered, he wouldn't be able to enjoy his morning scones anymore. Either way, he'd be sure to find himself in a stew of some kind."

"I never thought about that," Katherine replied. "It must be difficult to be a journalist."

Miss Harriet nodded. "Yes indeed, Dearie. I'm happy to stick to my tea shop."

Each morning, when Mr. James had been at his table for about an hour, a tall elderly lady would walk laboriously in with a book under one arm and ask in politest tones if the table at the back were available. Of course, it always *was* available, for Miss Harriet had given strict instructions that the seats preferred by the "dailies" be reserved for them, no matter how busy the shop might get.

Like Mr. James, this quiet lady always dressed neatly. She usually wore a wool skirt and blazer, in well-pressed, unassuming earth tones. Whatever the weather, she would walk in wearing plain, sensible heels with a small brown hat perched carefully atop her short grey hair, which curved neatly around her face. She always reminded Katherine of a little brown bird.

"Poor dear," Miss Harriet said quietly one day. "She's probably been up for hours. Doesn't sleep well, you see, and figures it's better to get up very early than stay in bed tossing and turning. That's why she comes in before most of the town is up and about. She hasn't much to live on, you know, and this is the one little indulgence she allows herself. Perhaps it's partly to make up for the trouble of having to wake up so early."

Once she reached her table, the lady—whose name was Penelope Wright, although everyone simply called her Mrs. Penelope—cautiously perched on one of the chairs, holding herself as stiff and straight as the chair itself. She somehow managed to seem at ease in that unbending posture, though, as she quietly ordered "Just a cup of black tea and three plain scones with jam, please." which she enjoyed with as much enthusiasm as her genteel nature would allow.

The scones Mrs. Penelope ordered each morning were quite different from the robust cheddar scone ordered by Mr. James. Miss Harriet's plain scones were small, round, and very fluffy, while the cheddar scones were dense, large, and triangular. They were so dissimilar, Katherine wondered how both could be called scones.

Miss Harriet said that the two types of scones came from different regions, and that, while the fluffy scones were her favorite, the dense scones were more like what scones originally would have been. "I make both kinds, you see, so that I can have the kind I like but still feel I'm being true to the historical side of things. Besides, this way none of my customers are disappointed, whichever type of scone they like."

And so, every morning Mr. James would have his biscuit-like cheddar triangle, Mrs. Penelope would have her three small fluffy rounds, and both would be equally satisfied.

Mr. James and Mrs. Penelope were not the only dailies, however. Round about mid-morning, as Mr. James worked away by the window and Mrs. Penelope sat engrossed in her book, Rosie would arrive. The self-appointed leader of the Luncheon Society disliked getting up early, but just like Mr. James, she wanted to see what people were up to first thing. Rosie's motive, however, was far from the professional and business-like interest of Mr. James. She just *had* to know everything happening around town so she could inform everyone else. The first time Rosie met Katherine, she had unashamedly introduced herself as the town gossip.

"If there's anything you want to know, I'm your gal. Not much escapes my notice around here, and there's always a tale to tell. Why, only yesterday, the mayor tripped going up the steps of the courthouse on his way to a meeting and got a black eye, or at least, that's what he said. *I* can't help but wonder if he ran afoul of one of his constituents somewhere, but didn't want to admit it. I've a nose for scandal, you see."

"Does the mayor often have violent conflicts with his constituents?" Katherine asked, trying not to smile.

"Well, no... at least, we can't be sure, now can we? It isn't the type of thing he would go around talking about."

Katherine soon noticed whenever Rosie came in sight, she was in for a tale of dramatic proportions. Not that much ever happened in Harborhaven which would merit such proportions, but that never stopped Rosie from framing every little detail of Harborhaven life in the most harrowing light possible. And in case nothing occurred to suit her thirst for shocking news, she carried around a sheaf of tabloids in her capacious handbag, "For when I need a good read while out and about," she would explain.

Her favorite topic of study from those tabloids was that of the British Royals. And since Miss Harriet herself had come from England, of course Rosie felt her day incomplete without apprising Miss Harriet of the latest news.

She would bluster through the door each morning, wearing a bright, garish coat with a large matching hat, ringed around the brim with a puffy layer of tulle and a few jaunty feathers fastened on one side. "Like the Queen wears, you know," she would say with a knowing nod. She would plunk herself down nearby the right window (often to the dismay of Mr. James), and talk, peer out the window, and eavesdrop on Mr. James' conversations by turn.

Each Wednesday, Rosie would come a little later than usual, and with a group of ladies in tow.

"The Luncheon Society," as they liked to call themselves, met each week to chatter, eat, and giggle over another of the Dailies, a tall, thin man with grey hair who came in promptly at noon.

Walking quietly in, the tall man would sit near the window across from that in which Mr. James was typically still installed, ordering Earl Grey tea and one of Miss Harriet's homemade Cornish Pasties, which he would then politely eat with fork and knife. This extremely proper man's name was Edward Patten, and he managed the town's only bank, which had been named "First Bank" by some optimistic town founder.

Katherine quickly observed that the reason this dignified man was doomed to be giggled over by Rosie and her "Luncheon Society" was because Mr. Patten was unmarried—and so was Rosie. And despite the garish red rinse Rosie used to disguise *her* gray hair, one could easily tell that they were about the same age.

This unfortunate circumstance had been intensified by Rosie's belief that Mr. Patten was "enormously rich, you know." When asked how she had ascertained this detail, she would lean in and say mysteriously, "I have my sources," punctuating her statement with a serious but vigorous nod of the head which made her hat feathers bob. The whole table would be still for a moment, conscious of the gravity of Rosie's statement, then erupt into a fresh wave of giggles and teasing as Rosie blushed and pretended to look shocked and embarrassed.

But regardless of Rosie's efforts, Mr. Patten had no interest whatever in her, and tolerated the cry of "Oh, hello there Mr.

Patten!" hollered across the quiet tea shop with a cold and dignified nod, trying his best to ignore the resultant clamor of the cluster of women at the table. Katherine always felt sorry for the man, and wished Rosie and her friends would leave him alone. She said so to Miss Harriet one afternoon.

"They're not so bad as they seem, dear." she had replied in an undertone, leaning on the counter as she surveyed the scene. "All hat and hairspray, that's what they are. There's no substance whatsoever behind their tittle-tattle. Mr. Patten knows this, and has the happy ability not to be offended by the chatter of silly schoolgirls—even when they're schoolgirls with wrinkles and grey hair."

Katherine did observe that on the days Rosie dined alone, she appeared hardly to notice Mr. Patten's arrival at all. Only when she had an audience did she greet him so boisterously. Katherine thought she liked Rosie much better without her entourage.

One week, Miss Harriet and Katherine noticed that Rosie seemed subdued and uncharacteristically quiet. This lasted for days, and Miss Harriet began to be concerned for her. On Wednesday, she asked one of the Luncheon Society ladies if anything was wrong with Rosie.

"Oh, I know what's wrong with her. She decided to take on the Captain over at the Harborside."

Katherine, clearing a table nearby, slowed her work to listen as Miss Harriet replied,

"Oh, yes? And what happened?"

"Well, we had been talking last week, you know, about how no one could get anything out of him about where his sister had gone to, and you know that Rosie has her theories."

"Yes?"

"Well, Maybelle got exasperated with Rosie, like she does, and said, 'why don't you go ask him about it, if you're so sure.' and then she said she would. The next day, Maybelle ran into Rosie on the street in such a state, she told Maybelle everything before she could even stop to think what she was doing."

Miss Harriet patiently nodded. "And what did she say?"

"She said she went to the Harborside, and walked in all lofty like. When the captain came out, she said she was interested in looking at some tea—which she wasn't, of course—and he asked which kind. She, thinking herself so smart, said she couldn't remember the name, and that his sister had recommended it. Right off the bat, he looked her over and said the name of a tea.

Since Rosie really hadn't ever gone into the store for tea before, she couldn't say it wasn't the right kind, and had to buy some. As he got the tea from the jar, she asked about his sister, and he just said she was doing all right where she was, like he always does, you know."

"And what did Rosie do next?"

"What she's best at, of course. She stuck her nose in a little further. She said, 'and where *is* she, exactly?' trying to sound all innocent. The Captain turned red, and shoved the package of tea into her hand, saying angrily 'She's where she is, and it's none of yer business!' Well, Rosie just flew out of there fast as she could go, and that's when Maybelle found her."

Miss Harriet listened sympathetically to the tale, and waited on the Luncheon Society with the utmost decorum, but as the afternoon wore on, Katherine noticed that the corner of Miss Harriet's mouth would twitch now and then, as though trying not to laugh.

As soon as the door closed on the last customer of the day, Miss Harriet walked composedly into the kitchen where Katherine had been tidying up, carefully pulled the curtain across the doorway, then burst into laughter.

"Can't you just see it! Oh, good for the Captain!!" she said, laughing until tears streamed down her face. When she finally recovered, she explained, "Rosie's a generous old thing, and she can be ever so kind on occasion, but people *do* tend to allow her to be impertinent, and it will do her no end of good to have been taken down a peg or two."

At first, Katherine didn't know what to think of this outburst, being so unlike Miss Harriet's usual gentle composure. She had to admit it was funny, the thought of Rosie challenging the captain to a battle of wits and losing so decidedly. She began to laugh as well as she pictured the scene, and soon the two were merrily washing the dishes, chuckling now and then as the scene resurfaced in their thoughts.

"I only wish I had been there when it happened." Katherine said. "It would have been so interesting. I wonder whether Captain Braddock had any idea he had won so substantial a victory against the forces of small-town gossip."

"It certainly would have been interesting to witness, but I think it's better we weren't there." Miss Harriet said, with a mischievous grin, "This way, we have all the fun of imagining the scene, without any of the responsibility of disapproving of either party's actions, since we only have it on hearsay what passed between them."

Katherine looked over at Miss Harriet with a sly grin. "I

thought you were always ready to disapprove of the actions of Captain Braddock."

Miss Harriet pretended to be affronted. "Why, me? Never!" then, becoming more serious, she added, "I do admit that it is sometimes *very* easy to disapprove of the captain, or at least of his opinions and manners. But then, we can always find fault with others if we've a mind to, and I daresay he has about as much to find faulty with me as I do with him."

A tone of finality had slipped into Miss Harriet's voice, and Katherine decided to drop the topic. After a moment's pause, Katherine asked, "Miss Harriet,"

"Yes, Dearie?"

"Do you think Mr. Patten is really as rich as Rosie supposes?"

"Why do you ask?"

"Just curious, I guess."

Miss Harriet looked at her for a moment before replying. "Well, I know he's no billionaire, that's for sure. It's natural to assume he would make a decent wage at the bank, and he seems to live quite frugally, so I daresay he's got a good sum saved up. But, Katherine, something tells me this is no idle question. What are you thinking of?"

Katherine blushed. "Well, he's about the same age as Mrs. Penelope, isn't he? And didn't you say her husband died several years ago? I would say she's a much better match for Mr. Patten than Rosie, any day."

"Yes, well. I should not be encouraging you, but I have to say I agree. It would be nice to see Mrs. Penelope well off, but I don't think she'd ever consider anything of the kind, especially at her time of life."

Miss Harriet gazed absently into the dish water as she mechanically scrubbed a teacup. "Mind you, she does seem a bit lonely, with her children far away, and no grandchildren coming to visit. It would be nice..." Bringing herself back to reality, she turned to Katherine. "But we mustn't be such gossips. If we're not careful, soon we'll be carrying tabloids around in our handbags like Rosie!"

They both chuckled and resumed their work, but Katherine couldn't keep from thinking about the little old woman and the quiet banker and how nice it would be for them to have a happy ending.

6

Beginnings at the Harborside

Captain Braddock stood up from his desk and stretched. Looking up at the old clock on the wall, his heart started to beat faster.

It's almost time, he thought.

Over the last three weeks Katherine had made her weekly pilgrimage to the Harborside, he had watched her carefully. She seemed to be respectful and conscientious, and listened most intently to anything he had to say about the history of the Harborside.

She always had some question or other about the teas on the shelves; why they looked the way they did, how they differed from other kinds, where they had come from—but she hadn't tried to pry into his personal life like the other townspeople were always trying to do.

To a man as private as the captain, hiring a potentially nosy employee seemed risky, indeed, but Katherine appeared to have her inquisitive nature under control. Besides, he found he liked her curiosity; it made her teachable.

Yes, the captain thought, *She's the right one. She'll be good for this old place.*

The only difficulty was, could he get her to come work for him? He had made some casual inquiries into her working schedule and determined that he could only ask her to come twice a week. To tell the truth, that was just as well, since it was also all he could afford to pay her for. But whether she would be willing to give up two of her days off, he couldn't quite tell.

Well, he thought as the clock began to chime, *There's nothing for it, but to ask her.*

* * *

Katherine walked in the door of the Harborside, full of anticipation. She had been looking forward to this errand all day long. But today the captain seemed distracted.

"Hello, Captain Braddock!" She called out cheerfully as the old man limped in from his office and stepped behind the counter.

"Hello. Is that yer list?" he asked.

She nodded and handed him the piece of paper she had brought from Miss Harriet. To her surprise, he turned and walked over to the sea chest without a single disparaging remark. As she watched him transferring boxes from the chest to a paper bag, she wondered what could be wrong.

He seemed different—nervous, almost. That was certainly a change from his usual blustery confidence.

Once the bag was full, the captain labored to his feet and held it out to her. As she reached to take it, he took a deep breath and spoke.

"I was wondering... well..." his voice trailed off, as if he couldn't think how to finish his sentence.

"Yes?" Katherine smiled encouragingly.

"I wanted to know... that is... How would you like to come work at the Harborside?"

Katherine's eyes sparkled. "Oh, I'd *love* to!... but..."

Now it was Katherine's turn to look nervous. She desperately wanted to say yes. After all, to spend whole *days* in a place where history and adventure permeated the air, oh, it would be lovely! Yet, she had to be honest.

"There's one problem," she said.

"And what would that be?"

"I could only come on Tuesdays and Thursdays."

The captain studied her anxious face for a moment, then burst out heartily, "Just the days I could use yer help!"

He gave Katherine a smile she had never seen on his face before, a real smile –a happy smile. It lasted just a moment, then, returning to his accustomed seriousness, he continued with what Miss Harriet would have called "the particulars".

"You'll arrive by eight o'clock, and leave when the work's done. The shop closes at five-thirty, and I'm always headed home by six, but some days I may be able to let you go sooner than that. Other days the work might go a bit later. It just depends on how much there is to do and how quickly we get it done. You'll get a break for lunch, of course. I can't afford to pay you as much as that woman does, but I'm not opposed to payin' you more if the shop does well. Sound okay to you?"

Katherine, too delighted to speak, only nodded happily.

"Well, then," said the captain, "I guess I'll see you Tuesday morning, at eight o'clock—sharp."

* * * *

Katherine walked back to Miss Harriet's, her heart all aglow with excitement. When she arrived, the shop was full of customers. There had been a rush while she was gone, and she could tell that Miss Harriet needed her help right away. She set the package in the kitchen and threw her frilly floral apron over her head. She tied it quickly and smoothed her hair before walking calmly out from behind the kitchen curtain to welcome a woman and her granddaughter who had just come in.

Katherine spent the rest of the day hurrying from table to table, cheerfully taking orders and delivering food. She kept so busy that the afternoon flew by, in spite of her impatience for the day to be over so she could tell Miss Harriet her news.

At last, it was closing time. She helped Miss Harriet clear the tables of their dishes and teapots. Finally, unable to keep her excitement to herself a moment longer, she exclaimed to Miss Harriet,

"You'll never guess what happened at the Harborside today!"

Miss Harriet laughed. "Well, now, I did wonder. Whatever

it was, it's had you fairly floating ever since you came back!" Katherine grinned, trying to stand still, feeling she might burst with excitement.

"All right," Miss Harriet pulled out a chair and sat down, motioning for Katherine to take a seat in the chair across from her. "Let's hear all about it."

Katherine quickly sat down and began her tale.

"Well, when I got there today, the captain was so preoccupied and strange, I wondered what could be wrong. And then when he was done filling the order, he asked if I'd like to work there! It would only be twice a week... on Tuesdays and Thursdays." She searched Miss Harriet's face for signs of disapproval, unsure how her employer would feel about her taking on a second job, especially considering the town's view of the two shops as rivals.

"Well. And you accepted the position, I hope?" was her reply, to the astonishment of her young friend.

"You're okay with me working there? Really?"

Miss Harriet smiled. "Yes, I am. Truly." She leaned back in her chair and sighed. "Goodness knows I don't pay you near enough for all the work you do here, and while your room and board are covered, you'll want to be saving up. This will help you do that, although I can't imagine he'll be able to pay you any more than I do." A sly sort of smile twitched around her mouth. "Besides, it will give you an excuse to go over there more often."

Katherine blushed and looked down. "Is it that obvious?" She asked as she raised her eyes again.

"Only to me. And if I weren't such a generous soul, I might

be a bit jealous." Miss Harriet said teasingly. "Now, just to satisfy my curiosity, why is it that you enjoy your visits to the Harborside so much?"

Katherine sat silent for a minute or two, thoughtfully considering the question. "I don't know for sure... It's partly that there's so much to learn, and everything seems to be tied to history —you know history was always my favorite subject in school, as well as my major in college. And then there's the feeling I got when I walked in that very first day. You know, it's odd, but I just can't shake it. Whenever I'm at the Harborside, it feels... well, like...like..."

"...like home," finished Miss Harriet gently.

"Well, yes, I suppose so. It seemed strange to say it out loud. How did you know?"

"For the simple reason that I recognize in you the same glow I had when I first found this place." She looked up and surveyed the shop into which she had put so much time, effort, and love.

"You may have heard the story of when I first arrived from Rosie's Luncheon Society. I'm well aware it's one of their favorite tales when someone new comes into the shop. I had been looking up and down the downtown blocks at every vacant space, and nothing seemed right, somehow. But then I walked down this last block and as I turned to look at the realtor's sign in the window, I just knew it was the right place.

Of course, I had certain features I was looking for, and a budget to keep to, but as I looked through the dingy window at the counter with its horrible peely paint, and the floor you could hardly see for the dust and grime, it hit me. All of a sudden, for the first time since leaving Mother's cottage in England, I felt I was *home*—and so I was. Even now, when I walk in the door each morning, I feel like I've come home."

"I suppose," said Katherine thoughtfully, "That's why everyone who comes here feels so comfortable. Maybe your 'at-home' feeling transfers to all the people who walk through the door. Like the day I came, for example. I don't quite know if it was the shop itself or just you, but I know I felt welcome right from the start, and I've never felt otherwise since."

Miss Harriet leaned over and gently squeezed Katherine's hand. "And so you are, Katherine. I'm ever so happy you came." There was a moment's pause as the two smiled, enjoying the new depth of their friendship, then Miss Harriet broke the happy silence with, "Well, now. Let's get this place tidied up!"

7

Katherine's First Day at the Harborside

The following Tuesday, Katherine awoke while the soft light of morning was just beginning to peek in at the window overhead. She looked through her clothes, trying to decide what an employee of the Harborside should wear. With a mixture of excitement and nervousness, she got dressed, ate some breakfast, and set off in plenty of time for her first day of work.

Upon arrival, Captain Braddock handed her a heavy navy apron, plain and stiff, with one large pocket in the front.

"Yer gonna want this on whenever yer in the store... it can be a dusty place to work in." he explained. Then, motioning for her to follow, he began to show her around the store. "Yer already familiar with the shelves, and behind the counter, here's where you'll find bags and scoops for measuring the tea, and then there's the scale on the end of the counter to measure the bigger orders with."

Katherine looked at the old-fashioned scale. It looked Victorian, with a shiny brass bowl on top and ornate brass metalwork surrounding the large dial on the front. She smiled and touched the top of the scale as she walked past, watching the needle bounce with the lightest pressure. How she would enjoy using such a piece of the past!

The Captain continued his tour, showing her where the empty jars were stored in some cupboards built into the back of the counter.

Then, he led the way through a doorway into his office. An old rolltop desk stood against the back wall, and she noticed a rectangular wooden table in the center of the room, with various orderly piles of paper on it, along with what looked to Katherine to be an old brass oil lamp, fitted with an electric bulb. Behind this resided an antique captain's chair on wheels, which Katherine thought particularly appropriate. There were glassed-in lawyer's cases and bookshelves around the rest of the walls, and above the rolltop hung an oil paint-ing of a clipper ship, tossing triumphantly on stormy waves. To the left of the doorway into the office stood another door, painted the same shade of green as the shop's front door.

"There's not much in here you'll need, except this—" he reached over and pointed to a clipboard hanging to one side of the door. "This will be yer' most important job. You'll be in charge of inventorying the tea shipments as they come in. Let me show you where you'll take the boxes when they arrive." He opened the green door and led Katherine down a short flight of steps into a cavernous space, flipping a switch on the wall to turn on the few antique lights that lit the center of the room.

"This is the storeroom." He said, walking over to a stack of boxes. "Now, see, some of these boxes will have labels in other languages. They're organized on the inventory sheet by the country they've shipped from. Make sure you compare them carefully and ask me if there's any you can't figure out. You may be able to find the name of the country somewhere on the shipping labels."

Katherine nodded and looked around the room, wondering how such a large room had come to be used for only a few small stacks of boxes. Along the far wall, away from the light, she could just barely discern some shadowy shapes that looked like some sort of large boxes or trunks.

The Captain caught her peering off into the shadows, and moved towards the door, saying gruffly, "The Harborside's got many little cracks and crevices, and I hope I don't have to tell you to mind yer work and not to go nosin' about."

Katherine nodded, with a faint twinge of disappointment. Now that she'd been *told* not to nose about, she certainly would have to be careful not to. She looked back at the storeroom with a quiet sigh.

Since it was only Tuesday, with more shipments expected to arrive before unpacking on Thursday, Captain Braddock set Katherine to work dusting.

"It's very important that the jars stay clean," he said, picking up a dust rag and working with her. "The customers don't seem to mind a dusty counter—although we wipe that down almost constantly—but they do hate having dust on the jars. Makes them squirm, see."

He and Katherine dusted the jars, then she set about dusting the various nautical knick-knacks and pictures. She paused as she took down a model of a clipper ship that looked remarkably like the one in the painting in the captain's office.

She turned around and saw the captain standing behind the counter, surrounded by jars from which he was measuring out tea for the Grand Hotel's order.

"Captain Braddock," she began,

"Yes?" The captain looked up sharply, as if he were startled to hear a voice other than his own in the usually deserted little shop.

"This ship... what's her name?"

The captain put down the jar he had been measuring from and stepped out from behind the counter, wiping his hands on his apron. "Ah, that's the *Anne*. She was named for the wife of the very first Captain Braddock, who built this place."

Katherine's eyes widened. "And this was his ship?"

"Yes, indeed. And it had its adventures, that's for sure." He took the model in his hands and stroked it lovingly, while Katherine leaned carefully against the shelves, sensing the beginning of a story.

"You know what kind of ship this is, then?" He asked.

She shook her head.

"It's a clipper. Built for speed, plain and simple. See how she has three masts, and all these sails? Clippers carried more sails than any other kind of ship back then. And the masts, see how tall they are? That helped the ship to be more aerodynamic. The sails were arranged carefully to best catch the wind and that helped the ship to be fast—a hundred knots a day faster than other sailing ships at the time. Speed was the crucial factor, because the *Anne* was a merchant ship, you see. She sailed to China and brought back the Harborside's first tea shipment in 1847. They unloaded it onto the wharf out yonder, and brought it right into this very room."

Katherine gave a puzzled frown. "But... I thought this building went up with the rest of the old downtown buildings, in 1890?"

"Ah, I can see you know yer local history. That's right, the brick of the outer walls and the storerooms were built in 1890, but because the Harborside was already such an important part of Harborhaven, the Braddocks faced a dilemma. They wanted the Harborside to stay the same, but they knew they needed to build on.

After all, they didn't want the Harborside to be a dumpy little wooden building amidst a sea of towering Victorian brick, and they needed more room. Business had been good, and they had to build storerooms for the cargo the *Anne* would be bringing back. So, being a family of resources and ingenuity, they decided to do both: they would build up, but keep the store the same."

"How could they do both?" Katherine asked with a puzzled frown

"By building their Victorian brick storerooms *around* the original building." The captain watched Katherine's face, enjoying the changes in her expression as she processed this revelation.

"So... the brick in your office, and this storefront with the windows in it, are all from 1890, but the wooden walls in here are from..."

"1846. You see, the first of the Harborside Braddocks,

Captain Jeremiah, for whom I'm named, he and his wife Anne and their three sons built the Harborside from scratch, just as the town was being settled.

"Anne and the boys sold off what stock they had been able to bring with them while Captain Jeremiah went off to China in the *Anne* for more. Tea had just gotten to be a big thing out here, and the Braddocks knew there would be other merchants selling it, but they were determined to get a foothold here in Harborhaven, since it was such a good place for shipping. Strategically placed, that's what they said about it at the time.

"Well, the *Anne* made the Braddocks a fortune, and there was money enough for grand improvements by the time the town was really getting going, so, they decided to improve."

Katherine hardly heard this last part of the captain's story as she stared at the walls in wonder. She was standing in the very room in which the first Captain Braddock and his wife Anne had unpacked the very first Harborside shipment! And now, centuries later, she would be doing the same job. A thrill went through her at the thought.

"But, you know," continued the captain, "It wasn't an easy trip, that first one. No, not by a long shot."

Katherine snapped back into focus at this, leaning forward in her excitement to find out what adventure had befallen the *Anne* on her maiden voyage.

"They had good weather on the way there, and they were able to get quite a good cargo. Captain Jeremiah even had been able to get ahold of an ornate box of tea so precious, he had to keep it with him at all times while ashore lest it be stolen. Someone had seen him with it, though, and the *Anne* wasn't two days out from shore before the lookout spied a ship coming towards them. They soon heard a warning shot fired across their bow, and sure enough, if it wasn't pirates!"

Katherine raised her eyebrows skeptically, but the captain continued.

"Now, then. These weren't pirates like in the movies. These were the real thing, and they had been hired by another merchant to steal the captain's precious box of tea. They boarded, and searched the ship, but the box was nowhere to be found. The pirates were furious, but Captain Jeremiah calmly told them that he had thrown the box into the sea when he saw them coming. They made another search, and eventually left, having found nothing."

"And had Captain Jeremiah really thrown the box into the sea?" asked Katherine, once again absorbed in the tale.

"Yes and no," he replied. "He was a sly one, Captain Jeremiah was. He had thrown the box into the sea, but the contents he had carefully sealed in a bag of waxed cloth and sewn it into the hem of one of the curtains in his cabin before they had even left the harbor."

"And the pirates didn't suspect a thing?"

"No. You see, the box was made out of wood, and he made sure he threw it over just as the pirate ship got close, so they would see it still floating near the ship. When they saw that, they gave up. They didn't leave peacefully, though."

"What did they do?"

"Well, they beat several of the crew, trying to get information out of them, and in their fury upon seeing the box floating in the water, they struck the captain and threw him overboard, unconscious. But the cabin boy, who had been hiding behind the lifeboats in terror, saw the captain go overboard and threw a rope over the side of the ship. He climbed down, and quietly eased himself into the water. The pirates never noticed a thing!

"Now this boy, you see, he happened to be a strong swimmer, and made his way to where Captain Jeremiah was floating. The boy kept the captain's head above water until the pirate ship was far enough away the crew could safely bring them aboard. Needless to say, that cabin boy was well looked after from then on."

He put the model back on the shelf and said with a hint of reluctance in his voice, "Well, now, I suppose we'd both best get back to our work."

Katherine turned and began to vigorously dust the shelf behind her, not wanting the captain to regret having taken time for the story. She somehow knew that there were many more he could tell, and she began to pay closer attention to the things she dusted, wondering what story each one would reveal.

8

Secrets and Stories

Wednesday had never seemed longer to Katherine. It was no different than any other Wednesday, with the Dailies each coming in at their appointed time, and the Luncheon Society's ever-present chatter throughout the noon hour, but to Katherine, it all seemed to drag along at a snail's pace.

Even the dishes seemed to take longer than usual, despite Miss Harriet being as cheery and talkative as ever. Katherine enjoyed giving her an account of her first day at the Harborside and Captain Braddock's tale of the *Anne's* first voyage, but all the while, she had a bubbling sort of impatience inside. She wished the evening would fly just a *little* faster, for tomorrow was Thursday, and she would be spending the entire day at the Harborside again. There was no telling what she might learn or discover!

Katherine did manage to sleep that night, although somewhat fitfully. When she awoke, the sun was smiling in, sending bright beams through the round window overhead. Katherine jumped out of bed, eager to begin the day.

As she hurried down the sidewalk to the Harborside that morning, the sun had already begun to warm the sticky air. Katherine looked up at the cloudless sky, thinking how glad she would be to work in the dark, cool storeroom most of the day. A slight breeze drifted in off the harbor, bringing a hint of freshness to the humid morning. Katherine smiled and breathed deeply, her heart full to bursting with gratefulness for the new day—a day which just *might* turn out to be an adventure.

She knocked on the door and the captain hurried to open it. After a quick greeting, he carefully informed her of the tasks he wanted her to finish that day. Having received her marching orders, Katherine eagerly took the clipboard off the wall and opened the door into the storeroom.

She savored the cool, musty air, which she now noticed smelled the same as the rooms above, but slightly staler, and with a bit of the earthy smell that always seemed to permeate old brick structures.

She flipped on the light and approached the first stack of boxes, looking carefully at the labels and trying to match them with the countries and addresses on the inventory sheet. It reminded her of a matching game she liked to play as a child. She took her time, determined to figure out every label on her own. Once the last shipment on the list had been checked off, she took out the boxcutter Captain Braddock had handed her when she arrived and set to work unpacking the boxes.

Thursday flew past with all the quickness Wednesday had

lacked. Before she knew it, the mid-afternoon sun was streaming in through the tiny porthole window high up on the back wall of the Captain's office. She had finished unpacking, had filled up the few empty jars on the shelves of the little shop, and stowed the rest of the teas in the larger jars kept behind the counter.

"Tea needs to be kept fresh; you see." The captain had explained as he showed her how he wanted the lids carefully tightened down with the rubber gaskets just so.

Katherine placed the last jar behind the counter and straightened up. She noticed a woman outside one of the big shop windows. She had met a friend on the street, apparently, and seemed lost in conversation with her, while a small boy stood near them and looked around with boredom plainly evident on his face.

He was a cute little thing, about five years old or so, Katherine thought. She felt sorry for him, and when he turned his gaze inside the shop, she smiled and waved through the window. He waved back, and turned around again, tugging on his mother's hand.

Captain Braddock came into the storefront carrying a jar he had been fitting with a new gasket and spotted the little boy outside. He told Katherine he would finish with the jars and instructed her to go fetch the broom beside the storeroom door and do some sweeping up.

Katherine quickly found the broom, but as she neared the doorway into the shop, she stopped short, shocked to see that the little boy had actually ventured inside! She shot a glance towards the window and saw his mother still deep in conversation, seemingly oblivious that her boy had wandered away.

Curious how the captain would handle this tiny customer, Katherine stood by the doorway, just out of sight, to see what he would do.

"Well, hello there, my little lad. And how are you today?"

Katherine had never heard the captain use such a gentle tone before, and watched with what could only be called shock as the little boy walked right up to the counter and began chattering away. He didn't seem to be at all afraid of the old sea captain.

The boy rattled off something about the hot weather, and being bored outside. Then, catching sight of the captain's hat on the old-fashioned coat rack, he exclaimed with wide-eyed admiration, "Are you a *real* captain?"

The captain looked grave and reached out his hand as he said, "Yes, I am. My name's Captain Braddock. What's yours?"

"Tommy. I never met a *real* captain before!" He gave the captain's hand a hearty shake.

Captain Braddock opened one of the many small drawers in the back of the counter and fished something out, saying, "Well, now, Tommy, I suppose it must be awfully hard to stand and listen to the grownups gab out there in the heat, so here's something to keep you occupied while you wait," and with that, he reached down over the tall countertop and handed the boy a peppermint candy, adding, "Now, you make sure you ask yer mother before you eat that, and whatever you do," he leaned further towards the little boy and dropped his voice to a solemn whisper, eyes twinkling, "don't ye go telling yer little friends I gave that to yer."

He ended with a quick wink, and the boy nodded in equal

solemnity, turning to leave, then stopping at the door with a bright, "Thank you, Cap'n!" and a boyish salute as he left.

Katherine waited a moment, then walked in and began sweeping as if she hadn't seen or heard a thing, but she did look over at the captain now and then with a secret smile.

We all keep a favorite picture of the ones we love squirreled away in our hearts, to be taken out and remembered again and again over the years. Katherine thought that this would be her favorite picture of the captain: leaning over the counter, dropping his persona of the grumpy old man, just for a moment, to make a small child feel important.

Katherine kept the Captain's well-guarded spirit of benevolence a secret from all except Miss Harriet. She knew she could trust her friend to keep it to herself. They had come to a place of mutual confidence, and felt the freedom to discourse about any topic, without fear of their words being "bandied about the town", as Miss Harriet once put it.

Miss Harriet found the intelligence concerning the captain's interview with little Tommy surprising indeed, and replied by setting her teacup down on the table and gently exclaiming, "Well! So he's got a heart after all underneath all that bluster. I always suspected as much, but I've never been able to discover just what the chink in his armor might be."

"I guess now we know." chuckled Katherine. "Although, I wonder when he first started keeping candy in that drawer? I suppose he must have gone out and bought it on purpose, for I've never seen him eat any."

"It's a tradition left over from when Serena was there." Miss Harriet said with a sudden tinge of sadness in her voice.

"Really? Did she keep candy in a drawer for kids that came in?"

"Not exactly. She had it in a lovely cut glass candy dish atop the counter. She told me one day that she kept the candies in a dish with a lid so that the children had to ask her for one. Otherwise, she said, they would just reach right in, and then their parents would be embarrassed. She said having to ask discouraged her young customers from being quite so greedy."

"I suppose when the captain took over the shop, he must have just swept it all into a drawer to get it off the counter. I've noticed that he's very particular about what gets put out on that counter."

The two agreed that must have been what happened, and Katherine resolved to keep her eye out for that candy dish.

They walked into the kitchen and began the nightly ritual of washing up. Katherine got out a dish towel and leaned on the counter by the sink while she waited to dry the first dish.

"It's odd that Tommy walked right in without his mother. I suppose it's all right because she was nearby, but she never even noticed when he came into the shop. When I was little, my parents wouldn't have dreamed of losing track of me long enough to slip into a shop by myself and have a chat with a shopkeeper they'd never met."

"How did you like growing up here?" asked Miss Harriet.

"Oh, I loved it." Katherine answered with a happy smile "We would spend summer days on the beach, walking up and down, gathering all sorts of little shells and pretty rocks. Sometimes we would even find sea glass, although that was pretty rare. I loved the freedom, the light, and in the fall and winter, I loved the storms. I used to stand by my window and watch the waves crash over each other out in the harbor. We could see it from our house, you know, and we would gauge the changing of the seasons by the color of the water."

"It sounds like you had a lovely childhood" Miss Harriet said, handing Katherine another dish to dry.

"I did. But, then again, it was the only childhood I knew. I never thought to compare it with other peoples' childhoods. But then, we left, and nothing was ever the same."

"And why did you leave?" Miss Harriet asked gently.

"Christmas night, we were all in the living room when the phone rang. My father went to answer it, and Mom and I knew right away something was wrong. Dad's face turned a funny grey color, and he rushed up to my attic room, where we could see over the trees and houses towards the harbor. We ran upstairs and found him staring out the window. The mill had caught fire, and we could see the flames in the distance." Katherine took a deep breath before continuing.

"It was a terrible tragedy for the whole community, and many people lost their jobs, not just my dad. But when we had to move, it felt like my whole world had disappeared. We went from our lovely house with the view of the harbor to an apartment in the city with a view of a grimy brick wall. Then Mom had to take a job, and there just never seemed to be anyone at home. I was old enough to understand why we needed to move, why my parents both had to spend so much time at work, but it didn't change the fact that I felt so...*abandoned*."

Both ladies worked silently for a while, then Miss Harriet said softly,

"You know I grew up in England, but did I ever tell you about *my* childhood?" Katherine shook her head eagerly, inwardly preparing for a good story. All Miss Harriet's stories were captivating, and Katherine always loved to listen to her tell them in her lilting accent.

"I grew up in a little village in Surrey, England. I spent my childhood there, much as you spent yours here, only instead of the shore, we wandered the hills, and brought back treasures from the fields and streams.

I thought we were the happiest of families, my parents, my brother and I. We lived in a beautiful little cottage, with just the smallest little patch of a front garden. Despite its size, Mother had managed to plant a variety of flowers, so that it seemed to be perpetually bright and fragrant. Just as you marked your seasons by the harbor, I marked mine by those flowers." Here she paused, as if savoring the memory of that long-lost flower garden.

"Is that why you fill your shop with flowers?" Katherine asked with a smile.

"Perhaps...Yes, I suppose it must be. I had never thought about it that way." After another pause, Miss Harriet continued somberly. "When I was still but a little bit of a girl, my father left quite suddenly. I remember seeing him at dinner one night, and the next night it was just us three, my brother and I not really understanding that Papa had gone for good, and Mother trying so bravely to keep us from the sickening shock of it."

"Oh, how awful!"

"Yes. It was. But Mother was so wonderful. She never complained, never spoke ill of Papa before us. But she didn't excuse him, either. She took a job to support us and came home each evening tired, but determined to be the mother we needed her to be. I can only imagine how exhausting it must have been for her. But she had such strength."

"And she *really* never said anything bad about your father?" Katherine asked, astonished.

"No, never. But I know that she *did* pour out her sorrow and hurt to the only One who could heal them. When we went to bed each night, she would go to her room and kneel by her bed. Then she would pray, lifting up her heart, and sometimes her voice, although she did try to be careful not to disturb us. I only know about it because I would often hear her muffled sobs and creep to the door to check on her. My brother never dared, but I just had to.

"'I would stand softly outside in the hallway while she cried, voicing her hushed words of grief and pain to God alone. But then, her pain and grief would give way to words of forgiveness and pleas on behalf of the man who had so wronged her, abandoning her and leaving her to care for two small children who just couldn't understand why Papa would have gone away.

"Once these prayers of forgiveness began, her sobs would gradually begin to subside, and I knew she would be all right. I would then go back to bed, stopping on the way to reassure my brother. Then, we went to sleep feeling secure, certain that it would all come out right somehow, because Mother was praying."

"And... did he ever come back?" Katherine asked.

"No, we never saw him again—but don't you think for a moment that it made the rest of my childhood dreary. You see, because Mother handled the whole thing so splendidly, we were surrounded by love and concern, and had the attitude of forgiveness and hope fostered in us. We prayed every day for Papa, that God would protect him and bring him home safe one day, and we were taught to pray those prayers in a tone of love and from a heart full of longing to forgive and to restore. Our home was never a place of anger, bitterness, or despair. No matter how hard things got, Mother just never gave up.

"The whole village rallied around us, and it seemed as if every old lady thought it their responsibility to mother us while our own dear mother was at work. We were well-fed, well-petted, and well-scolded when we did wrong. In all, we were surrounded by people who loved and cared for us, so that we never had reason to feel sorry for ourselves—except we *did* often wish that Mother didn't have to work and could have spent time with us like our friends' mothers did. But even so, she would make the time she did spend with us so special. She always had some treat planned, whether a simple picnic, or a walk in the twilight, or just reading a book to us. What a good mother she was!" Another long pause followed, in which Miss Harriet seemed engulfed in visions of the past. Then with a deep breath, a quick shrug, and a gentle smile, she brought herself back to the present and resumed her task of scrubbing the plates.

"She's still alive, you know", she continued brightly. "She lives with my brother in one of the larger villages, not too far from the hills we so loved to wander as children. My brother takes good care of her, and I call her up a couple times a week just to chat."

****

When Katherine climbed the stairs to her apartment that night, she took with her a heart and mind full to the brim. She couldn't fathom the kind of love and devotion that could cause someone to forgive an offender who never changed or asked for forgiveness.

As she contemplated all this, it occurred to her just how much her own parents had sacrificed to give her the peaceful, stable childhood she had enjoyed and how much she had taken for granted their presence in her life all those years.

Katherine closed the apartment door, picked up her phone, and stood frozen for a moment, a torrent of feelings raging against itself inside her. She knew what she needed to do. Part of her even *wanted* to do it, but struggled against letting down her guard, even a little. Finally, she took a deep breath and dialed.

"Mom? Yes, it's me. I'm fine. I ended up staying in Harborhaven. Yes, I'm working at a tea shop. I just..." She gulped back the flood of emotions that threatened to steal her voice, "I... I wanted to say thank you, for... for everything, I guess."

9

Cliff Top Memories

It was Saturday. Katherine had the day off, for which she was glad, although she always wondered at Miss Harriet's choice to work the busiest day of the week all by herself.

"It's mostly just tea and scones anybody wants on Saturdays, and besides, I need the reminder of what a rush every day was before you came. It keeps me grateful."

Katherine had her suspicions that perhaps one reason for Miss Harriet's generosity in making Saturday her day off was really because she secretly enjoyed the challenge of the Saturday rush and wanted an excuse to be out among the people more than she would have with Katherine there to wait tables.

This particular Saturday, the weather was fine, and Katherine decided to take her library book and a few scones and go looking for a good place to read outdoors. Miss Harriet thought this a wonderful idea, and insisted on adding a small thermos of tea and a couple sandwiches, "In case you find you're hungrier than you think you'll be."

Katherine stepped out onto the sidewalk and looked up into the lofty blue of the sky. It was cool enough for a sweater, but walking would warm her, and as the sun climbed higher, it would be just right for sitting and reading outside.

Now, she thought, *Where shall I walk to?*

She knew the area well, particularly the little neighborhood atop the cliffs, and she tried to think of a place where she could sit and enjoy her book and tea undisturbed. She began to walk towards the center of the downtown blocks where Main Street crossed First, which ran between the buildings from wharf to hillside. There, a long flight of stairs had been cut into the rocky slope of the cliffs.

As a child, Katherine had enjoyed racing her friends up these stairs, to see how far they could get without stopping. Now, she stared up them, gathering courage and energy: energy because it was a very long flight of stairs, and steep, too, and courage, because she had not been to the top of those stairs since she had moved away, and wasn't sure just what memories and emotions would be there to greet her at the top. She felt compelled to go, however, and placed her foot upon the first step. Soon, she was nearing the last step, all out of breath.

There at the upper landing, an arch of trees formed by two great weather-beaten oaks met her gaze. She had forgotten how lush and green Cliffton Park was in the early autumn. The trees were just beginning to turn, and the grass was bright, abundant, and soft, ringed with tall firs and the dark foliage of camelia and rhododendron bushes beneath them.

Even now, just past the driest part of the year, this park remained fresh and vibrant, partially due to the large ever-greens which threw the lawns into shade at the hottest part of the day.

Katherine decided to walk along the paved path to the edge of the park, where she remembered a gravel trail which led out of the park along the top of the cliffs. There was a tree somewhere along that trail, way out on a promontory.

That would be a good place to read, she thought.

She followed the trail for a while, then at last, rounding a bend, she spotted the promontory. The tree, which she had remembered as seeming small and spindly and a little too frail to be on its own out there on the promontory, was now strong and tall, with a thick, wind-twisted trunk and a spreading canopy that provided just the right amount of shade.

Katherine spread her large scarf, which she had worn for just such a purpose, over the grass beneath the tree, and sat down with her back against the sturdy trunk. She opened her bag and brought out the tea, sandwiches, and a copy of *Sense and Sensibility*.

How right Miss Harriet was about the sandwiches, she thought to herself as she unwrapped the first of the dainty triangles. The walk up the stairs itself had been strenuous, and she had walked pretty far along the cliffs to get to this spot.

The sun gently filtered through the leaves of the tree as she immersed herself into the trials and tribulations of the Dash-wood sisters. A light breeze was blowing up from the harbor, and when Katherine surfaced again from the enthralling story, it was mid-afternoon. She stood up, a little stiff from sitting so long on the hard dirt, and stretched. Then, packing her scarf and the remnants of her lunch into her bag, she set off down the trail back towards the middle of the park.

As she walked, she began wonder what her old house looked like now.

I suppose it might not even be there still, she thought, *It could have been torn down.*

Katherine wasn't sure if she wanted to see the house if it was much different, but by the time she neared the stairs, curiosity had gotten the better of her fear. She turned away from the cliffs and walked along the paved path towards the entrance to Cliffton Park.

Katherine hesitated a moment at the entrance, then strode out of the park and into the neighborhood. Turning down a familiar street, she looked with unexpected delight at the houses around her. They were almost exactly as she remembered.

The neighborhood had an interesting history. It had begun as a collection of little white farmhouses, each with a large enough lot to accommodate a substantial kitchen garden, in addition to an outbuilding or two. Katherine remembered having seen them in an old painting of the neighborhood on a long-ago school trip to Harborhaven's small museum.

Beyond the cluster of houses had been an expanse of fields. As time went on and the shops and businesses below had become more successful, the inhabitants of the houses above had become more affluent, and nearly all of the original farmhouses were pulled down, with grander houses in various styles erected in their places.

The Victorian period especially had brought a boom of development to the cliffs, as the town's industry and businesses flourished, and farming went out of style for the more affluent citizens of Harborhaven. While all this development was occurring, new arrivals to Harborhaven began to fill in, buying up some of the old farmhouses or building new ones, some between the grand houses, some in small clusters beyond, until the fields disappeared, and the neighborhood reached halfway to the next town. Katherine's steps began to slow as she turned a corner.

Among the grander buildings along the street was nestled a little blue house, resembling the style of the original farmhouses, though a bit bigger, and having been built much later. It was carefully situated, so as to have a view of the harbor from its second-story windows. There was a porch out front with three steps, and a walkway which led between two white fenceposts at the sidewalk.

Katherine stopped before the house and stood pensively, taking in the scene. There were different curtains in the window, the old porch swing was gone, but yes, that was the same house she remembered. That was the walkway where she had played hopscotch with her friends, the three steps where they would sit and eat popsicles in the summer, the window, way up at the top of the gable, where she would look out at the harbor every morning. How she missed those days!

She stood and gazed for a while, then turned back the way she had come. She walked back to the park and down the stairs, reliving old memories—good memories, mostly—of a time when all the world seemed so simple, so fresh and new.

Now those days were gone, the people scattered; and life was so very different than she had imagined when she was still a child, eating popsicles on the front steps in the sunshine.

* * * *

Still deep in reverie, Katherine arrived back at Miss Harriet's just before closing. She walked up to her apartment, unpacked her bag, and then returned to the shop. She entered the kitchen and quietly slipped an apron over her head.

Miss Harriet, just about to start the washing up, looked at Katherine in surprise.

"Well. And did you have a nice afternoon?" Miss Harriet asked gently, sensing something was amiss.

"Yes. I read for a while under a tree, and then I walked around Cliffton." Katherine picked up a dishcloth and prepared to dry the dishes as Miss Harriet washed them.

"Did you, now? And how was Cliffton? I hardly ever get up there myself, but there are some very fine houses to see. The Historical Society has a walking tour now, you know. They have maps at the museum that tell you all about the houses up there."

Katherine just nodded. The two washed dishes in silence for a while, then Katherine said softly, "I walked by my old house today."

Light dawned in Miss Harriet's eyes. "Is that why you're so quiet tonight?"

"I guess so. It just brought back lots of memories from my childhood, and I'm not sure what to make of them yet."

Silence reigned for a few moments more, then Miss Harriet asked, "Do you want to talk about it?"

Katherine looked up at her friend and smiled weakly. "No, not yet. As you always say, 'sometimes all the world needs is a good nap to set it right'. I think a good night's sleep is all I need—but thank you, anyway."

Miss Harriet returned her smile and said, "Anytime, my dear, anytime at all." She handed the last dish to Katherine and said in a brighter tone, "Well, then. I suppose you'd better get on up to bed. I'll finish up in here. Pick you up in the morning for church?"

Katherine nodded. "Of course. I'll be ready by eight-thirty."

She turned and walked up the stairs to the little apartment that had become her home. Then, closing the door behind her, she wandered listlessly over to the window seat and basked in the fading light. Her mind whirled with pictures of the past, of her home and family in Harborhaven. Oh, how her heart yearned to return to those days of peace and happiness!

Better get some rest before church tomorrow.

She reached up to close the curtain, but paused for one last lingering moment with her hand grasping the heavy folds of fabric. This was the time of year when she hated to close the windows at night. Everything stayed so beautifully luminous, even after dark. With a sigh, she twitched the curtains closed, then walked to her room where the small round window let in just a bit of the pale blue twilight.

As she lay in bed, trying to fall asleep, a memory surfaced —one she hadn't thought about in years. She remembered the pink curtains of that long-ago attic room in Cliffton, and could see in her mind's eye the familiar scene: her mother, coming in on such a night, pulling the covers up little closer to Katherine's chin with a motherly caress, then walking soundlessly over to the large window to pull the curtains shut. She always left a little sliver through which the morning light would peep, so Katherine wouldn't have to wake up in the dark. How young her mother looked in those memories! How young and lithe and unhurried! A tear trickled down Katherine's cheek.

How can I be here, home in Harborhaven at last and still not be free from the misery of the past? If this can't free me, is there anything that can?

* * * *

The next morning, Katherine awoke to another sunny morning. She got up and dressed hurriedly for church, grabbing some leftover scones for breakfast from the kitchen downstairs.

She rode to church with Miss Harriet every Sunday, and knowing how her employer liked to be punctual, always tried to be careful not to make her late. This morning, however, she was ready a little early, so she sat at one of the tables by the door in the empty tea shop and basked in the soft sunlight which filtered through the lace curtains as she ate her breakfast.

Soon, she saw Miss Harriet's little blue car pull up to the curb. She quickly locked the shop door and hurried out to the car. When she got in, Miss Harriet smiled happily.

"I see a rest *did* do you some good! I'm glad to see you a bit more chipper."

Katherine blushed a little and smiled back. "I do feel a bit better this morning."

They drove up the winding road which travelled around the edge of the harbor before turning inland towards the outskirts of Cliffton. Katherine always enjoyed the drive, and this morning it was particularly glorious, with all the beauty of a high blue sky reflected even bluer in the waters of the harbor. The leaves were just beginning to turn on the trees along the road, and Katherine wondered if anything could be more beautiful than Harborhaven in the autumn.

As they drove up to the church building, Katherine took a deep breath. Her visit to her childhood home had brought other memories to the surface, and although she had been to church many times since returning to Harborhaven, she had not experienced such a flood of memories and emotion as she did this morning.

The little white church with its hard wooden pews, smoothed by hundreds of years of use, and its tall old-fashioned belltower that still rang out on Sunday mornings to call the community in to worship was the same church she had attended with her parents as a child.

It was here she had gone to Sunday school all those years ago and heard for the first time that Jesus died to pay for her sin. It was here as a child she had prayed, asking Him to forgive her sins and be her Savior. It was here she had been baptized, and it was here she had learned so many truths that now seemed lost in the hazy far-off days of childhood.

As she walked up the steps and through the arched doorway, she remembered how it had looked the last service her family attended before they moved. They had sat in the back, looking around at the empty places on the pews where other families used to sit who had also moved away because of the fire. The pastor had looked so sad that day, as if bearing the hurt of the whole community on his own heart.

He had given her small hand a hearty squeeze as they said goodbye after the service, saying, "God will go with you, Katherine." She had clung to that promise through the first dreadful year or so. Thinking back, she wondered exactly when she had let go of it.

Taking her place in the pew next to Miss Harriet, Katherine looked around, lost in memory. Soon, the service began, and she was brought back to the present by Miss Harriet's voice singing along with the first hymn. She quickly reached for a hymnal and turned to the page Miss Harriet had opened to, searching to find her place.

When the pastor began the sermon, she got out her notebook and pen and determined to listen, instead of letting her mind wander back down the path of memory. He was reading from the book of Jeremiah.

"Thus saith the Lord, Stand ye in the ways, and see, and ask for the old paths, where is the good way, and walk therein, and ye shall find rest for your souls"

The pastor read on, but Katherine was lost in thought.

Rest. That's what I want. Rest for my soul.

Silently, she began to pray, reading the verse again and letting its words sink deep into her aching heart.

As the two drove away from church after the service, Katherine asked timidly,

"Miss Harriet, what did the verse mean when it talked about the 'old paths'?"

"Well, I have always taken that to mean the way God designed us to live. You see, Jeremiah was speaking to the people of Israel, who had strayed from following God, and had stopped obeying the things He had commanded. Through

Jeremiah, God was inviting them to come back to Him, so He could give them rest."

"So, if we do what the Bible says, we will find rest?"

Miss Harriet took a quick glance at Katherine's face before answering. "I suppose that is essentially what that Jeremiah meant. Can I ask why that verse in particular stood out to you?"

Katherine hesitated. "Well, I guess I just don't feel like I have that rest it was talking about."

Miss Harriet considered for a few minutes before answering in a thoughtful tone, "Katherine, do you pray?"

"Well, not very much anymore." Katherine admitted, a bit sheepishly.

"If I might be allowed to suggest it, that might be a good start down the 'old paths'—that, and reading what the Bible says. After all, you can't follow the old paths if you don't know what they are. And Katherine, God does say we are to cast all our care on Him, because *He cares* for us."

Katherine looked out the window and said quietly, "Might as well try..."

Her voice trailed off, and, although neither woman said a word aloud as they drove along, both were speaking silently to the One who could hear the cries of their hearts.

10

Miss Harriet at Home

"My, that was quite a day! Busy right through, and we had just enough of everything. There's not a crumb left of what we cooked today." Miss Harriet sat down in a chair with a sigh. "Now, then. Since there's nothing left for your dinner... How about you come over to my place?"

Katherine looked up in surprise. "Well, I don't want you to have to go to any trouble. I'm sure I can run out and get something."

"Nonsense. It's no trouble at all. I like having company, and I so seldom get to have anyone over. Besides," Miss Harriet said with a wink, "you're practically family, so I won't feel I have to impress you."

A grin spread over Katherine's face. "All right, then! Just let me get my bag."

Katherine ran up to her apartment, brimming with curiosity. She had never seen where Miss Harriet lived, and she was happy for the excuse to go out after a long day. She always seemed to feel refreshed after spending time with her employer, and to be spending the evening at her house seemed like such a treat!

The two got into Miss Harriet's car and drove away from the downtown blocks which seemed to comprise nearly all of Katherine's world nowadays. They drove along a curving stretch of road which followed the edge of the harbor, until they were right out at the tip, where sea and harbor met. There stood a small lighthouse, built like a box with a tower poking out the top. It had been freshly painted and well-preserved by the ever-so-conscientious Harborhaven Historical Society. Just down the road from the lighthouse the colorful rows of ocean-view houses began. Miss Harriet slowed as she entered the neighborhood and pulled into a narrow driveway.

Katherine thought Miss Harriet's house was just like Miss Harriet herself. It was a prim and proper white Colonial, with bright shutters and an oval gable window. There was a tiny porch with a light pink swing. As they walked closer, Katherine noticed with a smile that the fabric pillows on the swing were of a pastel floral print. There was also a small white wicker table and a hanging basket of a flowering plant that released a dainty fragrance into the air as they brushed past.

Miss Harriet hung her purse on one of several hooks on the wall in the white entryway. Katherine noticed a narrow stairway, with a floral rug running down its steps like a cascade of blossoms. To the left was the kitchen, with a large window above the sink, which looked out on a charming window box of the same sweet-smelling plant that draped over the edges of the basket on the porch.

The older lady led the way to the "sitting room", as she called the large room at the back of the house which over-looked the garden, and the ocean beyond. Katherine gazed in silent awe at the view. Miss Harriet's garden was immaculate; though, when she would have had time to work in it, Katherine hardly knew.

They walked out the quaint old-fashioned back door onto a cobbled walkway. The wooden screen door creaked closed, then all was still, save the quiet roar of the ocean, the soft hum of bumblebees, and the faint cry of seagulls in the distance.

"Oh, Miss Harriet!" Katherine said breathlessly, once she could find the words. "It's beautiful! How do you ever bring yourself to leave it in the mornings?"

Miss Harriet smiled, and replied, "Well, I *do* have an equally lovely tea shop to lure me away, now don't I?" Then she turned down a side path that led towards a raised garden bed near the white fence. "I have a couple of leeks here, just ready to be picked. They'll do nicely!"

Katherine gave a puzzled smile. "Leeks?"

"Yes, they're sort of an onion, or at least, they must be related somehow. I grew up with them in England, and I always try to grow some myself. They're one of the foods I fix when I get to feeling homesick, but I think they'll be just right for tonight." She gave a sharp tug to a thick bunch of woody leaves, and the whole plant popped out of the ground.

"See?" Miss Harriet said, triumphantly holding the long plant above her head, "This is a leek, and you're about to discover how delicious it is." Miss Harriet handed the vegetable to Katherine, then turned and pulled up another. She led the way into the house, and as the screen door creaked and banged shut behind them, she looked fondly at the leek and said with an air of decision, "Leek 'n' bacon, I think."

For all her experience working in restaurants and now the tearoom, Katherine had never cooked much for herself. There were, in fact only a few foods she actually knew how to make. She watched eagerly as Miss Harriet rinsed the dirt off the leek and pulled out a cutting board.

"Now, my dear, they're a bit tricky. I'll show you how to wash this one, and then you can do the other yourself." Then she turned and deftly whisked an apron off a hook in the corner of the kitchen. "Here you go, Dearie, you'll want this by the time we're through." Katherine quickly slipped the apron over her head and tied the strings behind her.

"First, you cut the leaves and the roots off—so."

Katherine watched the woman's deft movements, trying to catalogue the steps in her mind. Miss Harriet then cut the long white stem into quarters, revealing that what looked from the outside to be a solid stalk was really a bundle of thin layers.

"This might just be the most important part." Miss Harriet said, handing two of the quarters to Katherine. "See how the layers fall apart so easily? Well, there's dirt between some of them, and we must be sure to get all of it rinsed out." The two washed the long bundles of leeks, then Miss Harriet showed Katherine how small they needed to be chopped.

"I'll just put the water on to boil and get a pan heating up for the bacon." Miss Harriet moved swiftly around the kitchen. It was well-organized and had obviously been arranged with care. Katherine could tell that her employer had put just as much thought into the management of her home kitchen as she had that of the tea room's much larger one.

"Miss Harriet," Katherine asked, running water between the layers of the second leek. "How did you come to live here? I mean, why did you leave England?"

"For the same reason many young folks first leave home, I suppose. I came to the States for school. I think Mother thought it would give me a grand adventure before settling down at home again to raise a family. She had some friends back east who had offered to take me in and let me live with them a year or two while I attended college."

Katherine finished chopping the leeks and put them into a bowl.

"What did you study at college?"

"Oh," Miss Harriet replied with a laugh, "this and that. I was so full of ambition then. One year it was culinary school, the next, a major in horticulture. I finally settled on a business degree. I suppose the practical side of my nature won out in the end."

"Well, *I* for one, am very glad you chose a tearoom over horticulture." Katherine said teasingly. "I finished these." She continued, "What's next?"

"Have you ever made a roux?" Miss Harriet asked.

Katherine frowned, then answered with a chuckle: "No. At least, if I have, I didn't know it."

"Well, then, we'll begin *your* culinary schooling." Miss Harriet replied laughingly.

She showed Katherine how to melt butter and stir in flour,

then let it bubble for a minute or two before adding the milk. The resultant sauce was a bit lumpy, but Miss Harriet encouraged Katherine by entertaining her with stories of disastrous sauces from her culinary school days.

"The leeks are boiled nicely, so we'll just fish them out and pop them into that bowl of cold water over there, so they stop cooking."

Katherine did as Miss Harriet had instructed, and then moved over to the stove to superintend the bacon, which had just begun to sizzle deliciously.

"This is really just a Welsh Rabbit, with bacon and leeks added in." Miss Harriet explained, stirring grated cheese into Katherine's sauce, while at the same time discreetly flattening out some of the bigger lumps with the back of her spoon.

"I've always wondered: why is it called Welsh *Rabbit* if it hasn't got any rabbit in it?"

"I don't know for sure. I've always heard that it was called that because the Welsh peasants were so poor, they couldn't afford meat. So, they called it rabbit, as a sort of joke, or perhaps because they enjoyed the irony of it. Some call it Welsh Rabbit, and others Welsh Rarebit, but I've never heard what rarebit means. I expect it's just a lazy way of saying rabbit." She shrugged her shoulders and kept stirring.

Soon the bacon was finished, and all the ingredients were combined. The result was a thick cheesy sauce with chunks of bacon and leek in it. Miss Harriet got out two plates and popped two thick slices of homemade bread in the toaster. Then she and Katherine carried the food into the "dining room", which was really just one side of the larger sitting room with a small dining table and four chairs.

Miss Harriet gave thanks, and the two began to eat. Katherine closed her eyes and savored the first bite.

"Mmm... that's delicious!" she took another bite before continuing, "Did you learn how to make this that year you spent in culinary school?"

"Oh, no, Dearie. I learned this recipe in my Mama's kitchen when I was about eight years old. We had this often when I was a girl." A smile spread over Miss Harriet's face, and Katherine knew she was remembering earlier days. Then, Miss Harriet took a breath and looked up at Katherine.

"I forgot to ask. Are you planning to visit your parents for Thanksgiving?"

Katherine looked down at her plate, suddenly intent on spearing a piece of bacon with her fork. Miss Harriet went on.

"It's just that I always close the tearoom that day, and I'm sure we can spring you loose for as many other days as you need if you'll be travelling."

"Well, I hadn't planned to. It's a long way to go, and there's not really anywhere for me to stay there."

"Have you been invited?"

"Yes, but I really don't see how—"

"Katherine," Miss Harriet interrupted, suddenly cheerful, "Did you know, we don't celebrate Thanksgiving in England like you do here."

"I guess that's because the Pilgrims' colony ended up American, instead of English." Katherine said with a shrug, puzzled, but relieved by the seeming change of topic.

"Yes, and remind me, what was it they were celebrating, those pilgrims of yours?"

Katherine's eyes lit up, as they always did when she talked

about anything to do with history. "Well, their first winter was very hard, and they had lost more than half the people. No one was certain they would even survive in the new land. But by the time the harvest was brought in the next fall, they had enough to last them through the winter and they had made friends with the Indians. So, they all had a celebration to thank God for all the good things He had provided."

Miss Harriet gave a sly smile and exclaimed unconvincingly, "That's right! Now I remember." Miss Harriet's studied her plate for a few moments, before looking thoughtfully up at Katherine and asking, "Do you believe God has provided good things for *you*?"

"Of course I do." Katherine began to squirm inwardly under Miss Harriet's kind but searching gaze.

"And," the older woman continued gently, "has God provided you with your parents?"

Katherine saw now where Miss Harriet's questions were leading, and looked away, replying quietly, "I don't know... I guess so."

Miss Harriet leaned forward and reached over the small table for Katherine's hand. "My dear, I know it might feel difficult or awkward or even painful to see them, but I also know that God doesn't make mistakes. He gave you those same parents for a reason, and I know it's probably not my place to say it, but I believe you should spend Thanksgiving with them, because *they* are part of what God has provided you *out of His goodness*."

"But.. how can you, of all people, say that?"

"Because I know that my parents—*both* my parents—were who God intended me to have. He knew my father would abandon us, but He also knew all the good He would do for and through my mother as a result of my father's wrongdoing. He knew the lessons of forgiveness, patience, and love He would teach us. He knew it all and planned it all for my good. After all, God says that He works *all things* together for good to those who love Him, and aren't the parents He chooses for us included in 'all things'? Some parents do choose to do terrible things, Katherine, like my Papa did, but God is bigger than all that. He can redeem even the worst situation if we will only allow Him to work."

Katherine looked down at her plate again and sat quiet, struggling inwardly, not wanting to admit that what Miss Harriet had said was true. Miss Harriet softly stood and began to clear away the dishes from the table. As she reached for Katherine's empty plate, she said hesitantly,

"Forgive me, dear, I shouldn't be telling you what to do...But would you do one thing for me?"

Katherine looked up, questioningly, tears glistening in her eyes.

"Will you promise you'll pray about where God wants you to spend Thanksgiving?"

Katherine took a deep breath and nodded.

Miss Harriet smiled, and said in a brighter tone, "Good. And if God leads you to stay here, I'd be just thrilled for you to spend your holiday with me. Otherwise, it will just be Whiskers and I."

Katherine gave a watery smile. "Whiskers?"

"Yes, he's my cat. He likes to roam around the garden all day and spends much of his time curled up under that little bench out there. Let me just set these dishes in the sink, and we'll go see if we can find him. It's nearly sunset now, anyway, and time for him to come inside."

Miss Harriet disappeared into the kitchen briefly, then the two went out into the garden. Miss Harriet called her cat's name and he came ambling down one of the garden paths, large, grey, and very fluffy.

"Hello Whiskers!" Katherine said as the cat sniffed her hand, rubbing his cheek against her with a purr. Miss Harriet smiled and picked him up.

"He likes you. You should be flattered, for he hardly likes anyone. There's days I think he doesn't like me very much." Then to the ball of fluff in her arms she said brightly, "Come on, then old boy, it's time to go inside."

The cat having been safely deposited in the house, Miss Harriet led the way back out to the garden so Katherine could watch the sun set over the waves in the distance. The two sat in companionable silence for a while then Miss Harriet drove Katherine back home.

As she waved goodbye and locked the tearoom door behind her, Katherine thought over the evening and what Miss Harriet had said about her parents. Leaving the lights off, she dropped her bag by the door and walked over to the window seat. She curled up with a pillow in her arms and looked out at the sky above the tall brick buildings.

She knew what she needed to do. Taking a deep breath, she began to pray.

Ok, Lord. Show me what You want me to do, and I'll do it.

11

Miss Harriet's Idea

The next morning, Miss Harriet unlocked the door and stepped into the tearoom. She called a cheery greeting up the stairs, then went back outside to fetch a large box from her car. Katherine was just coming down the stairs as Miss Harriet returned.

"Good morning!" Katherine said, yawning. "What's in the box?" Katherine knew she looked exhausted, but she felt more settled than she had when Miss Harriet had dropped her off the night before.

"Oh, just a few things to get this place looking a little more like autumn." Miss Harriet set the box heavily down on the floor by the counter and then turned towards Katherine. "Now, then, how's my favorite employee this morning?"

Katherine grinned, then yawned again. "Tired. I didn't sleep much last night. But I did what I promised."

"And?" Miss Harriet asked eagerly.

"Well," Katherine began sheepishly, "To be honest, I already knew what God wanted me to do, but I asked anyway to make sure, and then I bought a ticket right away, so I couldn't put it off." Miss Harriet gave a satisfied sigh, then gently taking Katherine's hand, said,

"Oh, Katherine, I'm so proud of you!" Katherine smiled a little, and Miss Harriet knelt and began pulling brightly colored leaves and flowers out of her box.

Katherine slowly sank to the floor beside her employer and sat, silent and uncertain, twirling one of the flowers between her fingers. Finally she spoke.

"I do feel better than I did last night, but oh, Miss Harriet, I still don't *want* to see my parents. I know it's the right thing to do, and I know there's really no excuse for me to avoid it, but I still can't help not wanting to go."

Miss Harriet's eyes softened and she gave Katherine an understanding smile.

"I know, Dearie. It's hard to do the right thing sometimes. It's even harder when the right thing is the one thing you would like the very least of all to do. Come on, let's put the kettle on and get some tea in you; then we can chat."

"What about the decorations?"

"Tea first. Then decorating. Mr. James won't mind if we're still finishing up when he comes, and you know there's no one else in town who would venture in so early."

The two finished the preliminary straightening and made everything tidy, apart from the overflowing box on the floor. Just as they finished making the shop ready for its first customer's arrival, the kettle began to sing. They sat down at one of the tables and sipped their tea. Katherine, curled up in the straight-backed chair, began to look a little less tired as she drank her tea, and soon her employer broke the silence.

"Katherine, what do you think makes you so dislike seeing your parents?"

Katherine sat, blowing gently over her tea, pondering the question. She answered slowly, "I think... I think it's because... I just...never quite feel welcome now. They were actually pretty good parents, and I know that I probably don't have any real right to complain, but that doesn't make me *feel* any better."

Katherine set her cup gently on its saucer and continued as Miss Harriet poured her some more tea. "I suppose it might be as much because of my own attitude than anything else. I just don't seem to feel like there's room for me. Not just in their home, although that's a fact, but in their lives, somehow. It's painful to feel like that, like I don't *matter* anymore."

"And what do you think would make you feel you do matter?"

"I don't know. I think that's part of the problem. I don't even know where to begin."

Miss Harriet took a sip of tea and looked thoughtfully out the window. Then she turned back to Katherine and said, "When I was a child, there was one day when a classmate got mad at me at recess and said something mean—something *very* mean—about Papa." She set down her cup, and Katherine leaned forward with a face full of sympathy.

"I was devastated, and it was all I could do to hold myself together until school was finished. I ran home and sobbed it all out to Mother when she got home from work. What my classmate had said hurt, and it had dredged up all the hurt of Papa's leaving all over again. I felt abandoned by Papa, rejected by him and by my classmate. That was the first time the full weight of it really hit me.

"Mother, as usual, let me cry myself out, and then gave me one of her gentle little talks. She told me that it didn't matter that Papa had left us—at least, that it didn't *have* to matter. I was shocked, and thought, *That can't be right,* but she took me to a verse in Psalms that said, 'When my father and mother forsake me, then the Lord shall take me up.'

"She explained that the only thing that *needed* to matter was that God loved me with a love that could never end. He had promised never to leave me, never to forsake me. She told me that even if everyone on earth abandoned me, God's love was big enough and strong enough to satisfy my heart. I listened, for I knew it was true; I had seen her live it out ever since Papa left."

Katherine's eyes glistened with tears, and Miss Harriet squeezed her hand and gently asked, "Could it be, dear Katherine, that what you're looking for from your parents may be something God is wanting to give you *Himself*? Could you make mattering to God what fills your heart?"

Katherine silently shrugged, unable to speak. The bell over the door jingled merrily and Miss Harriet stood to greet Mr. James. Then, leaning towards Katherine, she said softly,

"You just finish your tea, and we'll put the decorations up when you're ready." She gave Katherine another gentle smile, then hurried off.

Katherine sat for a while, thinking, trying to process what Miss Harriet had said. After a while, she got up, went upstairs to freshen up and remove the traces of the tears that had spilled out of her brimming eyes. Taking a deep breath, she came back down to the tearoom, ready to help Miss Harriet disperse the contents of her box.

The two did get the decorations up before anyone else arrived, much to the amusement of Mr. James, who watched them from his table in the corner. Katherine was surprised what a difference was made by just a few garlands and a scattering of orange and red throughout the room. It still looked like Miss Harriet's, but it now looked festive and cozy and fit seamlessly with the quickly changing autumn foliage dotted here and there throughout the downtown blocks.

Katherine hopped nimbly off one chair as Miss Harriet stepped gracefully down from another, having just put the last touches to the garland over the windows opposite the counter. The brilliant white of the lace curtains (which were always kept closed on those windows to hide the unromantic and very unlovely alleyway on that side of the building) made the bright leaves and flowers seem even brighter and cheerier, and gave a sense of completeness to the room.

Mr. James, perceiving that the decorators' efforts were now finished, applauded loudly from his table, proclaiming,

"Well done, ladies. It looks very autumnal. In fact, it looks fit for a celebration. You should throw a party."

"And so I shall, Mr. James." declared Miss Harriet, turning to face him, "and, if you please, I shall rely on you to help with it."

The reporter looked intrigued and answered politely, "Of course! And when shall this celebration take place?"

"On the fifth of November, of course!" Light dawned in the reporter's eyes.

"November fifth? What is there to celebrate on November fifth?" Katherine asked with a puzzled frown.

Miss Harriet flung out an arm and declared intensely, her eyes large and her voice dripping with uncharacteristic drama, "Gunpowder, treason, and plot!"

Katherine looked even more puzzled.

Mr. James chuckled and explained "Guy Fawkes day. It's an English holiday and usually includes something delicious to eat, if I remember correctly."

He concluded with a wink at Katherine, then turned back to Miss Harriet. "And what part can a humble reporter play in such a dramatic celebration?"

"Well," began Miss Harriet, returning to her normal down-to-earth self, "I want to do a *real* Guy Fawkes' celebration, and at home, we always had someone read the poem—you know, the one that begins 'Please to remember the fifth of November.'"

"I've heard of it." Mr. James replied, nodding.

"Well, I was wondering if you would be willing to be my reader? I don't have a dramatic enough voice to do it justice, and I don't want it to seem like just a publicity stunt for the shop. I think it would feel more like a *community* event if I weren't the only one up in front of everyone."

Mr. James made a show of checking his calendar, then looked up with a grin. "I suppose I could squeeze it in."

"Oh, I *am* glad!" cried Miss Harriet.

"It sounds like it will be quite the occasion! Do let me know if there's anything else I can do to help."

Miss Harriet smiled broadly. "I surely will!"

12

Harborside by Lamplight

The unusual warmth and sunshine of September shifted almost on the dot with the arrival of October. The puffy, white clouds which had drifted through the bright blue skies of September were suddenly replaced by a flat grey expanse, from which a light drizzle perpetually seemed to fall.

Katherine hummed softly as she dusted the jars, enjoying the cozy light from the large Victorian oil lamp which hung from the ceiling near the window. Another large oil lamp stood on the counter, and a third on a bookcase in the "Captain's quarters," as Katherine like to call the office room. Outside, the light—already gloomy to begin with—was fading, and the lamps, though they gave off a surprising amount of light, were beginning to lose their battle with the dusk which slowly crept in from the darkening pane of the storefront window.

Captain Braddock came in and set his ledger on the counter.

"Looks like it's about time to switch the lights on" he said, reaching behind the stiff sails of a model ship, strategically placed to hide the small black button-type light switches. Instantly, the room was filled with a rosy glow, as the round globes on the wall blinked to life. They were hung atop ornate brackets and had frosted glass shades that were white, but faded into pink towards the top.

Katherine turned from the shelves to admire the lights. "It's like a timeline of lighting in here."

The captain chuckled. "Why, I suppose it is."

He gazed at the light fixtures as Katherine asked, "Those lights on the wall. Aren't they old gas lights?"

"Yes, they are. You know yer lighting, Missie. And I suppose you can tell me just what kind of oil lamps we have?"

Katherine looked them over for a moment, then answered, "Are they Aladdin lamps?"

The captain seemed impressed. "Ah, but I'll wager you don't know what kind of lamp that is on top of my desk in the office."

Katherine looked at the captain, her eyes alight as she took his challenge and went into the office. She examined the lamp carefully, then turned to the captain with a half-smile and a humble shrug. "Nope. You've got me stumped."

The captain smiled, pleased that Katherine had admitted her defeat graciously. "Well, now, I don't suppose you've run across one like it before. It's a French pigeon lamp. It burned gasoline, but since that's not very safe, my father had it wired for electricity. It was originally billed as a 'non-exploding' lamp, which I suppose means that there had been a problem with some gasoline lamps exploding."

Katherine inspected the lamp more closely. "I never knew there was such a thing as a gasoline lamp. How fascinating!"

"The gas lights in the shop were put in during the time of the brick construction. They were the latest thing, you see. The Braddocks of the time, let me see... Edward, it was. Edward Braddock and his wife Helen. Well, they were an odd pair. He wanted everything new and fashionable, and she wanted it all to stay the same. She was great friends with her mother-in-law, you see, who of course was quite old by then.

"Helen wanted to honor her husband's parents by keeping things the same, and he wanted to honor them by demolishing it all and rebuilding bigger and better, from the ground up, a towering legacy in Victorian brick.

"Well, the Braddock siblings—I think there were three after Edward—they all got together with Helen and decided on a plan. They would keep the shop the same and build the brick around it. They had an architect draw up the plans and everything. But Edward was a stubborn fellow and wouldn't go along with it. The Harborside was his, he said, and he would do as he saw fit. But then, his wife grew ill—gravely so, and Edward promised to keep the original building, for she made it her dying wish.

"It was said that the gas lights were some she had picked out for her sitting room in the home he had built for her up on the cliffs, and that he installed them, saying then it was like a part of her lived on in the Harborside. Personally, I agree with the siblings' account of it, which was that he just wanted the place brought up-to-date, and used Helen's having picked the lamps out as a sneaky excuse to put them in."

"And did Helen never see them?"

"No. She died the day before the work was to begin."

"How sad."

"Yes, Helen was a great favorite of all who knew her. She was the only one who could have saved the Harborside, and it took her dyin' to do it." The captain stood, gazing at the lamps, lost in thought. Katherine finally broke the silence with another question.

"And when were the lamps converted to electricity?" The captain smiled.

"That was a ruckus of a different kind. Edward, you see, never had any children, and when he died, the shop was left to his nephew Albert. Well, Albert had a wife, stylish, they say, and wanted everything fancy. When she heard her husband had inherited the shop, *she* was all in favor of selling it off and buying something grand with the proceeds.

"Now, Albert never had been one to put his foot down when it came to his wife, but the rest of the clan kicked up a fuss. He'd all sorts of Braddocks to deal with by now: one sister and her grown children, a younger brother and his children, also grown, and several of Albert's own grown children and grandchildren and great-nieces and nephews who all had been brought up at the Harborside, so to speak. It was really a *family* business, with everyone in and out all the time— except that Albert only came rarely and his wife Lucy had never been here at all.

"Somehow, he convinced her to at least see the place. One

of the youngsters later wrote in a diary about her visit. He said they drove up to the door, and he handed her out of the motorcar (which was itself quite new and fashionable at the time). She was dressed in all sorts of finery, with a big hat on her head and as much sparkle as she could find space for on her fingers and around her neck. She was quite a sight. She stepped into the shop, held her skirts to her and sneered at everyone and everything she saw. She took a particular dislike to the gas globes, saying they were dreadfully old-fashioned and outdated. She went on and on about how gas fittings were soon to be a thing of the past and how electricity was the new mode of lighting for "civilized" people.

"Albert eventually scraped together enough of a spine to stand up to his wife. He told her that he would not sell the Harborside, and that was that. Apparently she could tell this was one battle she wasn't going to win, but by way of a parting shot, promised to say no more about it if only he would do something about those 'horrid gas lights.' So, he did. But much to his wife's chagrin, what he did about them was have them converted to electricity.

"She pouted about that for some time, for not only had she *not* succeeded in getting rid of what by now had become a symbol of Helen Braddock and her love for the Harborside, she had actually succeeded in bringing the Harborside more up to date than her own house, for Albert didn't have electricity installed there for a good ten years after."

"I wonder whatever could have made her so horrid." Pondered Katherine, gazing dreamily off into the darkness beyond the windows. Then she looked up at the captain, her curiosity freshly kindled by a new thought. "Were her children just as awful when it came time for *them* to inherit the Harborside?" The captain grinned and shook his head.

"No, if they'd all been as bad as her, there wouldn't *be* a Harborside anymore, now would there?" Then, with a glance at the clock, he assumed a veneer of his old gruffness, saying, "But that's enough yarnin' for now. It's time I was locking up and you was gettin' home for yer supper. I won't have that stubborn Englishwoman accusin' me of keepin' you past yer hours."

Katherine smiled and took off her apron, sad to be leaving, but glad at the prospect of more Harborside generations to explore another day.

13

The Captain's Idea

The next day, Katherine bustled into the Harborside to collect Miss Harriet's order.

It must have been a slow day, Katherine thought to herself as the Captain hurried in from the other room.

"Oh, it's you... Hello, Katherine. I thought a customer had come in." Katherine, not a bit offended at this odd statement, bantered back cheerfully,

"That's because today I *am* a customer. At least, I represent one. Here's Miss Harriet's order." And with that she handed one of the papers in her hand to the Captain, who looked it over with a grunt, before turning to walk towards the large sea chest. He began almost mechanically taking boxes out and placing them into a bag which Katherine had fetched from behind the counter. He didn't seem to be quite as open or friendly as he had the day before, but Katherine figured he must have something on his mind. She decided to try to snap him out of it.

"Captain," she asked as he put the last box in the bag and stood creakily up from the floor where he'd been kneeling.

"Yes'm?"

"Did you hear that Miss Harriet is throwing a party?"

"No. Whyever would I have heard that?"

"Because you're invited! The whole town is. It's to celebrate Guy Fawkes day." She put on her brightest smile and handed the captain a flyer.

"The whole town, indeed!" muttered the captain, with a dismissive glance at the paper. "And isn't Guy Fawkes the man who tried to blow up the government over there in England? Why is she throwing *him* a party?"

Katherine tried to face the captain's bluster undaunted. "She isn't throwing *him* a party at all. Guy Fawkes day is the day they celebrate the fact that he was caught and *didn't* get to blow up parliament." The captain grunted again and shook his head.

"Won't you please come! It sounds like it'll be so much fun, and there will be good food, and everyone will be there." Katherine stopped, judging by the set of the captain's jaw that she had been as unsuccessful as Mr. Fawkes.

"I thank you, but I've my own good food and company to enjoy. I don't need to be goin' off to that woman's shop for a party, 'specially if the whole town's gonna be there. And aren't American holidays good enough for her? After all, she does live *here* now. I'll bet she won't be throwing the town a Thanksgiving feast, now will she?"

"Why, Captain, that's the *best* idea I've heard all day! I've just got to go tell Miss Harriet!" Off Katherine went out the door, remembering just as she reached the doorstep that she hadn't picked up the bag of tea, and quickly wheeled around to take the well-packed sack from the bewildered captain. Then, she ran down the street, towards Miss Harriet's.

When she neared the shop, she slowed down and walked the last little bit, so she wouldn't be so out of breath when she arrived. She knew Miss Harriet didn't like her to burst in the door as she was prone to do. Self-control and gracious composure were paramount. Katherine had even been trying to learn to move about between the tables quietly and gracefully as her employer did.

Once she had herself sufficiently under control, she walked in, smiling happily at the customers as she walked back towards the kitchen.

"Oh, Miss Harriet, I've had the most *wonderful* idea!" Katherine exclaimed in a whisper as she joined her employer behind the counter after depositing her sack in the kitchen.

Miss Harriet looked at her, all pleasant surprise and curiosity. Then with a quick glance round the tables and down at her watch, she leaned over and whispered,

"I can't wait to hear it, Dearie, but it's only a half hour till closing, and as you can see, we've quite a few tables filled; may I suggest that we can make it the topic of our dishwashing discussion tonight?"

Katherine grinned and nodded, then whisked away to take the orders of customers at three newly-filled tables.

Finally, the customers had gone, the tables had been cleared, and what little food was left over had been put away. Miss Harriet changed her light floral apron for a plastic one (which was just as floral) and began to fill the sink, while Katherine stacked the dirty dishes on the counter next to her.

"Well, now. What's this grand idea you've had?" asked Miss Harriet, swirling the hot water to distribute the soap.

"It was Captain Braddock's idea, really." Katherine began eagerly.

"Captain Braddock's? And what kind of idea might he have had that got you bursting with excitement? He hasn't stolen you away from me completely, now, has he?" Miss Harriet interjected with mock sternness, shaking a sudsy finger at Katherine.

"No, nothing like that. He didn't realize he'd had the idea, and he was actually being quite rude at the time. By the way," Katherine said in an aside, "he won't be attending your Guy Fawkes Day party."

Miss Harriet did not look surprised at this revelation, and Katherine continued, thinking it wise to overlook the details of the captain's tirade.

"Anyway, he said something about Thanksgiving, and I thought, since I'm going to be with my parents, and I just can't *bear* to think you'll be alone with just Whiskers to keep you company, why don't you have Thanksgiving dinner with the town?"

Miss Harriet looked both intrigued and puzzled.

"But, my dear, won't 'the town' be having Thanksgiving with their own families?"

"Not the whole town. There must be people with nowhere to go and no one to visit. Think of poor Mrs. Penelope, for example. You yourself said that she never sees her children. Wouldn't it be nice for her to have somewhere to go for

Thanksgiving dinner?" Miss Harriet rinsed a teacup thoughtfully, then looked up at Katherine with a growing smile.

"I do believe that old grouch *has* had a good idea, after all!
I had never thought of throwing the shop's doors open to the
'lone and forgotten' like myself. I like the idea exceedingly.
But how shall we feed them all? I've never cooked a Thanks-
giving meal, and you'll be away, so I won't have any help."
Katherine had been thinking of this.

"You could ask Mr. James to help you. He's been so happy
to help you with Guy Fawkes' Day, and I don't think he has
any family to go visit. And you could ask people to bring
food, like a potluck. That way everyone gets their favorite
Thanksgiving dish, and you only have to cook a little!" Miss
Harriet handed a saucer to Katherine, then stopped, thinking
it over.

"Katherine, dear, I *knew* you'd be good for this place! I'll
do it. I really will! I'll talk with Mr. James about it first thing
in the morning."

* * * *

Katherine went to bed that night with a happy heart. She
had become somewhat resigned to visiting her parents but
had been bothered by the thought of leaving Miss Harriet
alone, even though Thanksgiving was not a holiday that
meant much to an Englishwoman. It would be good to be
able to leave for her parents' place with the knowledge that
Miss Harriet would be well looked after.

She knew that Miss Harriet enjoyed serving people more
than anything and that Mr. James would make sure it all ran

smoothly. Besides, it would be good to have something to look forward to hearing about after her trip. She nestled her head into her pillow with a satisfied sigh.

Now, she thought, *If I could just figure the Captain out.*

* * * *

The next morning was Saturday, and Katherine awoke later than usual, since it was her day off. Hearing voices down in the shop, she quietly peeked out her door and saw Miss Harriet standing near Mr. James' table, and both of them talking excitedly. She knew they must be discussing Thanksgiving. Unable to resist, she quickly got dressed and went downstairs.

"Good morning, Miss Katherine!" Mr. James cheerfully exclaimed as she approached the table.

"Ah, yes. Good morning Dearie!" Miss Harriet said, turning around to greet her.

"Good morning! You two look like you're in full planning mode."

"Yes, Miss Harriet was just telling me about your very excellent idea for a Thanksgiving town-wide feast. I think it will be just the thing, because so many of our people stay here and don't have anyone to share the holiday with. Statistically speaking, it's far more likely that people will stay home at Thanksgiving, to save their funds for a Christmas visit to family that live far away."

"How interesting! And—" Just then the kettle began singing from the kitchen, but Katherine was already halfway to the kitchen before Miss Harriet had turned around.

"I'll get it, Miss Harriet." Katherine called over her shoulder.

When she returned, she had a larger pot of tea than Mr. James usually ordered, and there were two cups and saucers on the tray.

"I figured since this is an official chat, you should join Mr. James in a cup of tea, so he can be spared the dilemma of whether to be impolite and drink his tea in front of you, or whether to suffer through a cup of cold tea after you're done."

Miss Harriet began to protest, but one look at Katherine was enough to tell that her protestations would be in vain. "Well... as long as Mr. James doesn't mind..."

Mr. James stood and pulled out a chair for her. "Not at all. In fact, I was just considering asking you to join me, and Katherine has just very graciously removed my only scruple. Of course, I couldn't monopolize your time while you were the only hand on deck, so to speak, but now that Katherine's arrived, we can take our time and discuss our plans thoroughly."

Miss Harriet sat down graciously, then popped up again with the exclamation, "Oh, but Katherine, it's your day off! I couldn't ask you to—"

"You're not asking. I'm volunteering. This is *exactly* how I want to spend my morning, so just sit down and relax. I'll take over until your conference is finished." And with that, Katherine whisked back into the kitchen to attend to some scones which were just beginning to fill the shop with the wonderful aroma of being just about cooked.

Thank goodness she had the baking in already! thought Katherine. She had not yet mastered the art of baking and was heartily glad not to have to try her skill this morning. She peeked around the curtain in the kitchen doorway as the two at the table erupted into hearty laughter.

Katherine smiled. It was nice to see Miss Harriet enjoying herself. She spent so much time thinking and doing things for others, Katherine considered it a treat even to do something little for her.

* * * *

That evening, Katherine joined Miss Harriet in the kitchen. She tied on an apron and picked up a dishcloth as Miss Harriet looked up with a pleased smile.

"Well, now! Here you are, working again on your day off. I should start paying you to work Saturdays as well!"

Katherine smiled and reached for a saucer. "Nonsense! I wanted you to have a chance to relax and talk over details with Mr. James."

"Aren't you a dear!" Miss Harriet said, handing Katherine a plate to dry. The two chatted about the day, then fell into a companionable quiet.

After a while, Katherine hesitantly asked, "Miss Harriet, forgive me if this is too personal a question, but...why did you never marry?"

Miss Harriet handed her a teacup and kept washing as she replied, "For the simple reason that I never loved, not really anyway. There was a young man once, and we did talk of marrying, but I wanted from love what I expect all young girls want: to be looked after, adored, to have my own needs and wants considered as the most important thing in the world. He wanted the same thing, however, and when two selfish beings try to impose their will on each other, it never goes well. So...we parted."

"How sad." Katherine looked at Miss Harriet in sympathy. Miss Harriet looked up at Katherine and smiled.

"Sadder if we hadn't," she replied. "I needed to learn what love is, and so did he."

"But," Katherine looked puzzled, "Isn't love just something you instinctively *know*? I mean, something you feel."

"Ah, well, that *is* the prevailing opinion nowadays, but feelings are only a part of it: they ebb and flow, while true love chooses to behave the same, even when feelings are changeful. It chooses to put the other first, even when doing so runs contrary to its own inclinations or interests. That's why my chap and I parted, because neither of us were willing to give up our own selfish wants and wishes in order to put the other's first."

"I hadn't ever thought about it that way."

"Well, I suppose I hadn't, either, until one day, I was reading in the Bible about how God is love. Then I read another passage that listed qualities of love. You see, the Bible says that love doesn't seek its own, doesn't boast, isn't prideful. It keeps no record of wrongs; it is longsuffering and kind. That was all missing from the love I thought I had in my heart. That love was all about *me*; true love is all about the loved one."

"That's a pretty tall order."

"Yes, it is." Miss Harriet wiped a plate and rinsed it before continuing, "Katherine, the real test of love is sacrifice. Just as Christ Jesus died on the cross to pay for my sin and yours even though He could have just let us die in our sins and go to hell, He expects *us* to love one another with that same kind of love with which He loves us. Of course, that applies to any relationship, but most especially to marriage. That willingness to sacrifice daily, constantly, with no end in sight, in order to achieve the happiness or comfort of the one you love: that is what makes a marriage work. The emotions are wonderful, but I've seen far too many friends and relations base their marriages on feelings, only to have them fall apart when the feelings falter."

Miss Harriet dried her hands on her apron and turned to Katherine, looking earnestly into her eyes. She took both Katherine's hands in hers, saying soberly, "Your young man will come; I feel certain of it. But promise me one thing, Dearie: when he does, don't let impatience or a rush of emotion blind you to what true love is. Let the love of Christ be what defines your love for others. *That* will be a love that stands the test of time." Miss Harriet squeezed Katherine's hands once more before dropping them and continuing to wash the last few dishes.

Katherine worked on, surveying the remarkable lady next to her, so confident, happy, and full of joy. She seemed utterly and completely happy, and not the least bit dissatisfied with the life she led. The more Katherine learned about Miss Harriet, the more she wanted to be like her; to be at peace with the past, the present, and the future.

That night, Katherine lay awake, thinking over what Miss Harriet had said. Moonlight streamed through the little window above her bed as the moon began to rise over the trees on the Cliffs. Finally, she got up and knelt on the floor in the pale light and began to pray.

Lord... make me like Miss Harriet. Show me how to begin to have the peace she has.

As she sat still on her knees in the quiet, a verse came to mind—the same verse that had been tugging at her heart ever since the day she had heard her pastor read it:

"Ask for the old paths, where is the good way, and walk therein, and ye shall find rest for your souls."

...Oh, Lord, she prayed, *help me to find the old paths that will give me rest for my soul."*

14

A Blustery Day

"Oh, Katherine, I have something for you," said Miss Harriet as Katherine hurried down the stairs. "I know you're on your way to the Harborside, but this won't take but a moment."

Katherine wound her scarf around her neck as Miss Harriet hurried into the kitchen and returned with a book in her hand.

"I ran across this on my shelves last night and thought you might enjoy reading about Guy Fawkes. Then you'll be able to *fully* appreciate our celebration."

Katherine took the old volume and ran her hands over the embossed gold decoration on its worn fabric cover. Then she turned it and read the title aloud from the spine:

"*A Child's History of England*, by Dickens... Charles Dickens?" she asked looking up at Miss Harriet inquisitively.

"Yes. That's what made me think of you. I remembered that

you had enjoyed *Bleak House* so much and thought you might enjoy Dickens' narrative of the Gunpowder Plot as well. I've marked it for you, but in case the bookmark falls out, it starts on page 328."

"Thank you, Miss Harriet! I can't wait to read it!" Katherine had already opened the cover and was scanning the table of contents.

Miss Harriet chuckled, gently pushing Katherine towards the door.

"Now, don't you go reading it on the way to work. I'll never hear the end of it if Captain Braddock thinks I've made you late!"

Katherine reluctantly stowed the book in her bag and started off down the street. The wind blustered in off the harbor, ambushing Katherine as she crossed the spaces between buildings. It lashed her hair around her face and her skirt around her ankles as she hurried across the street.

No leisurely walk home along the wharf tonight, she thought, holding tightly to her scarf as the wind tried to blow it away. She was glad to reach the Harborside block and have a little relief from the biting cold of the wind. Stepping into the doorway she saw the Captain hunched over on a little three-legged stool in front of the old wood stove.

"Good morning Captain!" she said cheerily. Without looking up, he replied,

"Good mornin', Missy," and continued to stare into the stove, blowing gently now and then and adding kindling.

Katherine had never seen the wood stove in action. The fall had been so mild that until this morning, she hadn't even thought about how the old part of the shop would be kept warm in the winter. She took off her coat and scarf and smoothed her hair, using her reflection in the shop window as a mirror. Then she quietly slipped on her apron and stepped behind the counter to get a clean dust rag.

Usually, several rags sat in a neatly folded stack on one of the shelves. Not seeing any there, she straightened with a question at her lips, but seeing the captain so engrossed in tending the fire, she abruptly disappeared behind the counter again. This was her chance to "snoop" without snooping.

She quickly surveyed the rows of drawers next to the shelves, wondering which to open. She knew she might only have one chance before the Captain asked what she was doing. She looked at the drawer which had held the candy.

No, I know what's in that one, and he does open it sometimes, so I might get to look in it another time.

Finally, she decided to open the drawer directly below it. To her disappointment, she only found a ball of string and some scissors. Emboldened by her attempt, however, she pulled on the next drawer down.

It stuck, and the faint thud caused the captain to look up from his task with a gruff, "What're you looking for back there?"

Katherine quickly jumped to her feet, trying not to look as if she were up to anything. "I needed a rag, and didn't see any on the shelf," she said, inwardly cringing at her half-truth.

"Oh, yes, I forgot to put the clean ones out. I'll get one for you." And with that, he disappeared into his office and returned with two rags, carefully folded. He handed them to Katherine, who put the extra one in its place on the shelf. "And next time you need something, you can ask me, instead of rummaging around in drawers." The captain had a note of warning in his voice, and Katherine could tell he had seen through her excuse.

"Yes, sir. I'm sorry. I know I should have just asked."

Captain Braddock seemed taken aback by such a prompt and open apology and, not knowing just what to do with it, turned back towards the stove with a confused, "Yes, well... about yer work, then."

Katherine quickly began dusting the jars. Now and then she looked over at the Captain, still bent over the stove. Finally, she asked, "Captain, does that stove heat the whole building?"

"Nope. Just the old bit. The rest had radiators put in with the brick. They don't work very well, but the rest of the building doesn't need to be as closely looked after as the shop does."

"Is that because it's old?" asked Katherine, looking at the walls and trying to remember any facts she might have read about preserving old buildings.

The captain shut the door of the stove and stood up with a groan. He held his back and peered at an old thermometer on the wall before answering.

"Not really, although I guess it might be a good thing for the wood to be kept from extremes. It's because of the tea. You see, if tea gets too hot or too cold, its flavor will be damaged, and then the tea's no good. It has to be kept at a constant temperature."

He looked to the thermometer again, then, as if something had just occurred to him, he turned and beckoned her over. Pointing at the thermometer, he said, "If you ever see the mercury above 77 or below 68, you just shout for me right away."

Katherine nodded solemnly, feeling as if she had been given a grave responsibility.

"But what if you're not here?" she asked, thinking of how Captain Braddock would often leave her to mind the shop while he went on errands.

Considering, he rubbed his chin and finally replied, "I suppose it would be good for you to learn how to tend the stove...but you're not to go messin' with it without permission, you hear?"

Katherine did hear—and what was more, she silently resolved to heed this order more faithfully than she had his earlier prohibition of "snooping".

He opened the door and let her peek in so she could see what a proper fire looked like. Then, he laid out kindling on the floor and showed her the process of building the fire.

"How do you know how much wood it will take to keep it up to temperature?" Katherine asked.

The captain scratched his head. "Well, you kinda just know. It comes with doin', I suppose. Tell you what, I'll have you help me whenever the fire needs tending today, and tomorrow when you come for that woman's order, you can peek in and tell me what you think it needs. Then I'll know how much yer soakin' in of what I've told you."

Katherine liked that idea. Once the fire had been set in order, she went back to dusting. Her hands moved deftly, though carefully, as she picked up the jars and knick-knacks. She was just itching to get to the book Miss Harriet had loaned her, and that shabby little chair by the stove beckoned, being just the place to sit and read on a dark, blustery November day.

She wondered if the captain would let her read while she watched the door if her work was done.

I guess I'll never know if I never ask.

She still felt awkward and nervous whenever she had to ask the captain anything. She told herself she felt that way because she had been enjoying her time at the Harborside so much, and didn't want to do anything that might jeopardize her position there.

But whenever she dared to take an honest look into her heart, she saw (but did not yet have the courage to admit—even to herself) that she enjoyed her time at the Harborside largely because of the time she got to spend with the captain. He had begun to be more open with her, and above all, she feared offending him and causing him to close up again.

Unbeknownst to Captain Braddock, he had become an important part of Katherine's life, just as Miss Harriet had. Somehow, with all his gruffness, he had found his way into Katherine's heart, and she often found herself wondering if he was at all like the grandpa she had never known.

What the captain did know, was that he liked having this bright young girl around the shop. She did her work well, and that was a help, for sure, but he had to admit it was nice to have someone to teach things to, who would listen so attentively to his stories.

The captain's experience with children had not been extensive, and he had never known the joy of having a youngster around the shop, since he and his sister had been the last of the Braddock children. Seeing Katherine there reminded him of his own childhood, and, if he had known what to call it, he would have admitted to feeling a fatherly sort of delight in being listened to and respected by such a smart, capable young girl. (For "young girl" she was to the captain, who thought of her as being yet a child, even though she was in her twenties.)

Pushing aside her nerves, Katherine finished dusting the last shelf, blew the dust off the sails of one more model ship, and laid the dust cloth in its place. She walked up to the captain's desk, where he was poring over an inventory sheet.

Clearing her throat so she wouldn't surprise him, she began tentatively, "I've finished the dusting, and there are no packages to sort today. All the jars seem to be topped up as well, so I wondered... while I watch the shop, can I read?"

As she spoke, she searched the captain's face for an answer. Unable to tell what he was thinking, she rattled on. "Of course, I'll be careful to pay attention, and I'll put the book down the instant anyone comes in—"

The captain smiled, and Katherine breathed a sigh of relief as he answered, "Of course. In fact, I often read while watching the shop. So long as yer work's caught up, and there's nothing more important to do. Why don't you sit by the stove? There's a chair there that's pretty comfy, and there's a light right overhead, so you won't hurt yer eyes."

Katherine took a deep breath feeling she had confronted a dragon in its lair, and found it instead to be a lamb.

"Oh, *thank you!*" she said delightedly, "I had been hoping you would let me sit there. It does seem like just the right place to read, and I have a book I brought today that I'm just dying to get to!" The captain chuckled as she hurried out into the shop and fetched the old volume of Dickens out of her bag. Then, he turned back to his work.

Silence reigned over the little shop while the wind blew outside, rattling the windows in the captain's office and whirling the fallen leaves down the street. Katherine finished the passage about the Gunpowder Plot, and, remembering her newly-bestowed responsibility, she checked the thermometer before curling up in the chair again and turning back to the beginning of the book.

A little while later, the captain came in to check the fire. Katherine laid her book on the little table with a contented sigh and leaned forward to watch what the captain was doing. He poked at the fire, expertly gathering the coals together and adding another small log on top. He looked up at Katherine.

"Well, is it as good as you expected?" he asked, nodding towards the book.

"Oh, yes. It's very interesting. It's a history book by Charles Dickens."

"Oh, and what part of history are you reading about?"

Katherine began to explain to him about Guy Fawkes and his plan to blow up the parliament building with the government and the king inside. He listened with interest, then gave the fire one last prod before closing the stove door and standing up.

"That does sound like an interesting plan. It's probably good he didn't get away with it," he said, moving towards his office again. Stopping in the doorway, he turned and said thoughtfully, "I can see why they celebrate. It's not quite like our Independence Day, but I can see why they made it a holiday." He went back to his desk, leaving Katherine to pick up her book, secretly feeling she had made some progress with the captain.

15

Guy Fawkes Day at the Harborside

November 5th dawned as grey and drizzly as ever, but Katherine woke with sunshine in her heart. She had been looking forward to this day ever since Miss Harriet had mentioned her idea of throwing the town a Guy Fawkes Day celebration.

When she had gone to bed the night before, Miss Harriet still bustled energetically about in the kitchen, trying to work quietly. Sitting up and stretching, Katherine wondered if Miss Harriet had gotten any rest.

By the time Katherine was dressed, she had already begun to hear the comforting sounds of someone working in the kitchen. As she pulled her sweater off a hanger and grabbed her shoes, she noticed a delicious aroma beginning to waft through the front door of the little apartment.

A little thrill ran through her heart when she thought about the evening and helping to host a whole town—but there was no time for daydreaming, she reminded herself, because today was Thursday, and she needed to get off to the Harborside. She picked up her coat and scarf from the chair she had dropped them on the night before and opened the door.

The dark drizzle of the outside world made the cozily lit interior of the shop seem to glow with color. Miss Harriet had brought in fresh bunches of leafy branches to add to the orange and yellow chrysanthemums on the tables, and air was filled with such a delicious mixture of baking smells, Katherine couldn't resist popping into the kitchen on her way by, secretly hoping for something to snack on as she walked.

"Good morning, Dearie!" Miss Harriet said, cheerful as ever, though, from the looks of all the baked goods cooling on racks around the kitchen, Katherine was sure her employer had not slept much, if at all.

"Good morning!" Katherine replied. "You've sure been busy! I should have stayed up longer to help you."

Miss Harriet shook her head with a smile and bustled over to the oven to put in another tray of what looked like some sort of brown cake. "Nonsense. I knew you would need your rest, especially since you're working all day and then helping with the party in the evening. You're bound to be exhausted by the end. I'm glad you got your rest."

"But you're working all day and then *running* the party, and I'm sure you hardly rested at all!"

"Ah, but *I'm* not working with Captain Braddock all day, now, am I?" she winked at Katherine as she closed the oven door and set the timer. "Now, I know you're just off, but how about something to take along with you?"

Katherine's eyes lit up. "Oh, yes please!"

Miss Harriet cut a big slice of one of the brown cakes cooling on the counter and deftly wrapped it in a napkin. She handed it to Katherine. "It's still piping hot, mind, so give it about half a block before you try to eat it."

"Thank you, Miss Harriet! What is it?"

"Parkin. It's a treacle cake we used to only have on Guy Fawkes Day."

"It smells delicious." Said Katherine, then looking around at all the sheet pans full of cake, remarked, "Looks like you'll have enough for the whole town!"

Miss Harriet laughed. "Almost. I've one or two batches left to whip up, and I should finish just in time to get Mr. James his morning tea. He's coming early to put up some fairy lights before we open."

Just then there was a rap at the door.

"I'll let him in on my way out. Thank you for the cake!" Katherine buttoned her jacket with one hand, while holding the slice of cake in her other as she hurried towards the door. Mr. James was waiting outside, a roll of lights under his arm and a hand on his hat to keep the wind from blowing it away. Katherine unlocked the door and let him in.

"Good morning, Katherine. Is your illustrious employer around?"

Katherine grinned. "Try the kitchen. She's been in there baking for at least an hour already."

Mr. James held the door open for Katherine and noticed the napkin-wrapped bundle in her hand. "I see she's favored you with a sample! I might try my hand at procuring one of my own before I begin."

Katherine waved goodbye and walked briskly through the whirling leaves that played around her ankles. Her long coat was instantly covered with tiny droplets of rain, and she pulled her scarf up around her head as she walked. She always thought this made her look like an old grandmother from a fairy tale, but it did keep her ears warm when she forgot to wear a hat.

About halfway down the block, she unwrapped a corner of the steaming cake and broke off a chunk. As the took her first bite of the moist, springy morsel, she reveled in the warm comfort of ginger and spices. It seemed like the perfect thing to eat in November. She was glad of the napkin, for it was a bit sticky to eat.

She broke off another bite and looked down at the last chunk of cake in her hand, contemplating whether to save it for the captain. Deciding that he probably wouldn't eat it, she finished it off as she stepped onto the sidewalk at the beginning of the Harborside block.

"Good morning!" Katherine cheerily called out as she walked in the door. The fire in the stove had already been lit, and the room was cozy with the electric globes shining and both oil lamps lit.

Katherine traded her jacket and scarf for the stiff canvas apron and walked into the office. Grabbing the clipboard from the nail on the wall, she looked around the empty office and began to wonder where the captain could be.

She heard a noise in the shop, and walked in, expecting to see a customer at the door, but instead, she saw the captain coming down the last few steps of the spiral staircase in the corner. Her eyes alight with curiosity, she was about to ask the captain about the staircase when the bell over the door really *did* ring and in bounced little Tommy, in a balloon-like green jacket which was several sizes too big and obviously brand new.

Captain Braddock sent her a glance that said, *don't ask,* and then turned to Tommy with the usual mock-gravity in his voice.

"Well, then. Who might you be?"

Tommy giggled and pulled down the zipper, releasing the collar which had been zipped up till it nearly reached his eyes. "It's me, Cap'n!" he said with the best salute he could muster with so much fluff about his person.

The Captain chuckled in spite of himself and said, "I thought it must have been a grownup, in such a fine coat."

"It's new!" said Tommy proudly.

"I can see that."

"Mom bought it for me yesterday at the store. It was on sale. She said it'll fit me for two whole years!"

Katherine and the captain both stifled smiles and listened to the boy's tale, told in all seriousness, of the shopping trip and his coat. After a while, Tommy's mother came to fetch him, and the Captain slipped a candy into the little boy's hand.

On his way out, Tommy turned and cried, "See ya tonight Cap'n!"

Katherine shot a glance at the captain's face. She couldn't tell whether he were amused or worried, but she was sure that he hadn't actually told Tommy he would go to the party.

Seizing the opportunity to capitalize on Tommy's influence, Katherine turned to the Captain as the little boy's happy face disappeared from the window.

"*Are* you coming to the party tonight?"

Captain Braddock shook his head fiercely and bent to check the fire.

Katherine tried again. "You know, Miss Harriet has been baking all week, and last night she made this special kind of cake that they only have on Guy Fawkes Day. She gave me some to try and—" Captain Braddock whirled around with thunder in his face and said in a restrained tone,

"I ain't goin' and that's final. Now, get about yer work."

Flinging the poker back onto its stand, he went into his office and began to agitatedly sort the papers on his desk. He didn't even look up when Katherine walked quietly through to get to the storeroom door.

She was glad to have the excuse to be out of sight for awhile. The captain's reaction had stung: Katherine hadn't expected such a strong rejection.

Perhaps whatever he was doing in that room has put him out of sorts, she thought, remembering how sad his face had looked in that brief second before he saw her. *I do wish I could have asked him what was up there.* She knew it would not have been the right time, though.

Katherine unpacked slowly, dreading going back into the shop. She had begun the morning with such bright hopes for the day, and now she felt as if there were a heavy weight pulling her down. Finally, unable to find any more excuses to linger, and feeling chilled from spending such a long time in the only slightly heated brick storeroom, she walked towards the steps. Pausing with her hand on the knob, she listened for some clue of the captain's mood, but hearing nothing, she took a deep breath and opened the door.

The captain looked up as she came in and, with a nod at a brown teapot on his desk, said, "I figured you'd be a bit cold after bein' down there so long, so I made a pot of tea."

"Thank you." Katherine said shyly, pleasantly surprised by this softening of the captain's earlier manner. As she returned the clipboard to the wall, the captain said,

"Why don't you pick a couple tea bowls from the shelves and I'll have a cup with you."

Katherine looked puzzled, "Tea bowls? Is that what those are?" She had noticed the clay bowls interspersed with the ships and nautical artifacts and wondered about their significance.

"Yes. That's how tea was originally served, in bowls. In fact, those are very old, so be careful carrying them."

Katherine went into the shop, took two bowls down, and went back to the table. The captain poured the tea out and handed her a bowl. Then he motioned for her to sit in the chair by the stove.

"We have tea cups, of course," he continued, "but the bowls warm yer hands better."

"It *was* a bit cold down there. I'll have to remember to bring some gloves next week." Katherine sipped her tea, then asked, "How come the storage room can be colder than the shopfront, when there's tea in both places?"

The captain leaned against the end of the counter. "The packing materials provide a bit of insulation." He explained. "In the old days, of course, tea came in crates full of hay, which insulated very well. Now it's packing foam and bubble wrap." He looked down into his tea bowl thoughtfully before taking another sip.

"What kind of tea is this?" she asked, her hands curled around the warm tea bowl.

"Assam," the captain replied, somewhat absentmindedly.

"From India," Katherine murmured, taking a sip and staring dreamily into the fire.

Captain Braddock stared at her in surprise. She certainly was picking things up quickly. Perhaps he should begin teaching her more about the teas, teaching her what he had been taught at the Harborside in his youth. She did seem to have an aptitude for it.

She's not a Braddock, he thought, *but she's willing to learn, and bright... Maybe I should.*

The rest of the morning ran smoothly, and soon it was mid-afternoon. Katherine had been busy filling up some jars and had just put the lid on the last one when Captain Braddock walked into the room.

"Are you finished there?" he asked.

"Yes, sir. I just filled the last jar."

"Good. Why don't you take off a little early today?"

Katherine looked up, holding her breath, unsure whether to take this as a favor or a punishment.

A slow smile spread over the captain's face. "You'll want time to get all prettied up for your party tonight."

Katherine let out the breath she had been holding and smiled. The sun had come out again.

16

The Celebration

Evening came, and with it the party guests. Outside, the rain poured down in large drops, and darkness descended even sooner than normal for early November. The biting cold and soaking downpours did not deter the townspeople, however. Soon the umbrella stands overflowed, and the cozy tea shop abounded with cheerful people, all of whom seemed happy to have a reason to celebrate on such a dreary day.

The shop's usual brightness was enhanced as much by the darkness of the weather outside the tall windows as it was by the cozy glow of the fairy lights Mr. James had installed that morning.

Katherine had offered to let Miss Harriet freshen up in her apartment before the guests came, though it was all she and Mr. James could do to persuade Miss Harriet to stop trying to fine-tune everything and take a few moments for herself.

Finally, Katherine had taken her friend gently by the

shoulders and turned her towards the immaculate and well-decorated shop, now cleared of most of its furniture.

Quietly, Katherine said, "Look how lovely the shop looks!"

Miss Harriet relaxed a little. "Yes, it does look lovely."

Turning Miss Harriet around to face her, Katherine reasoned, "Now, you don't want all your guests coming in and seeing how lovely it is, then being startled at you looking like you've been up baking half the night, now would you?"

Miss Harriet looked shocked for a moment at the bluntness of her friend's argument, then smiled. Reaching up to smooth her hair, she began to laugh.

"Yes, you have a point there, Katherine. Let's go see what can be done."

Mr. James, who had been watching the scene with interest, piped up. "I'll greet any guests that might arrive before your return. And I promise not to spoil the intricate way you've arranged the refreshments by eating anything prematurely."

"Thank you. I'm sure we won't be long."

The two ladies rushed up the stairs and began to get ready. Both changed into fresh dresses and tidied their hair. Katherine looked over at the older woman, admiring how tall and graceful she looked in her deep burgundy dress. It was probably the plainest thing Katherine had ever seen her wear, so different from her usual floral skirts and dresses with frilly pastel blouses and cardigans.

She usually had her sleeves rolled up, but somehow had an elegance about her, even when wearing a flour-covered apron. She looked even more elegant now, with the long sleeves fitted to her wrists and the soft folds of fabric falling from the beaded waistline almost to the floor.

Katherine had donned the simple navy dress she had bought to wear to church. It was the dressiest thing she owned, and she had put on a string of glass pearls to give the outfit a more formal look, but comparing herself to the tall, graceful woman before her, she wondered if she looked nice enough for the party.

Miss Harriet looked up just then, caught sight of the look on Katherine's face in the mirror, and turned to say, "Oh, Katherine, I'm *so* glad you wore that dress. It suits you wonderfully, and it's just right for this occasion. Now, what will you do with your hair?"

The two absorbed themselves in the delightful details of getting ready, and Katherine ceased to worry about her attire. Just before they went down, Miss Harriet took a chiffon scarf from her bag and, with a practiced air, flung it around her neck and tied it so it draped gracefully.

Katherine couldn't help but smile when she saw that the scarf had roses on it. Even with such an elegant dress, Miss Harriet couldn't keep from wearing something floral.

"Now," said Miss Harriet, her hand poised on the doorknob. "Shall we make our grand entrance?"

Katherine stood up as straight as she could, her nose slightly in the air, and her hands folded primly in front of her. "Certainly," she said in her politest tone, and the two burst into giggles.

Only a few guests stood in the cozy shop when the two ladies made their appearance at the top of the stairs, but they all turned to watch them come down. Katherine was suddenly nervous, but Miss Harriet seemed in her element. She greeted the guests each by name as she and Katherine descended the stairs together.

Katherine looked around for Mr. James and noticed him by the front door, where he had been greeting the guests as promised. She left Miss Harriet's side and escaped to the kitchen door, where it would be less obvious that she wasn't interacting with the guests. She would do her part when the time came for her to help, but for now, she just wanted to stand by herself and watch for a while.

Mostly, she watched Mr. James. No matter who he was talking to, his eyes inevitably ended up fastened on Miss Harriet. Katherine smiled to herself and decided that Miss Harriet should be encouraged to ask Mr. James to help more often. He was obviously taken with her, although she appeared not to have noticed.

Seeing that the room was full of guests, and the main event was about to begin, Katherine went into the kitchen and worked on filling extra trays so she would be ready when the food on the counter began to dwindle. As good as Miss Harriet's parkin cake was, the trays were certain to be emptied soon after the guests began eating.

As she finished filling the last tray, the din of voices in the other room grew suddenly quiet, and she heard Mr. James welcoming everyone to the party. Ducking out from behind the kitchen curtain to listen, she found to her dismay that she had ended up next to Rosie.

Mr. James was just finishing up his opening remarks. "This is sure to be a fantastic evening, and before we begin the festivities, I would like you all to welcome Miss Harriet, who will tell us all about the delicious treats she has prepared for us tonight."

Miss Harriet stepped carefully up onto the sturdy wooden crate they were using as a platform and addressed her guests.

"Oh! *Such* an exciting evening, isn't it, dear?" Rosie said to Katherine.

Katherine nodded, and pointedly turned her attention back to Miss Harriet, who had already begun to speak.

"Thank you all for coming! Before I tell you about the food of which Mr. James is so eager for you all to partake..."

Laughter rippled through the room, and Mr. James chuckled as well, shouting, "Hear, hear!" and looking as hungry as he could manage.

Miss Harriet held up a hand and quieted the crowd. "As I said, before I tell you about that, I would like first to tell you why I have invited you all tonight. In England when I was a child, Guy Fawkes, or Bonfire Night, as we sometimes called it, was one of my favorite nights of the year. It was a welcome change from the cold, dreary days of November, which I assure you were just as rainy there as they are here.

"It gave us something to look forward to, something to celebrate, and an excuse to gather with family and friends. That is why I wanted to share this celebration with all of you tonight: to give you each a bit of joy and warmth and an excuse to gather with family and friends."

A round of applause (led enthusiastically by Mr. James) interrupted Miss Harriet's speech, and she smiled and nodded until it began to die down, and then silenced the room again by saying loud enough to be heard over the din, "Now, about that food!"

She described the parkin and treacle candy, then invited the crowd to form a line near the counter to fill their plates. Happy to get away before Rosie could corner her for one of her shocking tales, Katherine hurried off to her post behind the counter, where she presided over the food.

While Katherine kept busy going to and from the kitchen with platters, Miss Harriet presided over the large tea urns, whose unsightly appearance had been made up for by the addition of garlands of leaves which served somewhat to disguise their utilitarian look.

As she entered the kitchen to refill a platter, Katherine saw Rosie near the door. Setting the platter down, she turned to grab a spatula and found that Rosie had actually followed her into the kitchen. Feeling more than a bit exasperated, Katherine forced herself to smile and say sweetly,

"Is there anything I can get for you, Rosie?"

The older woman smiled back and nodded, her garish orange hat feathers nodding along. "I just wanted to ask you if you're expecting that Captain Braddock to come this evening?"

"I don't think so. He wasn't planning to attend."

"Oh." Rosie looked relieved. "I was just wondering." She stood by the kitchen door and watched as Katherine refilled her tray. Finally, trying to sound casual, she asked hesitantly, "I don't suppose you've gotten the Captain to open up to you any, you working there and all."

So that's her game. thought Katherine.

"Oh, yes. He's ever so much kinder than people think," she replied aloud, carrying the tray towards the door. As

Rosie moved to let her pass, Katherine couldn't resist saying innocently, "You should come by again some time!"

Rosie rushed off through the crowd, her face bright red. Katherine knew she would be interrogated no more, at least for the evening.

Perhaps that was a bit unkind, she thought. *but at least she won't be following me around now.*

It wasn't the first time Rosie had tried to pry information about the Captain out of her, and she knew it wouldn't be the last.

Soon, the refreshment line dwindled and Miss Harriet came over to Katherine with a basket full of sparklers. "Would you please pass these out at the door as people go out? Mr. James and I will stand outside and light them."

"Of course." Katherine replied. She had been looking forward to this. Nearly the whole town was there, and Mr. James had arranged for permission for the street to be blocked off so they could all stand outside with their sparklers.

"It's the next best thing to a bonfire" Miss Harriet had said.

Soon, they were outside and the sparklers were lit, each person helping to light their neighbors'. As the street was filled with the smoke and smell of gunpowder from the sparklers, Mr. James stood on the crate (which had been relocated outside) to recite the famous poem.

"*Please to remember the fifth of November...*" he began.

"Oh, isn't it *so* exciting!" said Rosie's voice in Katherine's ear.

"Mm-hm" Katherine replied, her eyes still on Mr. James.

"I just love the sparklers!"

Katherine said nothing.

"I *do* hope the sparks don't light anything on fire. You know I read somewhere of that happening at a fourth of July party. This isn't July, though, and things are much wetter, but you never know."

"Maybe it would be safer if you were to stand away from the crowd. You wouldn't want any sparks to land on your hat." Katherine said coolly.

Rosie raised her eyebrows and reached a hand up, as if to make sure her hat was still there, then looked around. "Oh, well, I suppose Miss Harriet has considered the safety of it. And the fire chief is just over there, so we should be safe enough."

She stopped to take a quick breath, then continued, jabbing Katherine in the ribs with her elbow. "My, doesn't Mr. James look handsome up there on his box! If I were just a bit younger, you know, I might be quite taken with him. But he's too young for me. Not like some others I could mention... but then, he does have such a *nice* nose. Not like that horrid Captain. His nose is quite atrocious. You can tell a lot about people by their noses, you know. I have this theory..."

Katherine sighed. She had been looking forward to the poem, read in Mr. James' sonorous voice, but Rosie was clearly determined to talk her way through the whole reading. Katherine didn't want to be rude to one of Miss Harriet's most faithful customers, so she listened just enough to know when to nod and tried to catch as much of the poem as she could.

Soon, the sparklers had died out and the reading was over. The crowd dispersed, calling merry farewells to each other as they did. Katherine and Miss Harriet went inside and began to clean up.

"That was such a delightful evening!" Miss Harriet said, rolling the cart out of the kitchen so they could collect all the dishes. "And just one broken teacup! Quite remarkable, given how many people we had here."

Katherine smiled to herself. How like Miss Harriet to be happy that *only* one teacup had been broken, instead of being upset that it had happened at all.

"Did you enjoy the party, Katherine?" Miss Harriet asked.

"The party was wonderful! I like parties when I have something to do, so I can just watch everyone instead of having to talk to people."

"I did see you talking to Rosie quite a bit."

Katherine rolled her eyes. "Yes, she talked through Mr. James' whole reading!"

"Well, I'm proud of you for bearing with her. I know it must have been difficult."

"It was. Have you heard her theory about noses?"

"No, that's a new one, but not surprising. Her last theory was about eyebrows!" Miss Harriet replied, and both ladies burst into giggles.

Just then Mr. James walked in carrying an old coffee can full of sparkler ends. "Well, you're a merry pair! I must admit it's quite a happy thing to walk in on such fun."

"We were just talking about Rosie's theories. Has she told you the one about noses?" Katherine asked.

"Thankfully, no. But forewarned is forearmed, or so they say. I shall now know to avoid the topic with all due diligence." Winking at Katherine, he set the can on the floor and began pulling tables away from the wall.

The three worked quickly and cheerfully, despite how tired they all were, and soon Katherine and Mr. James had the shop back to normal and Miss Harriet had put the last clean dish back in the cupboard.

"I think that's everything" Miss Harriet said, coming out of the kitchen with a tin-foil package. "Mr. James, you've been just wonderful this evening. Would you like some Parkin cake to take home?"

"What a silly question!" he said, eagerly taking the package. "And might I say, I have been ever so glad to be a part of your celebration. I sincerely hope it will become an annual event!"

Miss Harriet smiled happily in reply, and Katherine thought that perhaps the evening had been worth having to listen to Rosie's annoying chatter, after all.

17

Thanksgiving

After the Guy Fawkes celebration, the days flew by. Katherine kept so busy with preparations for Miss Harriet's town-wide Thanksgiving, she could almost have forgotten the upcoming trip to her parents' house. That is, she could have forgotten, were it not for the heavy feeling which welled up in the pit of her stomach whenever something brought it to mind.

But time flew by anyway, and suddenly, she found herself in the kitchen with Miss Harriet, doing the last of the washing up before leaving the next day.

"I know you're not looking forward to it, Dearie," Miss Harriet said "but what is it you dread so much?"

"I think it's the pretense of being a happy family, together for the holiday, when I don't even feel like I belong. It's not home, it won't feel like Thanksgiving, because all my *real*

Thanksgivings were spent here. But my parents can't see that, and I just feel awkward."

"Have you prayed about it?"

"Yes. And I know that going to see them is what God wants me to do, but while that made the decision easier, it doesn't make the trip any more appealing. To tell you the truth, I'm afraid. Not of my parents, of course. But I'm afraid that I won't be or do or say the right things—that I'll just make the rift worse."

Miss Harriet dried her hands on her apron and reached over for Katherine's.

"You don't have to be perfect, Katherine. God says that He knows we are but dust. He knows our limitations and still chooses to work through us.

"I told you once that God gave you your parents for a reason, imperfect as they are. Well, He also gave your parents *you* for a reason, knowing full well what your imperfections would be. It's not about being perfect. It's about following God's leading as best you can, and leaving the rest up to Him.

"Don't focus on yourself, Dearie. That will only add another layer of bricks to the wall you've built between you and your parents. Focus on what *God* has said. Focus on truth, and let truth tear down the wall. Let them back into your heart, Katherine. You won't have them forever, and we cannot have that "rest for our souls" until we have forgiven."

* * *

Early the next morning, Katherine came down the stairs with a backpack slung over one shoulder. Miss Harriet met her at the bottom of the stairs, her keys in one hand and a small tin in the other.

"Is that all you're taking?" she asked, as they walked to her car.

"Yes. It's only one night at their house, and then travelling most of the next. Besides, It'll just be me and my parents the whole time."

"I suppose so. Packing light has never been my strong suit. I'm forever trying to shove in twice as much as I need, just in case. You should have seen me trying to wind my way through the airports with all my suitcases when I came over from England. It must have made quite a sight!"

Katherine laughed in spite of herself and clicked her seat-belt into place.

Miss Harriet tossed the tin into her lap, saying, "I thought you might need some breakfast on the way to the airport."

"Thank you!" Katherine opened the tin and savored the comforting aroma which rose from the warm scones.

Miss Harriet switched on the headlights and the two drove through the darkness in silence for a while. As they neared the airport, Miss Harriet asked, "Did you rest well last night?"

"Yes, eventually. I thought about what you said, and prayed about it. You know, it had never occurred to me that I needed to forgive my parents. And I definitely hadn't considered the possibility that they might need to forgive *me*. But as I prayed about it, I decided to try to talk to my parents while I'm there, instead of just shoving it all beneath the surface and pretending. It's not going to be easy, but it's what God wants me to do."

Miss Harriet nodded.

They arrived at the airport and Miss Harriet got out of the car to say goodbye. Tears trickled down Katherine's face as Miss Harriet wrapped her in a motherly embrace.

"Pray for me." Katherine whispered, then picked up her backpack and turned to walk into the airport.

* * *

Miss Harriet often prayed while she drove or worked by herself in the kitchen of the little tearoom. But never had she pleaded so fervently, so constantly for Katherine as she did that day. She got back to the shop, mixed up an extra batch of scones, then went about all the everyday ritual of preparing to open the doors and welcome the customers who would soon arrive.

But throughout the day, Miss Harriet kept up a conversation with God. While her hands worked, her heart followed Katherine on her journey, marking the miles with the hours, and praying about what she might encounter at each step of the way.

* * *

As Katherine walked out of the airport, she felt stronger than ever before, but, when her parents suddenly appeared on the busy sidewalk in front of her, she had to fight the sudden urge to turn around and walk right back into the airport.

"Hi, Sweetheart!" her mom said as she rushed up to hug her. "Ed, take her backpack. You must be so tired after getting up so early to fly here. You're gonna need a nap for sure!"

"Hi, Mom. Hi, Dad," Katherine said, still a bit shocked to see them. "I... I wasn't expecting you to pick me up. I could have taken a cab."

"Oh, yes, but we wanted to surprise you. Ever since you called and told us you were coming, we've been so excited, and I just decided I couldn't wait a minute longer to have you here." Katherine's mother led the way to their car. "You must be hungry... we can stop on the way back and get a bite to eat. Ed, what restaurants do we have around here?"

Katherine's father scratched his head. "I think there's a nice place just across the way, over there."

"I guess we'll try that one, then." Katherine's mother said merrily as she got into the passenger seat of the car.

Katherine opened her door and looked over at her dad. He popped the trunk open, swung her backpack in, then grinned at her and winked. "We sure are glad you're here, honey." he said, warmly, and something sprang up inside Katherine— something she hadn't felt in a long, long time.

She smiled back, feeling that a bit of the wall had begun to crumble.

The restaurant was indeed a "nice place", and Katherine smiled to herself as they entered. She couldn't remember going to such a fancy restaurant with her parents before. As a child, the ice cream shop in Harborhaven had been about her family's level of indulgence when it came to eating out.

There was much discussion between Katherine's parents about what they should order, and while they were engrossed by their decision-making, Katherine watched them.

Strangely, she hadn't taken time to really *look* at her parents in years. She was shocked by how much older they both seemed. She thought of Miss Harriet's words from the previous night, *"You won't have them forever."*

Memories once again began to rush through her mind like waves on the harbor, surging in and out, one on top of another, until she was startled back to the present by the arrival of a tall waiter in a stiff white apron.

"May I take your order?" he said loftily, raising his eyebrows and looking imperiously down at them. Katherine's mother looked a little intimidated, but her father went right ahead and ordered, not a bit daunted by the waiter's attitude of superiority. Katherine had always admired that quality in her father, his ability to be comfortable and confident with anyone and everyone. Seeing it now, it reminded her a bit of Miss Harriet.

Once the waiter had gone, the three looked awkwardly around the room, trying to think of what to talk about next. Katherine finally spoke up.

"Mom, Dad, I have something I want to talk to you about. This might not be the right time or place, but I need to tell you that...that I know I've had a rotten attitude ever since we moved from Harborhaven, and I'm sorry. I know it was wrong, and it must have hurt you that I've been so distant and resentful. Will you please forgive me?"

Katherine's parents gazed at her, stunned by their daughter's sudden contrition. Then, her mother reached across the table and took both Katherine's hands in her own. Tears brimmed in her eyes. "Yes. Yes, of *course* we forgive you."

Then they lapsed into silence for a while, but this time there was no awkward surveying of the room. Instead, they looked into each other's happy faces, savoring the clearness of the air between them.

* * *

"Katherine! Over here!" Katherine spotted Miss Harriet's graceful arm waving a handkerchief above the throng of people which filled the small but unusually crowded airport. She squeezed between the clumps of people and hurried towards the older woman.

"Oh, Miss Harriet! I'm so glad to see you!"

"And I you, dear. Let's get out of this crowd, and then we can get all caught up!"

As soon as the car doors closed, Miss Harriet turned and scrutinized Katherine's face.

"Well? And how are you? Was it as dreadful as you expected?"

Katherine smiled the happiest smile Miss Harriet had ever seen on her young friend's face. "Oh, no. It was actually a very good visit. All these years, I'd been feeling sorry for myself because I felt like my parents weren't interested in having me around, when really, *I* was the one pushing *them* away.

"I didn't realize that until I saw how happy they were that I had come at last. They actually drove out to the airport to surprise me, because Mom couldn't wait to see me. And when we got to their house, I found out they had bought a brand-new hide-a-bed sofa so I would be more comfortable."

"And did you get to talk to them like you'd wanted to?"

"Yes. We went out to eat on the way to their house, and

I apologized then, but when they showed me the sofa, I just couldn't hold it in anymore. We all sat down, and I told them how I'd been feeling and asked them again to forgive me for pushing them away. We all cried, even Dad. They really had no idea what it was that had come between us, because I never told them. They only knew something was different. I guess they just figured it was part of my growing up and becoming my own person."

"And how do you feel now?"

"It's strange. I do still have that longing for how things were, and it still saddens me to think about the miserable last Christmas we spent together, but now that I'm not holding onto it, the hurt has slipped away, and I feel... some-how... free."

Miss Harriet smiled, her eyes shining as she quoted, "'and ye shall know the truth, and the truth shall make you free.' I do believe you've found one of the old paths, my dear."

"Yes, I think I have." Katherine said, with another happy smile.

* * * *

The journey back to the shop in the early morning light seemed to fly by. Katherine looked out the window at the early morning fog and could just make out the bare branches of the trees that lined the highway. Past that, all was white and still.

"You know, when I got to that big city, it was like a differ-ent world," she said to Miss Harriet. "It hasn't taken me long to get used to the slower pace of Harborhaven. The noise and rush of people everywhere was quite a shock."

Miss Harriet laughed. "I suppose it would be. I haven't been away from Harborhaven since I moved here, and I must admit, I enjoy the pace. I would probably find the city jarring as well."

When they arrived at the shop, Katherine noticed that Miss Harriet had gotten everything ready for the day. "You must have been up early to get everything done before driving to pick me up."

"Oh, no, not that much earlier. Harold—Mr. James, that is—helped me do some of it last night after the meal."

Katherine couldn't help but smile at Miss Harriet's slip, and the blush that came after it. "And how did it all go? Did many people come?"

"Oh, yes. I'd say there were about half as many people as were here for Guy Fawkes, which is about as many as Mr. James had expected. I don't know what I would have done without his help. He organized everything and helped me figure out how to get everyone seated. We pushed all the tables together to make a big, long dining table and we were going to pass everything around like a family meal, but everyone brought so much food, we ended up just putting everything on the counter like a buffet.

"Speaking of which, there are enough leftovers in the kitchen to last us for days! And that's after letting people go through and fill up a plate to take home. Mr. James said that leftovers were just as much a part of Thanksgiving as the turkey."

"You and Mr. James sure seem to be getting along well."

"Oh, he's been quite helpful. Quite helpful, indeed. And did I tell you that the Dailies came? Every one of them. Mrs. Penelope showed up, and so did Mr. Patten. And do you know, I think Mr. James has the same idea we've had about those two? He met each of them at the door and made sure they ended up seated across from one another, and at the opposite end of the long table from Rosie, too. Rosie, of course, was in rare form, bustling around, noticing what was on everyone's plates. She's come up with a new theory, based on people's dietary choices."

Katherine laughed and rolled her eyes. "I'm sure. And Captain Braddock? Did he come?"

"No, Dearie," Miss Harriet said with a sigh, "and it wasn't for any lack of trying on my part. I went to pick up the tea order Wednesday afternoon, just like we'd arranged. He was not nearly as blustery as usual, and asked if you had gotten off on your trip all right. He said you had been quite a help these last few months, and that he guessed he owed some of that to me, for giving you the days off instead of keeping you all to myself.

"We were actually getting on quite well, but as soon as I extended the invitation to have Thanksgiving at the shop, his bluster returned, and he declined with as little civility as one might expect from a rough old sailor. On my way out the door, I made sure to mention that he could change his mind at any time, that we'd be happy to have him join us, but he just turned and stomped into the next room without a word."

"How sad. And I suppose he spent his Thanksgiving by

himself." Katherine sighed. "I should go see him..." she said, trying hard to stifle a persistent yawn.

"Not 'til you've had some sleep. As much as I'm sure a visit would cheer up that cantankerous old man, you've been up all night, and I'm going to turn mother bear and insist you rest."

"Yes, ma'am." Katherine said, starting up the stairs. Stopping halfway, she turned to say, "By the way, my parents said to tell you they think you've done wonders for my baking skills. I made rolls for Thanksgiving dinner, and they both agreed they were the best they'd ever had."

"Good work, Dearie." Miss Harriet said with a smile. "Now up to bed."

18

Home Again at the Harborside

"Captain Braddock," called Katherine as she opened the door of the Harborside.

The old man limped in from the back wearing one of his rare smiles. "Well, hello there! I see you got back all right. How was your trip?"

"Wonderful!" Katherine replied, flinging her coat and scarf onto the coatrack. "How was your Thanksgiving?"

"Oh, just fine." He answered. Katherine thought she caught a brief flicker of sadness in the captain's face as he spoke, but he quickly turned and stooped to tend the wood stove. Glancing back up, he asked, "What brings you around today?"

Katherine walked around him and plunked herself cheerfully down in the chair by the stove. "Oh, I just wanted to see how the Harborside had gotten along without me." She said playfully, with a scrutinizing glance around the room.

"Just fine, thank ye, but I think the jars missed your attention. They're a bit dusty, as you can see."

"Well, it's a good thing I came in, then. Do you want me to dust them while I'm here?"

The captain looked back up at her with an amused twinkle in his eye. "Well, seein' as it's your day off, I don't think that'll be necessary. Just you sit there and talk a bit, like company."

Katherine smiled and curled up in the chair. She gazed at the captain, who was still kneeling on the floor, carefully poking at the fire in the wood stove. She sighed a happy sigh, then asked cheerfully, "What does company talk about?"

"Well, now. I'm not sure. It's been quite a spell since the Harborside's seen any real company. Why don't you tell me what you thought about the city?"

"It was loud and busy. After being here for a few months, I couldn't help but wonder why anyone would want to live there."

"I know what you mean. The last time I was in a big city was when I brought my ship into port for the last time. I won't pretend for a minute I was sad to leave it behind. Wasn't my kind of place at all."

"Did you always plan to come back to the Harborside?" Katherine asked.

Captain Braddock stood up, stretching his back with a quiet groan. "That's quite a question. When I left, I knew this place was in good hands. I used to come visit now and then, but, as I moved up in the ranks, I spent less and less time here. I don't suppose I ever meant to leave for good, but I sure didn't plan on coming back for good, either."

Katherine considered a moment, weighing the risk of asking another question. "What happened to bring you back?"

The sadness Katherine had noticed earlier passed across his face again as he answered, looking around at the shop as he spoke. "The old girl needed me. While the Harborside was in capable hands, there was no need for me to be here, but then those hands went away, and I came back. That's all."

Katherine wanted to ask about where the capable hands had gone, but the note of finality in his voice warned her that any further inquiry would only make the captain close up again. She stared down into the woodstove, watching the flames flicker and dance. Then, after a while, she spoke up quietly.

"When I came back to Harborhaven, I came because I wanted to feel I was home again."

"And did you?" Captain Braddock asked, eying her thoughtfully as he picked up a rag and began dusting the counter.

"Not at first. I came back expecting everything to be exactly the same as I remembered it, and it wasn't."

The captain nodded, and Katherine continued. "But then I went to Miss Harriet's, and she was so kind, she made me feel welcome. And when I came here to the Harborside –" Katherine paused, gathering courage and choosing her words. "When I came here, I felt for the first time that I actually *had* come home."

Captain Braddock looked up from his dusting with a tender smile. "I thought so. That first day, I could tell the

Harborside had worked her charm on you. I suppose that's why I hired you."

"Really?"

"Yes. You know, sometimes it almost seems as if the Harborside chooses people. Like Great-Aunt Lizzy, for example."

Katherine's eyes lit up and she leaned forward. "Who was Great-Aunt Lizzy?"

"My Great-Aunt, of course." He said with a chuckle. "She was born back east somewhere and came to Harborhaven with her parents in the twenties.

"She was from a wealthy family, the type that had someone to do their shopping for them, you know. Goodness knows why they chose Harborhaven as their place to spend the summer that year, but they did, and one day Lizzy and her sister decided to have the chauffer drive them about the town.

"Folks said it was quite a sight, that great fancy car, all polished till it shone and sparkled. And then in the back, (it was a convertible, of course,) were the two young ladies, looking like they had stepped out of a fashion magazine. They giggled and pointed and generally had a good time at the town's expense, until suddenly, Lizzy told the driver to stop.

"They were just outside the Harborside block then, and she insisted that her sister come with her to see what was in the shop with the 'charming green door.' They sent the driver away for a bit, and in they came, only to find the shop empty, and the shopkeeper nowhere in sight. Nothing daunted, Lizzy began to nose about amongst the jars while her sister trailed nervously behind her.

"My Great-Uncle Isaac, now, he walked through the doorway right in time to find Lizzy taking the *Anne* down off the shelf for a closer look. He was instantly struck by her beauty, and also by the gentleness and respect, almost reverence, with which she held the ship, as if she had instinctively felt its importance.

"Lizzy turned at the sound of that one creaky floorboard in front of the doorway over there, and their eyes met. There was a stunned silence as they each pondered what they beheld. Accustomed as Lizzy was to being surrounded by lively, immaculately-dressed young men, there was something that drew her to this serious-eyed fellow who looked every inch the shopkeeper's drudge. He had his sleeves rolled to his elbows, his hair was ruffled and untidy, and the apron he wore, as well as his trouser legs, were very dusty."

"It must have been Thursday." Katherine said dreamily, settling down more comfortably in the armchair.

"Aye, so it must. He had been working down in the storeroom, unpacking crates. Well, Isaac finally managed to stammer out, 'I'm sorry, I didn't hear you come in.' To which Lizzy, (just as dazed as he was,) replied, 'You should get a bell for the door, so you can hear when it opens.' They both smiled, then Lizzy realized she was still holding the *Anne*.

"'Such detail. Is it handmade?' she asked, and soon he was telling her all about the shop's beginnings. When the car appeared to take the ladies home, Lizzy's sister (who was extremely bored by it all) was impatient to go. But Isaac was right in the middle of telling about Captain Jeremiah and the pirates, and Lizzy was determined not to budge until she had heard what happened next. Isaac very politely offered to see the ladies home if they wished to stay longer, since he would be closing the shop in an hour anyway, and would be delighted to escort them wherever they needed to go.

"Lizzy appeased her sister by sending her away in the car with a message to her mother, saying she wouldn't be home for a while yet. She laughed off her sister's disapproval, saying, 'It's the twenties, dear! And besides, I'm sure Mr. Braddock won't let me get lost on the way home.'

"Isaac finished his tale and locked up the shop, then the two took a leisurely walk along the wharf before heading back to the Grand Hotel, where Lizzy's family was staying. By the time they reached the door, each had secretly resolved to marry the other if they could.

"The next day, Isaac (looking much more like a gentleman and less like a shop assistant) couldn't wait to open the shop. Lizzy had indicated that she would be dropping by to learn more about the shop, and she was true to her word. She appeared mid-morning with a box in her hand, tied shut with a satin ribbon. Astonished, Isaac accepted the box, then laughed aloud when he removed the lid and found there a bell for the shop's door! 'Now,' she said, 'You'll always know when I am here.'" Captain Braddock nodded over at the door, "And there it's stayed ever since."

"And Lizzy?" Katherine asked.

"Ah, well, she spent nearly every day of her vacation here in the shop, and by the time the family went back home, Isaac had obtained permission from Lizzy's father to marry her. They were married for fifty-seven years, they were. Although I remember Great-Uncle Isaac saying that he never could quite tell whether she wanted to marry him or the Harborside.

Then Great-Aunt Lizzy would laugh her merry laugh and with a twinkle in her eye reply that she was just happy they came as a packaged set, so she didn't have to choose."

"Katherine looked over at the bell with a satisfied sigh. "How lovely it is to know the stories behind ordinary things. I think I shall remember Isaac and Lizzy every time I hear the bell ring or step on that creaky floorboard." She sat in dazed silence for a moment, then said thoughtfully, "You know, the way history comes alive here, I'm surprised the Harborhaven Historical Society isn't conducting tours!"

"Well now, that would be pretty difficult, since apart from you, I'm the only one around anymore that knows about the Harborside's past."

"What about your sister?" The words slipped out of Katherine's mouth before she could stop them. Captain Braddock stiffened, a jar in one hand and a dust rag in the other. His back was to Katherine. She wished she could see his face.

"Like I said, I'm the only one *around* who knows the old stories."

Katherine sat silent, mentally kicking herself. Things were so open, so friendly, and then she had to go and say something about Serena. Now the wall was back up between them, and she had no idea what to say or do to get him to take it down again. She watched him move around the shop, dusting and straightening, always with his back towards her.

Finally, he turned around and looked at her. His face softened as he said, "We'll need to be gettin' the Christmas decorations out from the storeroom when you're here on Tuesday."

Katherine's heart thrilled at this sudden change in the Captain's demeanor. "Decorations?"

"Yes," he said, leaning towards her with a grin, "*old* decorations. Harborside tradition, you know." He laughed as Katherine's eyes lit up. "By rights, I should have put them up yesterday, but I thought you might like to have a hand in it."

"Of course I would!" Katherine exclaimed, sitting up straight in the chair.

"Well, I supposed you wouldn't mind helping. I may need you to come in extra early, or else stay late, since we can't very well decorate while the shop's open."

"Just name the hour, and I'll be here!"

Captain Braddock chuckled and went back to his dusting, and Katherine settled back into the comfortable chair, basking in the warmth of the wood stove and the delight of being once more at *home*.

19

Rest for the Soul

The drive to church the next morning made Katherine even happier to be back in Harborhaven. Bright red leaves lay scattered across the road, and they swirled in graceful little curls after the cars as they passed. The road wound along through the mist that had rolled in from the harbor, and Katherine savored the view out the front windshield as Miss Harriet drove. The two chatted amicably as they wound their way through the mists to the little old church building.

When they arrived, Katherine got out of the car and walked towards the church, realizing that for the first time, she was looking forward to the service instead of looking back to memories of the past. With the rift between her and her parents beginning to heal, the memories that rushed in on her as she walked towards the building made her want to smile instead of cry.

She hadn't realized what a dark cloud her bitterness had

been. It had shut out the brightness of the joyful things in her past, making them shadowy reminders of how she wished life had gone instead.

She followed Miss Harriet in and the two took their usual place in one of the old wooden pews. As the service began, Katherine noticed that everything felt more vibrant: the words of the hymns they sang suddenly meant more to her, the sermon touched her heart more deeply, the times of prayer seemed more personal, as if she were suddenly *closer* to God, somehow, and could talk to Him about anything.

Her heart thrilled with fresh rejoicing as they stood to sing "Nothing Between My Soul and the Savior," basking in the fact that the words she sang were true: at long last, the walls were down, the rifts had been mended.

How different it felt from the previous Sundays since her return to Harborhaven, when church had been a constant struggle against her own memories and emotions. It had become something merely to be gotten through, because that was what she did on Sundays. But today everything seemed different. For the first time in years, she felt *free*.

After the sermon, Katherine slipped quietly out of her seat and knelt. Feeling she might burst with joy and gratitude, she began to pray.

Thank you, Lord. Thank you for showing me the "old path" of forgiveness and the truth of my own pride and selfishness. Thank you for restoring my relationship with my parents and for helping me to let go of the hurts of my past. Thank you for bringing this rest to my soul.

With tears brimming in her eyes, she stood and joined in as the congregation sang the closing hymn. Miss Harriet reached over and squeezed her hand. Katherine gave her a bright smile and whispered, "I've found it Miss Harriet—rest at last!"

* * * *

On the way home from church, Miss Harriet and Katherine were quiet. A joyful, holy hush had fallen over the two as they drove along the winding road. After a while, Miss Harriet asked gently,

"All right if we take a little detour? It's a perfect day to look at the harbor."

"Of course!" Katherine replied. "I haven't been up to the viewpoint in a long time."

When they reached the old viewpoint, Katherine was glad she had chosen a thick wool skirt and her warmest dress boots to wear to church that day.

The wind gusted icily around them, as they got out of the car, but what took Katherine's breath away was the view. The morning mists had cleared away and Katherine looked out over the harbor and the vast expanse of water beyond, reflecting the dull grey of the winter sky. The fierce wind gusting around them at the viewpoint also ruffled the surface of the harbor into waves that crashed against the wharf's sturdy sea wall.

"How could I have forgotten how beautiful the harbor is?" Katherine asked, bewildered. "I used to look out at it every day from my window growing up, but since I've been back, I've barely noticed it was there. I suppose I've just been too wrapped up in my own misery to notice anything else."

Miss Harriet surveyed her silently as they leaned on the old stone railing.

Katherine gazed out across the water for a while, then suddenly turned to Miss Harriet.

"I don't want to take this for granted, like I took my parents for granted, and the happiness of my childhood. I don't want to lose the wonder of this place, and I don't want to lose the closeness with the people I hold dear, or the sweetness of this new peace inside me. But how can I keep it all from getting lost in the day to day living of life?"

Miss Harriet drew in a long breath as she considered the question. "Well, Dearie, I suppose that's a question people have been trying to answer for many a long year now. And yet, I think perhaps the answer is much simpler than we might guess."

"What do you mean?"

"Only that, if we want peace, and joy, sweetness and wonder, closeness and gratefulness, we need to stay close to the One who created them." Miss Harriet took Katherine's shoulders and turned her towards the harbor.

"You see this view with fresh eyes today, because you are no longer distracted by the longings you've been clinging to. I read an old preacher once, who said that we will only be grateful to God for what He *has* given us when we have let go of the things He *hasn't*. You have given up the bitterness that was keeping you from being close to your parents and close to God. That is why everything seems so fresh and new. It only stands to reason that the way to keep things from becoming stale is to stay in that place of closeness."

Katherine nodded. "That makes sense. But... I feel like I should know this already: *how* do I keep myself close to God?"

"The same way you keep close to anyone, Dearie, by spending time with Him, and communicating with Him."

"You mean praying?"

"Yes, and reading the Bible with a heart ready to listen. As you do, God will show you how you can do the things that please Him, and as you obey, that closeness will not only remain, it will deepen."

Katherine looked back over the water and was soon lost in thought. Finally, a shiver jolted her out of her reverie, and she turned to her friend. "I'm getting cold, and I'm sure you are too. Do you want to go back now?"

Miss Harriet smiled. "Sunday dinner at my place? I made twice as much as I need, hoping you'd come."

"That sounds perfect!"

As they walked back to the car, Katherine turned to take one last look over the harbor. She smiled, and looking upward, silently prayed again.

Thank you, Lord. Please, help me to stay close to You."

* * * *

Soon, they had arrived at Miss Harriet's and were bustling around the cozy kitchen, putting the final touches on one of Miss Harriet's excellent "Sunday dinners." This week, it was a beef roast.

"Just big enough for two, with a bit to spare," Miss Harriet exclaimed happily as she pulled it from the crock pot. There were carrots and onions and rutabagas, which were fished out and piled into a china serving dish, onto which Miss Harriet popped the lid before whisking it away to the table. Meanwhile, Katherine peeled potatoes while she waited for the water to boil.

When all was said and done, Katherine thought it looked like Thanksgiving all over again. The small table loomed resplendent on one end of the long sitting room, covered with a dark green tablecloth and adorned with Miss Harriet's best china. Serving dishes covered much of the table's surface, and the smell of the feast they were about to enjoy mingled in with the scent of the evergreen garlands which Miss Harriet had draped over the long expanse of windows that looked out over her garden and the ocean far below.

They sat down to eat, and Miss Harriet prayed, asking God's blessing over the food. Then the two busied themselves with passing dishes and filling their plates.

"If there's one thing I enjoy, it's a good meal." said Miss Harriet, taking a delicate spoonful of mustard from a tiny glass bowl.

Katherine glanced up at her graceful companion, wondering how such a good cook could stay so slim.

"What's the mustard for?" she asked, eying Miss Harriet's plate.

"For the roast beef, of course! Sunday dinner just wouldn't be complete without it." Miss Harriet grinned and passed the little dish to Katherine. "Try it and see what you think."

Katherine gingerly spooned a little mustard onto a small bite of roast and popped it into her mouth. Her eyes widened as she chewed. "It *is* delicious! I see why it's a tradition."

They both laughed, and went on with their meal, chatting

about the food and the dishes and anything else that came to mind, until the cloud-induced gloom outside began to fade into darkness, and the small frilly lamps scattered around the long room filled the space with a cozy light. As the two sat over the remains of the meal, Katherine became suddenly pensive.

"What are you thinking about?" asked Miss Harriet.

"Just that, since my time with my parents, I've been so happy, and life has seemed so full of good things, but..." she paused, drawing her eyebrows together in a puzzled frown. "I wonder what it's all for. I mean," she continued hurriedly, "I don't wonder why God put me here. I know very well that I would have stayed miserable if it hadn't been for you and for all the things I've learned since I came. But...I can't help but wonder what's next."

"Next?"

"Yes. I can't quite explain it... but even though I still feel just as free and happy as ever, I have this sort of tugging in my heart, a sense that there's something more, something I can't quite put my finger on yet."

Miss Harriet smiled. "I know that feeling. Just pray about it, and ask God to show you what it is. I know He will."

20

The Christmas Trunk

As Katherine opened the door of the Harborside, Captain Braddock popped his head around the doorway.

"Ah, Katherine, just in time. Come back here and give me a hand."

Katherine quickly hung her jacket, hat, and scarf on the coat rack and followed Captain Braddock down into the storeroom.

He led the way past the piles of unpacked boxes waiting to be thrown out and towards the line of shadowy shapes along the far wall, which Katherine had been longing to explore since her first day at the Harborside. Her heart gave a little thrill as he stopped in front of several large trunks.

"Here they are. The Christmas things should be in one of these. Let me see..." He bent down and examined each, squinting in the dim light thrown from the bulb over the stairs. "I think it's this one. Let's have a look." He bent down with a groan and began to lift the lid.

Katherine held her breath in excitement as the lid creaked open. "Yes, this is it. Here, take these two boxes, for now, we can bring the rest in a bit." Katherine eagerly took the two large, old-fashioned hatboxes and followed the Captain up the stairs.

Katherine gingerly set the boxes on the counter. "Which do we open first?" she asked, her eyes wide and sparkling with anticipation.

Captain Braddock chuckled, "Whichever one you want, Missy. They're decorations, not Christmas presents!" Then, he added with a bit of his old seriousness, "we just have to make sure we don't get carried away. It's only an hour till we open."

Katherine nodded, then eagerly took the lid off the smaller box. "Oh, what beautiful bows! Where do these go?" She asked, untangling a large bow from the jumble of velvet ribbon.

"They hang from the gaslights. I'll get started on them; you open the other box."

Katherine opened the larger hatbox and found it was full of glass ornaments nestled together in a bed of ancient tissue paper, crumpled up around them.

"Will there be a Christmas tree?" she asked.

"Just a small one. It'll be here later today. I figured we could set it up tonight."

"I'm glad. I love Christmas trees." She was about to put the lid on the box when she noticed the corner of a fabric pouch sticking out from between the crumpled papers. Inside were some large but delicate silver hooks, with tiny sprigs of holly worked all over them.

"Those are to hang the garlands with."

"What garlands?"

"The garlands we're going to make while we wait for customers today." Captain Braddock replied, casting a sidelong glance at Katherine to catch her reaction.

"We're going to *make* them?"

"Yes. It's a Harborside tradition. We have to have *real* fir garlands in the window, shelves, and counter."

"Oh, that will be lovely!" Katherine said.

"The ornaments are only in the top of the box. There's a tray you can lift out," Captain Braddock said, turning to attach another bow.

Katherine lifted the tray from the top of the hatbox. There was another layer of crumpled tissue, with some mysterious shapes scattered throughout. Katherine lifted one gently and carefully removed its tissue paper covering. In her hand was an exquisite porcelain shepherd. She reached in again and unwrapped a wise man, then a camel, then Mary and Joseph, a donkey, and a delicate little sheep. Finally, she fished around among the tissue paper and found a manger, with a tiny baby to lay inside it.

"Where is this nativity from?" Katherine asked as the captain walked up to the counter.

"Great-Uncle Charles, that was Isaac's brother, you know, bought it in Italy. He was a great traveler, and always brought back presents for everyone. This was bought as a gift for Lizzy originally, but she put it out at the Harborside the first Christmas she had it, and here it's belonged ever since. She said it was too pretty to keep at home where no one would see it."

Captain Braddock pointed at the intricate detail of the tiny manger. "They're hand-painted, see, and worth quite a bit, so I've always been told. They go up there, on that shelf on the wall behind the counter." Captain Braddock picked up the shepherd, with a sad sort of smile. "Serena had such a way of arranging it. Somehow, when the pieces are all placed just so, it sort of draws you in. Makes you feel like you're really there."

Katherine looked down at the pieces, wondering if she could figure out how to place them "just so." The captain set the shepherd down and looked back over at the box.

"There should be an angel somewhere, too. Was it in the box with the other pieces?"

"No. I haven't seen an angel yet. Maybe I missed it somehow." She looked through the tissue papers one more time. "There's nothing left in the box but paper. Could it have gotten put away somewhere else?"

Captain Braddock shrugged. "I suppose so. I haven't helped with the decorations since before I went to sea. Can't imagine Serena mislaying anything, though. She was always so careful."

Katherine sifted through the papers again. "Maybe we'll find it later." She said, hopefully, thrilled that the captain was talking more freely about his sister.

"Likely so. Anyway, it's time to open up. Put the boxes back in the trunk for me while I unlock the door, will you?"

"Yes, sir." Katherine said, putting the lids back on the boxes.

* * * *

Back in the storeroom, she knelt on the floor in front of the open trunk. An aroma of ancient pine needles and cinnamon drifted out of the trunk as she gently set the boxes in their place. As she reached up to close the lid, she noticed something shiny wedged between the other boxes in the trunk. She moved them over and pulled out an antique picture frame.

Turning towards the light, she saw it was a black and white picture of two small children: a boy and a girl, sitting on the floor in front of a Christmas tree, engrossed in watching a small train wind its way around the tree.

Something about the scene seemed familiar to Katherine, but she couldn't quite figure out what it was. *I wonder who they were,* she thought. In a sudden fit of boldness, she decided to go back upstairs and ask.

* * * *

When Captain Braddock saw what she was holding, he reached out to take it with a look on his face she had never seen before.

"Well, now. I haven't seen this in ages," he said softly.

"I was wondering who the children in the picture were," Katherine asked cautiously.

"You'd never know it now, but that little tyke is me, and

that's my sister Serena next to me." The captain smiled and sighed. "Them were good days, when we were young. This was taken for my grandparents as a Christmas present. They set it on that shelf over there every Christmas. We were their only grandchildren, you see, and they doted on us."

Katherine gently took the picture from Captain Braddock. "I think we should keep it out." She said, walking over to the shelves. "Is this where it goes?" she asked, gently moving a tea bowl to one side to make room.

Captain Braddock smiled. "Yes, just there." He paused for a moment, then gave a heavy sigh, and said, "Well, I guess we'd best get to our work now."

* * * *

The clock chimed five just as Captain Braddock locked the front door and pulled down the dark green window shades. He poked at the fire in the wood stove, then turned and stood in the doorway to the office, watching his assistant.

Katherine sat on the floor, surrounded by piles of fragrant green branches, working busily away. She looked up and met the captain's gaze.

"What are you thinking about?" she asked, picking up another branch to tie onto her garland.

"I was just remembering the days long ago when *I* was the one sitting on the floor, tying branches together."

Katherine smiled and looked back down at the knot she was tying.

"You know, Katherine," Captain Braddock continued, "I sure am glad you came to the Harborside this year. I never would have had the heart to do all this on my own, and yet, Christmas wouldn't have seemed quite right without it."

"I wouldn't have missed this for the world," Katherine held up her garland. "Does this look right?" she asked brightly.

"Perfect. Now it's time to hang them. Let me show you where they go."

By the time they had finished, there were garlands over the windows and doorways, along the counter, and even along the top and sides of the shelves. The whole room was filled with the fragrance of the fresh branches.

The two stood back to admire their work. "It sure does seem like Christmas now." Katherine said.

"We haven't even put up the tree yet," Captain Braddock replied.

"Oh, I almost forgot about the tree. When is it coming?"

"Any minute now. I told them to deliver it at five-thirty. I'll bring in another chair, and we can both sit by the stove while we wait."

* * * *

At last, the tree arrived, and Katherine helped Captain Braddock set it up in the large shopfront window.

"It's the perfect size!" Katherine exclaimed. "I'm glad you got such a tall tree. It fills the window so well."

"I like a large tree, myself," The captain replied. "The last few years before my parents turned the Harborside over to Serena and I, they only had a short tree, over on the corner of the counter, but when I was young, we always had a tree this big." He motioned towards the picture of him and Serena.

"This is where that picture was taken, you know. Right in front of the window, with the tree."

"I wondered what was so familiar about it. I didn't even think to look at where it had been taken. I'm glad we're making it look just like you remember."

"Me, too. Now, let's get that box of ornaments from the storeroom."

Katherine found the box of ornaments and carried it back in.

"What was Christmas like when you were a boy?" asked Katherine, as they began to unpack and hang the ornaments.

"What was it like? Well, I suppose it was just as full of fun and wonder as any child's Christmas. We would decorate here and back at the big house, and when school got out, we would spend almost every day here with my grandparents. This was as much a home to us as anywhere, so I suppose it was just as much a part of my Christmas as my own home."

"It's strange how a place can have such a large part of someone's Christmas memories. When my family moved, I felt like I could never have a real Christmas again."

Captain Braddock looked over at her, his eyebrows raised, "And did you?"

"No, but I think I will this year."

"Because you're back in Harborhaven?"

"Not exactly." Katherine looked at the captain, trying to decide how much to say. It suddenly seemed very important to express herself clearly. Taking a deep breath, she began.

"You see, when my family moved, I felt angry and hurt. My parents took me away from the place I loved, from everything that was familiar to me. And then, they both had to work so hard, it seemed like they didn't have time for me anymore. I knew in my head that they were just doing what they had to, but in my heart, I felt they had abandoned me. For years I felt hurt, angry, and miserable."

"What changed?" asked the captain, his hand paused, holding an ornament in mid-air.

"I did," said Katherine simply. "I came here, hoping it would erase the hurt, but it only reminded me of it. Then Miss Harriet helped me find the old paths."

"Old paths? What does that mean?"

"I'm not quite sure how to explain it... In the Bible, God says that if we seek the old paths, the way *He* said to do things, we will find rest for our souls. That's what I wanted: rest from all the misery of how I felt about the past. So I began praying and reading the Bible, and God showed me that I needed to forgive my parents, and that *I* was the one who had built up the wall between us in the first place. All those years I had blamed my parents, but in reality, *I* was the one who had made it so that things between us were never the same again. It wasn't easy, but I knew I needed to forgive."

"And did it work?"

"Yes." Katherine smiled happily. "Yes, it did work. I talked with my parents at Thanksgiving, and I feel like I suddenly have them back again, though perhaps *I'm* really the one who's back. And what's better, I'm not miserable anymore! I feel like I'm finally free from all the hurt and the anger."

"And Christmas?" Captain Braddock finally hung the ornament he had been holding and reached for another.

Katherine smiled radiantly. "It's already shaping up to be the best I've ever had!"

Captain Braddock looked at her for a moment, hung his ornament on the tree, and then grinned. "Good."

21

Christmas Preparations

"Now, then. I think that's just about perfect!" Miss Harriet stepped back to survey the decorations they had just finished putting up. Mr. James had once again come early to help, and Katherine enjoyed watching the interaction between the two.

The reporter had become even more of a fixture at Miss Harriet's since Thanksgiving, and Katherine could tell the two were easily becoming what Miss Harriet would have called "*quite* good friends."

Katherine was thoroughly thrilled, and yet, she couldn't help but wonder how things would change were Miss Harriet ever to marry. The tea shop would surely continue, for it seemed inextricably intertwined with who Miss Harriet was. Katherine couldn't imagine a Miss Harriet without a tea shop. But the nagging question remained—w*ould* Miss Harriet continue to need her to work in the shop?

She shrugged, as if trying to shake off the thought, and turned her attention back to her fellow decorators.

"I think the lights made such a difference this fall! I'll admit to having been a little worried that it mightn't look different enough when we switched to the Christmas decorations, but I was wrong. The lights looked festive in the fall, but, with the Christmas garlands around the windows, they make it all look positively magical!"

Katherine couldn't help but smile. Miss Harriet was standing in the middle of the room, hands clasped under her chin in girlish delight, with Mr. James looking at her as if he thought *she* looked positively magical herself. And yet, she seemed to be completely unaware.

"I'll take the fall boxes out to your car for you." said Mr James.

"Thank you, Harold. Perhaps we can find a place to stack the empty Christmas boxes. It does seem silly to be carting empty boxes back and forth."

"I can take them upstairs," suggested Katherine. "There's plenty of space in that closet by the door."

"What a good thought." Said Miss Harriet. "You're sure you don't mind?"

"Not at all. I'll take them up, then get started on the dishes."

"Katherine, you're a dear! Thank you. I'll just see Mr. James off, and then I'll be right in to help you."

Katherine stacked the empty boxes and carried them upstairs. On her way back down to the kitchen, she caught a glimpse of Miss Harriet and Mr. James, chatting happily on the doorstep. She smiled and slipped quietly through the curtained doorway into the kitchen.

* * * *

She had already filled the sink and unloaded the dirty dishes off the cart by the time Miss Harriet joined her.

"Now then," said Miss Harriet, tying her apron strings and rolling up her sleeves. "Have you decided on your plans for Christmas?"

"Well, I talked to my parents last night about their plans. They told me that they had already booked a Christmas cruise months ago. I hadn't come for a holiday in so long, they had decided to give up and make the most of it. They offered to cancel, but I told them it was all right and that I would enjoy spending a Christmas here in Harborhaven."

"And how do you feel about a Harborhaven Christmas without your parents?"

"Surprisingly, just fine. When they told me about the cruise, I was actually *happy* for them. I know they must have been saving up for a long time to be able to go. It was obvious they were afraid it would upset me, and I halfway expected to be upset with them myself, but as they told me about it, there was this sort of... peace, I guess...and I just *knew* it was going to be ok."

"Sounds like God gave you grace to keep a good attitude." Miss Harriet turned to put a teapot away on a cabinet shelf, then turned back around with a smile on her face. "You know, Dearie, on the one hand, I am sorry for you to miss the chance to spend Christmas with your parents, especially since you've only just begun to rebuild your relationship with them. But on the other, I am delighted you'll be here, because...Katherine, how would you like to spend your Harborhaven Christmas with me?"

Katherine's eyes lit up, and she threw her arms around Miss Harriet, completely forgetting about the dripping dish-rag in her hand. "Oh, Miss Harriet! I couldn't think of anything nicer than to spend Christmas with you!"

"Nor I than to spend it with you, Dearie. And you must tell me all about your Harborhaven Christmas traditions, so we can do those, and then, if you don't mind, I'd like to show you what a real English Christmas is like. What do you think?"

"That sounds wonderful!"

The two grinned at each other for a moment, then went back to washing the dishes. Katherine looked over at Miss Harriet and asked mischievously, "And will *Mr. James* be joining us for Christmas dinner?"

To Katherine's surprise, Miss Harriet actually blushed. "No. He's heading out a few days before Christmas to spend the holiday with his sister's family."

"I see..." Katherine said teasingly.

"Now, Katherine," Miss Harriet said, "If you're implying that Mr. James and I... well, we're just good friends, and that is all."

"Are you sure?" asked Katherine.

"Quite sure. I admit that I have been enjoying his friend-ship very much, but that is as far as it goes. Besides," she continued, reaching for another saucer to dry, "I am content with my life. I have the shop, and with the shop I have my own little community of people to care about. I won't say I never think about what might have been, but I've learned to live at peace with my singleness. It's what God has allowed in His perfect plan for me."

"And what if Mr. James is also part of God's plan?" Katherine asked teasingly.

"Well, that would be a different matter." Miss Harriet put down her dishcloth and looked Katherine in the eye. "But I'm not going to go spoiling a perfectly pleasant friendship by getting myself all wrapped up in what-ifs and maybes."

"I'm sure he likes you more than you realize."

"You can be as sure as you like, but as long as he's content to be a friend, so am I, and that's that. I won't hear another word about it."

Stunned by the firmness of Miss Harriet's tone, Katherine nodded. "All right." The two worked on in silence for a few minutes, then Katherine spoke up again. "I'm sorry, Miss Harriet. I really don't mean to be a pest."

Miss Harriet's eyes softened, and she wrapped an arm around Katherine's shoulders. "I know, dear. And I do appreciate that you care about my happiness. I *am* happy, though. Really, I am."

"I know. I've always admired that about you. You seem to be happy no matter what happens."

"It's called joy, Dearie, and it can only come from being close to God and trusting His will."

"Like what happened when my parents told me they were going away for Christmas, and I was still able to be happy for them?"

"Exactly. When we know that God is at work in an area of

our lives, we can rest in His plan and timing, and be joyful in the knowledge that He is overseeing it all."

* * * *

The next morning, Katherine went from table to table as usual. There was a hum of excitement in the air, and it seemed everyone was full of anticipation. Rosie caught Katherine by the sleeve as she hurried past, and exclaimed breathlessly,

"Did you hear about what happened to me?"

Katherine braced herself for a long melodrama and asked politely, "No, Rosie. What happened to you?"

"Well, you know it's almost Christmas, and the mail has been full, I tell you, *full* of cards from all sorts of different places. I even got one from New Jersey." She paused, waiting for Katherine to grasp the enormity of a Christmas card all the way from New Jersey.

"That's very nice, Rosie. I—"

"Well, you'd never guess what was in one of the cards. It came yesterday,

"From New Jersey?" asked Katherine, slipping the question in when Rosie stopped to take a breath.

"Oh, no. Not in *that* one... although it was very nice, with sparkly gold around the edges, and— oh, yes, the other card. Well, it came yesterday in the mail."

"I've heard that cards do come that way." Said Katherine, in mock seriousness, causing Miss Harriet to raise her eyebrows at her in warning from across the room.

"Yes. So it came, and I got my letter opener—so elegant... it was a gift from the luncheon society, you know. Anyway,

I took the letter opener and slit the top. There was a card inside, and when I opened it, what do you think was in the card?"

"I can't imagine. What was in it?"

"A *ticket*. Yes, it was a plane ticket for the Monday before Christmas. Oh, dear me, that's just a couple weeks away!"

"That *is* a nice surprise. Who was it from?" asked Katherine, now genuinely curious.

"My kids sent it. They live in Colorado and haven't been out to see me this year, so they all decided to pool together and spring for a plane ticket."

"That's wonderful, Rosie! I'm sure you're excited to see them."

"Oh, my, yes. But even more so to see my sweet grandbabies."

"I never knew you had grandchildren!" Katherine said in astonishment.

"That just shows how you can never really know about people. Did I tell you my latest theory?"

"The one about noses?"

"No, sweetheart. That one went out weeks ago. My newest theory is about something quite different..." Rosie beckoned for Katherine to lean closer and lowered her voice to a stage whisper. "I have a theory that your beautiful and charming employer has *an admirer*."

Rosie nodded at the table where Mr. James was sitting. "I've been noticing how well they've been getting along lately."

"Now Rosie, you stop that." Katherine said firmly, keeping her voice low so no one else would hear. "Miss Harriet doesn't have any admirers at present, and I won't have you gossiping about her." Then, to soften the blow, she leaned in again and whispered, "Don't you think I've been noticing them, too? Just leave them be and you'll see how nicely things turn out if we just let them alone."

Rosie smirked and nodded, and Katherine could tell she had silenced the gossipy chatter on that topic—at least temporarily.

"All right then. Did you hear what the queen did last week?" And with that, Rosie was off into another long monologue about her beloved "royals".

Katherine slipped away as soon as she could and walked over to Mrs. Penelope's table, where the small elderly woman had sat staring at the same page of her book for quite some time.

"How are your tea and scones this morning, Mrs. Penelope?" asked Katherine gently. Mrs. Penelope was just as calm and composed as ever, but the sweet features of her wrinkled face seemed weighed down with sadness, and she had only nibbled at her scones. During Rosie's soliloquy, Katherine had glanced over just in time to see a tear trickle discreetly down her cheek.

"They are just as delicious as ever, Katherine dear. I'm just... not very hungry for them today, I suppose."

"Why, whatever's wrong?" asked Katherine.

"Oh, nothing very dire, I suppose. It's just...my family. They telephoned yesterday to tell me they would not be able to come see me this Christmas."

"Oh, Mrs. Penelope. I'm so terribly sorry." Katherine put her arm around the woman's tiny shoulders and gave her a gentle squeeze. "You will let us know if there's anything we can do to cheer you up, won't you?"

Mrs. Penelope nodded, and a tear dropped onto her napkin, which rested neatly in her lap. "You're very kind. Thank you. Just coming in and seeing you both each morning cheers me up some."

"I'm very glad." said Katherine with a smile. She turned to clear the dishes from another table just in time to see that Mr. Patten had been watching from his table by the window. She took the dishes to the kitchen, where she nearly bumped into Miss Harriet.

"Oh, Dearie. Would you mind taking Mr. Patten his bill? And here's Mrs. Penelope's, and Rosie's."

Katherine sighed heavily, and Miss Harriet took back one of the slips of paper.

"Alright, then. In the interest of you keeping a civil tongue in your head, I'll take Rosie's to her for you."

"You're the best!" Katherine said with a mischievous grin.

"Merry Christmas." said Miss Harriet, equally mischievous.

When Katherine laid the check down on Mr. Patten's table, he got out his wallet and said quietly, "Will you please allow me to pay Mrs. Penelope's bill as well? I see she is in some distress today."

Katherine smiled brightly. "Of course! Here it is." She stole a look at Mrs. Penelope to see that she wasn't watching and handed him her bill. When she turned to leave, he called her back and said, "Please, don't tell her I was the one who paid. Just say that it was... a friend."

Katherine nodded soberly and went back to the kitchen

with Mr. Patten's dishes before delightedly giving Mrs. Penelope the news that her bill had been paid by "a friend."

22

A Harborhaven
Christmas

Christmas morning, Katherine drifted awake to the soft sound of Miss Harriet humming in another room and the fragrance of something freshly-baked and full of spices. Her eyelids fluttered open and she gazed around the unfamiliar room. The ceiling and walls were white, and reflected the dimness of the dark, cloud-covered sky outside the pale blue curtains of the window.

Through the sleepy haze of a mind not quite ready to be awake, Katherine remembered that she was in the guest room of Miss Harriet's little cottage above the sea. She stretched beneath the luxurious fluff of the down comforter and settled back into her pillow with a satisfied sigh.

Just then, there was a gentle knock at the door and Miss Harriet's voice from the other side.

"Merry Christmas, Katherine! Time to get up if you want your Christmas breakfast before we head off to church."

"Coming!" Katherine called, and reluctantly got out of bed. She walked over to the window and looked out over the harbor. A flood of memories washed over her as she remembered looking out over that same harbor on Christmas morning from the windows of her old house. How long ago that seemed, and yet the harbor looked just as it had all those years ago.

There was another knock at the door.

"Katherine, can I come in?"

Katherine opened the door to find Miss Harriet standing there with a small package, wrapped in Christmas paper and tied with a ribbon.

"I wanted you to have this before you dressed for church." Miss Harriet explained.

Katherine took the package and sat down on the bed with a bounce. She gently untied the heavy silk ribbon before tearing the paper.

"Oh, Miss Harriet!" she cried, as she pulled the paper away, revealing a silvery grey scarf. She gently removed the silky folds of fabric from the paper and shook it out, admiring the richness of the light fabric.

"It's lovely!" she said, jumping up to hug her friend. "Will you show me how to wear it?" she asked.

"Of course, Dearie." Miss Harriet wrapped the scarf loosely around Katherine's neck and stood back to survey the results. "Well, now. If it can look that lovely with a nightdress, imagine how it will look with your other outfits!" The two laughed heartily and Katherine stood in front of the mirror to see how she looked. Turning suddenly, she exclaimed,

"I almost forgot! I have something for you as well." She opened her overnight bag and pulled out a very precisely-wrapped package. "Here."

She handed it to Miss Harriet and sat down on the bed. Miss Harriet sat down beside her and carefully popped the tape off the back and ends of the package. She drew in a long breath as she moved the paper aside and gazed on the contents. She held up the ornate book and said,

"Oh, it's Mrs. Beeton's! I love this book and have always wanted a nicer copy than that ratty paperback I have in my kitchen."

Katherine smiled happily. "I found it at the Antiques Emporium downtown, and it seemed like it should belong to you."

"Thank you, Katherine. It's a wonderful present!" The two hugged, then Miss Harriet stood up, saying, "I'd better go see to breakfast and let you get dressed. Happy Christmas, Dearie."

Katherine closed the door behind her and pulled off the scarf. Rummaging around in her bag, she took out the skirt and sweater she had brought for church and quickly dressed. She sat down at the antique dressing table and tried to drape her new scarf like Miss Harriet had done.

Wonderful smells from the kitchen wafted into her room as she brushed her hair, and her stomach was growling by the time she walked down the short, curved flight of stairs and into the kitchen. Miss Harriet was just pulling the last slices of bacon out of a pan.

"I'm all ready to go. Is there anything I can help with?"

"Yes, in a moment. Did you sleep well?"

"Oh, yes. You have the most comfortable guest room I've ever stayed in."

"Is it, now? Well, that's good. Would you just carry that in for me?" Miss Harriet motioned to a towel-enshrouded basket sitting on the counter.

Katherine picked it up and walked out into the main room of the house, where Miss Harriet had set the table with china and crystal.

"It all looks so beautiful!" Katherine cried, as Miss Harriet came in from the kitchen with the plate of bacon.

"Christmas breakfast." She replied merrily, "It was always one of our favorite things to eat off the fancy plates at Christmas, so we made a tradition of using them for breakfast as well as dinner on Christmas Day. Now, have a seat, and we'll say grace."

* * * *

"Doesn't it just feel *right* when Christmas is on a Sunday?" Miss Harriet exclaimed as they put on their jackets and walked to the car.

"What do you mean?" asked Katherine.

"Well, the whole point of Christmas in the first place is to celebrate God's gift of salvation to us, so doesn't it seem fitting to spend at least part of the day worshiping Him with other believers?"

"I guess so. I hadn't really thought about it before." Katherine looked out the window as they drove down the winding road. A few pockets of frost clung to the undergrowth beneath the fir trees that darted past.

"I wonder if the captain will come to church." Katherine said wistfully.

"Did you ask him to?" asked Miss Harriet, a little surprised.

"Yes. When I left on Friday, I asked if he would like to come. I offered for him to sit with us."

"And what did he say?"

"Oh, you know Captain Braddock. He just sort of grunted and walked away."

"That does sound like the captain. Still, you never know what people will do on Christmas. He might change his mind and surprise us after all. We'll save a seat, just in case."

* * * *

Inside the church, there was a hum of conversation as people milled around, exchanging Christmas greetings. The children excitedly compared tales of the presents they had unwrapped, while parents told each other how early their children had woken them up that morning.

The low rafters of the old church were twined with green garlands, and a large wreath hung at the front of the sanctuary. It all looked just as Katherine remembered from those years before the move.

The organ began to play and people made their way into the crowded pews. Katherine left an empty space at the end of their row, just in case the captain should come. She looked around expectantly, watching the doors so she could make sure to see when he came in, but when the first hymn began, she turned around with a disappointed sigh and joined in the singing.

The Christmas service was everything Katherine remembered it to be, and she thoroughly enjoyed it, even though the captain hadn't shown up. After the closing prayer, she and Miss Harriet stood and exchanged greetings with those around them before putting on their jackets and stepping out into the aisle. Katherine looked up and abruptly stopped. There, in the very last row, sat Captain Braddock!

She pushed her way through the line of people making their way towards the door.

"Captain! Oh, you came! Merry Christmas!"

Captain Braddock grinned as Katherine hurried towards him.

"I thought you weren't going to come," she said, her face alight with happy amazement.

"To tell you the truth, Missy, I wasn't. But then I got to thinking about what you said the other day, and... well," he leaned forwards and lowered his voice. "I thought I might try out some of those old paths for myself."

"Oh, I *am* glad!" Katherine said softly, tears swimming in her eyes as she smiled back at the old man.

"Captain Braddock! Happy Christmas to you," said Miss Harriet warmly as she walked up next to Katherine and extended her hand.

"Thank you. And the same to you as well." The captain said gruffly, but with a gracious nod of his head as he shook her hand.

"I was just wondering," Miss Harriet began, "Would you...

that is, Katherine and I would very much like it if you came and had Christmas dinner with us."

Katherine watched the Captain's face, expecting to see storm clouds gathering, but to her surprise, the old man paused for a moment, then gave a reluctant smile.

"I thank you. I had thought to take my Christmas dinner at home today, but... I may as well join the two of you—since it's Christmas and all." He looked at Katherine and winked.

* * * *

Dinner was as wonderful as Miss Harriet had promised: turkey and stuffing, homemade cranberry sauce, roasted potatoes, rutabagas, and another kind of root vegetable Katherine didn't recognize. There was gravy and a dense, spongy sort of bread Miss Harriet called Yorkshire Pudding. For dessert, a concoction of sponge cake and pudding sat chilling in the refrigerator, while a tin of mince pies waited on the counter.

Captain Braddock stood awkwardly in the kitchen doorway, as if he had intended to help, but found himself utterly at a loss as to how. Katherine set the table with an extra chair and Miss Harriet's beautiful china plates. Once the food was all transferred into its serving dishes and set on the table, Miss Harriet took off her apron, smoothed her hair, and led the way to the table.

"Captain Braddock, will you take the head?" Miss Harriet asked, motioning to the chair at the end of the small table, which was now a rectangle, due to the extra leaves Miss Harriet had put in it that morning to accommodate the feast.

"I, uh...yes, thank you," said the Captain, and he sat carefully down, eyeing the floral china plate and crystal glass at his plate with a degree of uneasiness.

"I'll ask the blessing, shall I?" Miss Harriet said, extending one hand to the Captain and the other across the table to Katherine. The captain grunted and nodded, reluctantly placing his hands in theirs.

"Lord God, we thank You for all Your many gifts. We thank You for this food and for friends with whom to share it. We thank You for bringing Katherine to Harborhaven, and for bringing Captain Braddock here to share our Christmas with us today. Most of all, we thank You for Your greatest gift of all: the Savior whose birth we celebrate as we share this meal. With grateful hearts, we ask Your blessing on our meal and our time together. In Jesus' name we pray, Amen."

Katherine opened her eyes and stole a quick glance at the captain. His eyes glistened as he raised his head, but he quickly shook off his emotion, clearing his throat and asking,

"What's that lumpy-looking gravy in the pitcher over there?"

Miss Harriet laughed heartily as she deftly carved thin slices of meat off the turkey and laid them on the plate Katherine was holding for her. "Oh, that. I suppose neither of you have had it before. It's called bread sauce, and *I* think it's delicious! It's meant to go on the turkey, but you can do what you like with it."

"You're right, I haven't ever heard of it. Why is it called bread sauce?" Katherine asked, drizzling some over her turkey.

"Because it's made with crumbled bread, to thicken it. I'm sure you remember that in medieval times, bread was the most basic thing they had to eat. It isn't very nice to eat stale, though, so they had to think of things to make with it after it had gone old. Bread sauce was something nearly anybody could make as a Christmas treat, and so it became a tradition. What do you think?" she asked as Katherine took a bite.

"I like it!" Katherine said. "It tastes like Christmas, some-how, and it's nice to think that we have something to eat that so many generations before us have eaten with their Christmas dinners."

"That's exactly why I make it."

Captain Braddock chuckled. "I can see why you two get along so well," he said. Cutting a small bite of turkey, he tried some of the sauce himself. "Say, it does taste good... sorta familiar." He took another bite and chewed thoughtfully. "Come to think of it, Great-Grandma Braddock used to make this for Christmas when I was a boy."

"Really?" asked Miss Harriet, "Why, that's quite remark-able. Was she from England?"

"No, but it may have been a recipe from the Braddock side, which did come from England to begin with. It was one of those holiday foods that everybody is expected to eat, because it's a tradition, but I don't remember how it came to be one. Strange, though. It's unlike the Braddocks to let a tradition die out like that."

"Well, I'm very glad I made it, and that you decided to join us. There's nothing like food for transporting us back to the good old days, especially at Christmas."

* * * *

Katherine was surprised to see Captain Braddock and Miss Harriet getting along so well, and when the meal was done and Miss Harriet began to clear the table, the captain stood and said with unusual politeness,

"Well, ma'am, thank you kindly for the excellent meal. I would offer to help with the washing up if I weren't so fearful I'd break some of yer pretty plates in the attempt. And since I can't be a help by staying, I'll be a help by goin' and letting the two of you get to it."

"Oh, Captain, you don't need to go so soon." Miss Harriet said, setting down the dish she was holding.

"No, I think it would be best for me to be getting back home before my old bones get too tired. A Merry Christmas to you, and thank you for giving a grizzled old curmudgeon a good meal."

"You're very welcome, Captain. And you're welcome any time, really." Miss Harriet said, shaking the captain's hand. Just then, Miss Harriet's phone began to ring in another room.

"Katherine, perhaps you could see the captain out while I run and answer that? Goodbye, Captain, and Merry Christmas!"

Miss Harriet hurried over to the phone while Katherine walked down the short hall with the captain and handed him his jacket and cap. He put his jacket on and felt for a pocket.

"By the way, I, uh, have something for you." He pulled a small wooden box out of his pocket and held it out.

Katherine picked it up and ran her fingers over the smooth wood before opening it.

"Oh, it's beautiful!" she said softly, as she gazed down at

an oval brooch nestled on a velvet cushion. It had a creamy color, as if it used to be white, but had yellowed with age, with a detailed image of a sailing ship.

"It's scrimshaw." The captain said, a bit shyly. "Made by Captain Jeremiah during one of his voyages. It's the *Anne*, you see. He brought it home and gave it to his daughter-in-law, Ophelia, as a wedding gift." He shifted his hat back and forth uneasily in his hands. "Anyway, I ran across it the other day and thought you might just like it."

"I love it!" said Katherine, giving the old man an impulsive hug. "I have something for you, too, only it's upstairs, because I didn't know if I would see you today. Stay right there!" she said, running up the stairs.

She was back in a moment with a little drawstring bag. Captain Braddock pulled open the top of the bag and looked inside.

"What's this?" he asked, reaching in with two fingers and pulling out a loop of ribbon, from which hung an intricately-carved wooden ship's wheel.

"When we decorated the tree the other day, I noticed that the ornaments all told a story." Katherine explained. "It seemed like there was a story from every generation of Braddocks, except yours. I thought you should have an ornament of your own, so the tree can tell your part of the story, too."

Captain Braddock's eyes glistened and his voice was husky as he took Katherine's hand and squeezed it, saying, "Thank you, Katherine. It's the most kind-hearted gift I've ever had."

He turned and opened the door to leave.

"Captain,"

"Yes?"

"I'm so glad you decided to come."

"I am, too, Missy. And you can tell that employer of yours she has my thanks for the invitation. She's quite a lady," he said, then leaned close and with a bit of his old gruffness, added, "but don't you ever tell her I said so, you hear?" he winked and patted Katherine's shoulder. "Merry Christmas, my dear, and thank you for making mine merry as well."

* * * *

Once Katherine and Miss Harriet had finished the washing up and put the last of the leftovers away, they settled into chairs in the "sitting room" end of the house, where Miss Harriet had a fire crackling cozily away in the little fireplace. Miss Harriet had brought out a pot of tea and two cups on a little tray, with some cookies and two small packages which looked to Katherine like large tootsie rolls made of wrapping paper.

"What are those?" she asked.

"Christmas crackers." Miss Harriet replied cheerfully, holding one end out towards Katherine. "Pull your end, sharply, as I pull mine. Ready? One, two, three, Go!"

There was a sudden loud snap, and a smell of fireworks as Katherine's end came off the cracker and the contents flew out of the cylinder. Miss Harriet gathered them up and handed them to her. There was a colorful wad of tissue paper, which unfolded into a flimsy crown, a folded piece of paper with an incredibly corny joke on it, and miniature game of horseshoes.

They repeated the process with the other cracker, and the

two giggled as they put the crowns on their heads and read their jokes to each other. Then, Miss Harriet poured the tea, explaining how her family always had crackers at Christmas.

"They're generally meant to be done at the table before dinner, but I couldn't imagine the captain would be any too willing to wear a paper crown, so I decided not to press my luck."

Katherine took the cup and saucer Miss Harriet handed her. "I think we may have witnessed a miracle today with the captain," she said, curling her legs under her and settling deeper into her chair.

"Yes, it certainly was unprecedented. I've never known of him accepting an invitation to anywhere, and I've certainly never seen him get along so well with people."

"I'm glad he did, though." Katherine said, staring into the fire as she sipped her tea. "It must be so lonely for him, with all his family gone, but with the memories of their Christmases together so alive."

"Yes. Particularly living in that great old house up on the cliffs all by himself, surrounded with so much tradition and history. I mean, history is all well and good, but when it's your own history, and there's no one to enjoy it with, it seems it would be more of a burden than a blessing."

"I suppose so." Katherine said thoughtfully.

The two sat silent for a while, listening to the sound of the raindrops pelting the windows as the wind blew in off the harbor and enjoying the warmth of the fire, until Katherine suddenly set her cup down and asked, "By the way, who was on the phone?"

"Oh, it was just Harold. He called to wish us Merry Christmas. He's with his sister in New York, of all places."

"That's nice," Katherine said, trying not to smirk. They returned to their companionable silence, but Katherine couldn't help but notice that Miss Harriet was blushing.

23

Quiet Beginnings

The week between Christmas and the New Year passed quietly at Miss Harriet's, with the Luncheon Club disbanded until its leader's return and many of the other regular customers out of town as well.

Mr. James was to stay with his sister until New Year's Day, and even Katherine had to acknowledge that the place didn't seem the same without him. Still, she was glad for Rosie's absence, for she would certainly have noticed how many times a day Miss Harriet remarked with a soft sigh and a glance at the empty table, "this place is so *quiet* these days." Katherine had never known Miss Harriet to complain before, especially about things being quiet.

There were two of the dailies, however, who had not gone out of town. The day after Christmas, Mrs. Penelope arrived at her regular time, carrying a book as usual. There was a quiet gladness in her nut-brown eyes as she greeted Katherine.

"Good morning, Mrs. Penelope. How are you today?" Katherine asked cheerfully.

"Oh, very well indeed!"

"Good! Scones and tea as usual?"

"Yes, dear. Thank you."

Katherine went to the kitchen to fetch Mrs. Penelope's order, which had been carefully timed to be ready when she arrived. When she came out again, she saw Miss Harriet standing at Mrs. Penelope's table. As she walked up, Miss Harriet asked,

"And how was your Christmas, Mrs. Penelope?"

Katherine was a little shocked at this because, last anyone knew, Mrs. Penelope had planned to spend her Christmas miserably alone. Miss Harriet always seemed to know the right questions to ask people, though, so she set the tray quietly down and waited for Mrs. Penelope's reply.

"Oh, it was wonderful, just wonderful!" Mrs. Penelope said with more enthusiasm than Katherine had ever seen her display.

"Really?" Katherine burst out before she could stop herself.

"Oh, yes. You see, someone (I don't know who) heard about my children not coming for Christmas. They must also have heard about how I couldn't go to them because a train ticket would have been so expensive, and I don't fly anymore, you know. Anyway, some kind soul left a round trip ticket in my mailbox that very night after I talked with you, Katherine."

"How extraordinary!" Miss Harriet exclaimed.

"So you got to spend Christmas with your family after all!" Katherine said, eyes shining.

"Yes, and they were so pleased! I wasn't sure if they would

be, with me just showing up like that, but they really were! They said that they had been wishing they could have come and gotten me to spend Christmas with them, and as it happened, it was the very best Christmas I've ever had!"

"Oh, I *am* glad!" Katherine exclaimed, with a silent guess at who the mystery purchaser of the ticket might be.

A little later, while Mrs. Penelope was still savoring her scones and reading at her table, Mr. Patten came in. After a quick glance at the quiet lady immersed in her book, he took his usual place at the front.

"Good morning, Mr. Patten. You're a bit earlier than usual today."

"Yes, well, I... I thought since I had the day off, I might see if an earlier lunch agreed with me. It's hard to change routines while I'm working, so I thought I should try to vary things a little when I have time off."

"That's nice." Katherine replied, trying not to smirk as she caught another glance in Mrs. Penelope's direction.

"Are we varying your lunch order as well?" she asked.

"Pardon? Oh, no. I think the earlier time is quite enough variety for today."

"Right. I'll be back in a minute or two, then."

Katherine walked back to the kitchen, where Miss Harriet was already preparing Mr. Patten's tea and Cornish pasty.

"Miss Harriet," Katherine said in a hushed voice

"Yes?" Miss Harriet replied, also hushed.

"I'm *sure* Mr. Patten is the one who bought Mrs. Penelope that ticket. And he came in so early today... and he keeps looking over at her."

"Does he?" Miss Harriet said calmly, pouring water from the kettle into a small teapot.

"Would it be wrong of me to suggest he go talk to her? He obviously wants to."

"Dearie, sometimes we just have to let things take their course. Mr. Patten is a grown man. He'll speak to Mrs. Penelope when the time is right."

"Then you think he likes her, too?"

"It's none of our business." Miss Harriet put the last of Mr. Patten's order on a tray and handed it to Katherine, saying, "Now, go out there and be your own charming self, but keep those matchmaking tendencies well in check."

"Yes, Miss Harriet." Katherine took Mr. Patten his food and tried to be content to let things "run their course."

* * * *

The week passed quietly at the Harborside, as well. The day before New Year's Eve, Captain Braddock looked up at the garland over the window and said,

"Well, now, I suppose it's about time to take all that down."

"I suppose so. It will seem so bare without it, though." Said Katherine, dust rag in hand.

"Tradition is to take it all down on New Year's Eve."

"That's what Miss Harriet does, too. She says it's a natural transition point, that it just seems right to have a fresh start on New Year's Day."

"Aye, that it is. Years back, the Braddocks always insisted that the decorations stay up till January 6. That's Twelfth Night, you see. You know about Twelfth Night?"

"Yes. It's a tradition from the Middle Ages, when people would celebrate Christmas for twelve whole days, ending on January 6 with the biggest celebration of all, commemorating the arrival of the wise men, as I recall."

"Right. I remember it was a big deal when we started taking things down sooner. Great-Grandma Braddock insisted over and over that 'Christmas isn't over till Twelfth Night' and generally raised a fuss. As you might have noticed, we Braddocks don't adjust well to changes."

"What was it that made you start taking things down on New Year's Eve?"

"Practicality, my dear. Plain and simple. The tree got too dry one year, and turned brown. We couldn't have a *brown* tree in the Harborside shop window, so we took it down, and the other greenery with it. To keep Great-Grandma happy, though, we always kept the Nativity scene up till Twelfth night. By the time she died, we had sort of settled into it, and that's what we did every year." The captain walked over to the tree, limping more heavily than usual.

"Is your leg worse today?" Katherine asked.

"No worse than normal for this time of year. It's the cold and damp, you see. Doesn't agree with it."

"We should take the decorations down today, then, while I'm here. It's only ten minutes till closing, and I don't at all mind staying late tonight."

"Well, perhaps we should at that. I suppose the tradition can bend that far for practicality. I don't much relish getting up on a ladder to take all that down."

"Besides," Katherine said, "the current tradition is *based* on bending the tradition for practical reasons." She thought for a moment before continuing cheerfully. "Maybe practicality is the *real* tradition, after all!"

"I'd have to think long and hard about that one, Missy, but you might have a point, at least in this particular case. Go and fetch the ladder, and I'll close up shop. Don't think we'll have any more customers tonight."

* * * *

On New Year's Eve, Miss Harriet closed the shop a little earlier than usual so she and Katherine could take down the Christmas decorations.

"Let's clear the last of the dishes off the tables first, and put everything away so that the only thing we'll have left to do after the decorations is the washing up." Miss Harriet suggested, surveying the room with folded arms, as if planning a military offensive.

"Good idea." Katherine replied. She brought the cart out from the kitchen, and the two got to work clearing the tables. The task went quickly, and soon they were bringing the Christmas boxes down from Katherine's apartment.

"My dear, I am so glad I have you to help. Otherwise, I might have been here all night taking this all down!" They both chuckled, and Katherine quipped archly,

"It just doesn't seem right to be taking the decorations down without Mr. James here."

To Katherine's surprise, Miss Harriet sighed and said, "I know. I'm beginning to wonder if I haven't been wise to make him so much a part of everything we do here."

Katherine was just opening her mouth to reply, when there was a knock at the door.

"I'll get it." Katherine said, and went to the door while Miss Harriet wheeled the cart towards the kitchen.

"Mr. James!"

"Katherine! Merry Christmas and the happiest of New Years to you! May I come in?"

Katherine shot a glance over to the kitchen doorway to see that Miss Harriet had safely retreated. Then she swung the door wide.

"Of course! I was just saying that it didn't seem right to take the decorations down without you, and now here you are to help!"

Mr. James chuckled and shifted a small bag between his hands. "Well, it's good to be thought of in one's absence, I suppose."

"Mr. James!" Miss Harriet stepped out of the kitchen, with a face carefully composed, but showing genuine gladness as she greeted her friend. "Why, I thought you weren't due back until tomorrow?"

"The weather report said there was a storm brewing, so I changed my flight a day earlier."

"I see."

Katherine busied herself with gathering up the Christmas centerpieces at the back of the room, to give the two space to talk.

"I'm just on my way home from the airport now. I was hoping to find you here still."

Katherine saw Miss Harriet's blush and downcast eyes

from across the room and joined the conversation again with a merry, "Oh, Mr. James, you know better than anyone that we're *always* here... More to the point, so are *you*—except when you're not."

"Yes, we've been noticing how... *quiet* it is around here without you." Miss Harriet had shaken off her sudden shyness and joined in the banter. "It made for a change, to be sure, but it really won't do to have an empty table right in the window like that, so it's good you've come back."

"This place certainly has become a fixture in my daily routine. You know, there's no place like it in New York. In fact, my sister hardly seemed to believe such a place existed anywhere at all! And even though I scoured the city looking for a cheddar scone, I only found one bakery that made them, and when I tried one, it was absolutely terrible."

"I'm glad to hear it." Miss Harriet quipped, "We like to have the corner on the market."

"There could never be a doubt on that score."

There was a pause then, just long enough to become awkward, as the two stood, trying to decide what to say next. Katherine decided to interject again.

"I suggested we name the table after you. That way, when you're a world-famous journalist, we can take advantage of your fame."

"Excellent idea!" laughed Mr. James. "Though I don't know if even world-famous journalists can survive without their cheddar scones." He shifted the bag in his hands again, and then started, as if suddenly remembering it was there. "Oh! Now, the real reason for my visit, apart from your charming company—"

"You mean you didn't come to help us take the decorations down?" Katherine said, eyes wide in mock disappointment.

"No, but I did come bearing gifts." He took a small package out of the bag and held it out to Katherine. "They're sort of Christmas and New Year's gifts... tokens of my esteem and appreciation... Honestly, I just saw them and thought of you." He spoke the last phrase with his eyes fixed steadily on Miss Harriet's face. Turning to Katherine again, he said impatiently,

"Well, go on. Open it!"

Katherine grinned. She could tell by the feel of the package that there was a book inside. She tore off the paper and exclaimed, "*David Copperfield!* I've been wanting to read this, but the library didn't have it."

"I remembered you mentioning that, and with your propensity to carry a book around with you at all times, I figured a pocket edition might prove useful."

"Thank you! I'm sure it will."

"And you'll have to tell me what you think of the story. It happens to be one of my favorite Dickens novels."

Katherine nodded. "I will."

Mr. James took another package out of the bag and held it out to Miss Harriet. "And this one's for you."

She smiled sweetly and took the package. Carefully opening one end of the wrapping paper, she pulled out a plain oblong box. Handing the paper to Katherine, Miss Harriet opened the box and gasped in delight. There lay two dainty gloves of deep burgundy leather, fine and soft, with a warm white lining even softer than the leather.

"Thank you." She said quietly, nearly speechless. She lifted one from the box and tried it on. "However did you know what size to buy? They fit perfectly!"

Now it was Mr. James' turn to blush. "Well, reporters *are* supposed to be observant, you know," he rushed on. "I saw them in a little shop my sister took me into. It was your kind of place. You would have liked it. Anyway, these reminded me of the dress you wore at the Guy Fawkes party."

Miss Harriet looked down at the gloves, an involuntary smile playing around the corners of her mouth. Mr. James took a step towards her and said, "Harriet, if you only knew—"

Miss Harriet looked up, a little alarmed, and he broke off abruptly. Changing tack, he forced a playful smile and said, "If you only knew how horrible that New York scone was, you'd have baked a whole batch for me, just so I could cleanse my palate."

With a smile that Katherine could only describe as relieved, Miss Harriet said brightly,

"Well now, I think I may just have one or two left in the kitchen. I'll go warm them up and make us all a pot of tea while you help Katherine with the lights and garlands."

She laid the gloves gently back in their box and retreated swiftly to the kitchen, leaving Katherine to wonder whether or not to follow Miss Harriet's advice about letting things run their course.

The two worked in silence for a while and were putting the lights and garlands back in their boxes at the far end of the room when Katherine felt she couldn't keep quiet any longer. She could hear Miss Harriet washing dishes in the kitchen, and she knew the noise of the water would keep her from overhearing anything they might say.

"Mr. James," she began, closing a box and turning around to face him. "Are you in love with Miss Harriet?"

"Katherine! What a question." Mr. James stammered, looking as if he weren't sure whether to feel relieved or affronted. Then he sighed. "Is it that obvious?" he asked, handing her another roll of lights.

"Just a bit." She said dryly. "Even Rosie has noticed."

"Ah, well, it *is* obvious then."

"Why don't you tell her?" asked Katherine, in exasperation.

"Because I wouldn't want to ruin the way things *are* if she weren't to return my feelings. It's too good a friendship to spoil."

"But it's too good a possibility to miss by being afraid." Katherine retorted. "I won't speak for Miss Harriet's feelings, but I will say that I think you should know she has been nearly as obvious about missing you these past two weeks as you were just now. It's a mercy Rosie wasn't here to see it, or the whole town would be talking."

Mr. James laughed in spite of himself. "I suppose so. But how do you explain the look of sheer terror on her face when I slipped just now and almost told her?"

Katherine shook her head. "You said it yourself. You're afraid to spoil what you have with her, and that look of terror was likely due to her being afraid of the same thing. I can't tell you any more than that. I just think you should try."

Mr. James was about to speak again when the sound of running water abruptly stopped and Miss Harriet came in, carrying a tray of tea and scones.

"My, don't you both look conspiratorial. Making plans for how to decorate for winter?"

"Not exactly." Katherine said, hurriedly. "Let's sit down and eat. I'm starving!"

24

A New Year

The new year dawned brightly, with a high, blue sky and a bone-chilling breeze. Katherine had stayed the night at Miss Harriet's cottage again, and the two stayed up till midnight to see the new year in.

Katherine's alarm woke her while the sky outside her window was still pitch black, and she hurriedly dressed and crept downstairs to the kitchen. As silently as she could, she began to make a breakfast of eggs, sausage, biscuits, and gravy. Miss Harriet came down just as she was taking the sausages out of the pan.

"Happy New Year, Miss Harriet!"

"Happy New Year, Dearie. What is all this?"

"Well, you've cooked for me so often, I wanted to surprise *you* with breakfast for a change." She chuckled as she added, "Don't worry: I've been practicing."

Miss Harriet smiled and hugged her friend. "I can tell!

Well, this *is* a good start to the new year! It all looks and smells delicious!"

"The table's all set and everything. I wanted to give us plenty of time to eat before we have to leave for church."

"Good idea." Miss Harriet said, as Katherine led the way to the table.

* * **

At church that morning, everyone seemed just as jolly as they had been at Christmas, only quite a bit more tired-looking. When the service was over, Katherine and Miss Harriet made their way to the back of the church, where Captain Braddock had again slipped into the very last row.

"Happy New Year, Captain!" Miss Harriet said.

"And a Happy New Year to you too, ma'am. And to you, Katherine."

"Thank you. It's been a happy year so far."

"Glad to hear it." The captain said heartily. "Well, if you'll both excuse me, I have my lunch to get to. I'll see you Tuesday, Katherine."

The captain limped off towards the parking lot, while Miss Harriet and Katherine exchanged smiles.

"I'm so glad he came again!" Katherine said, once the captain was out of earshot.

"Me too. If you achieve nothing else in life, Dearie, you've made that crusty old curmudgeon step foot in a church again, and that's quite a feat."

As they walked out into the parking lot, Katherine

suddenly tugged on Miss Harriet's sleeve and said, "Look! It's Mr. James."

"Why, yes, it is." She said, smiling broadly at the reporter as he strode towards them.

"Happy New Year, both of you! Bright and chipper as ever, I see."

"That's a nice thing to hear after staying up late to see the New Year in! And, you know, Katherine was up before the birds this morning, making me the most delicious breakfast."

"I'm glad to hear it. You deserve a little pampering now and then. Good thinking, Katherine."

He winked at Katherine, and then turned back to Miss Harriet again. "I wanted to see if you would like to come for a stroll with me. There's something I want to ask you about."

Miss Harriet hesitated, and before she could reply, Mr. James continued, "Of course, it is quite cold this morning. If you would prefer, perhaps you could join me at my table in the morning for tea and scones? My treat. I happen to know that you have excellent staff available to take your place for a while, and I also happen to know that said staff is also *willing* to do so, right, Katherine?"

"Very willing." Katherine replied, with an encouraging smile.

Miss Harriet still looked unsure. "Well, I suppose so... that is..." she stopped abruptly and let out a breath. "I'm sorry to sound so ungracious. What I mean to say is yes, thank you. Tea and scones at the shop would be lovely." She smiled at Mr. James, whose face turned instantly from anxiety to jubilation.

"Good. Tomorrow morning, then."

"Tomorrow morning."

* * * *

When Katherine came downstairs the next morning, she found Miss Harriet surrounded by bowls and baking sheets and racks full of baked goods.

"You've been busy. What time did you get here?" Katherine asked, putting the big brass kettle on to boil.

"Oh, I don't know, perhaps since four." Miss Harriet said distractedly.

"*Four*?" Katherine exclaimed, "Why ever did you come that early?"

"I was so flustered, I couldn't sleep."

"And so you came here to calm your nerves by baking?"

"Well, yes. I suppose you could say that."

Miss Harriet put one last pan of scones in the oven and turned around. Katherine looked admiringly at her friend. Despite the lack of sleep and the smear of flour across one cheek, Miss Harriet looked polished and put together. The frigid winter morning had prompted her to change her light floral skirt for plain thick wool, but she had paired it with a floral blouse and a long-sleeved cardigan of the same shade as the gloves Mr. James had given her. Katherine silently wondered if she had done that deliberately.

"And are your nerves calmed now? Or should I call in an emergency order for more flour, eggs, and milk?"

Miss Harriet laughed and wiped her floury hands on her apron. "I think it's safe now, although I don't exactly feel calm. Whatever *can* he have to talk to me about?"

"Many things, I would imagine. Talking to Mr. James isn't an unheard-of occurrence for you. Why are you so worked up about it?"

"It's the *way* he said he wanted to talk to me. One minute I'm convinced he's about to, well..." Miss Harriet broke off with a blush.

"Proclaim his undying affection?" Katherine suggested helpfully.

"Something like that, and then the next minute I'm convinced that it's just something mundane and ordinary and I'm making a fool of myself over nothing."

Katherine turned from the sink with a bowl in her hand.

"First of all, you're not making a fool of yourself." Katherine paused, looking around the kitchen at all the dishes and cooling pastries. "Ok... well, maybe just a *little*."

Miss Harriet looked around too, and they both laughed. Miss Harriet picked up a stack of mixing bowls and handed it to Katherine, who put them in the sink to soak.

"I can see why you're nervous. But think of it this way: if he *is* about to say something that will change things between the two of you, so much the better! And if not, you won't walk away from this breakfast date—"

"Meeting." Miss Harriet interjected.

"Meeting, then, with anything less than what you had before. Either you'll end the morning as good friends, or as something better."

Miss Harriet sighed and set a wooden spoon in the sink. "You're right. Have I ever told you how glad I am to have you here?"

"Yes, but it's been a day or two." Katherine replied laughingly.

As they worked together to get the kitchen cleaned up, Miss Harriet began to return to her normal calm and cheerful self. Soon, they heard the bell over the shop door ring brightly, and Miss Harriet turned to Katherine.

"Help me off with my apron, Dearie, and tell me if I look all right."

Katherine reached up and quickly brushed the flour off her companion's face saying reassuringly,

"You look lovely. Here, I'll take the apron; you go out and greet your guest. I'll bring the tea things in a couple minutes, once the water has boiled."

It was all Katherine could do to restrain herself from peeking around the curtain to see how the meeting was progressing. Unlike Miss Harriet, Katherine had no doubts as to the purpose of the meeting, and she was determined to give the almost-couple as much time to themselves as they needed.

The water boiled, and Katherine prepared the tea as slowly as she thought believably possible. Then she took the tray to the table.

"Tea for two!" She exclaimed. "Good morning, Mr. James. You'll be happy to know that these scones just came out of the oven. They're as fresh as can be."

"Thank you, Katherine." Mr. James smiled at her broadly. Miss Harriet had her "carefully composed" look on again, and Katherine assumed they hadn't gotten to discussing whatever it was Mr. James had wanted to ask her about.

"I have some cleaning to do in the kitchen, so just let me know if you need anything."

With that, Katherine turned and walked calmly away, fighting the urge to steal a look back to see what was happening. She surveyed the kitchen with a sigh. At least she would have plenty to do until the rest of the morning customers arrived. She grabbed a dishtowel and began drying and putting away the bowls and spoons she had washed earlier.

By the time the bell over the door rang again, Katherine had the kitchen looking as spotless as ever. She stole a glance at the two by the window as she walked over to greet Mrs. Penelope. They were leaning across the table towards each other, deep in earnest conversation.

"Good morning, Mrs. Penelope! How are you this morning?"

"Oh, I'm just fine, dear. Just three plain scones and a cup of tea as usual, please."

"I'll be right out with it."

Back in the kitchen, Katherine wondered how long the two would be able to talk undisturbed. Mercifully, Rosie wasn't due back until tomorrow, and the rest of the luncheon club only came in on Wednesdays. Mr. Patten would be fine, because he had his own affair of the heart to distract him. That just left the occasional walk-ins.

As she passed through the kitchen doorway, Mr. Patten walked in.

"I thought I'd see what breakfast is like here." He said casually, with another glance over at Mrs. Penelope's table.

"Ah, well, we do happen to have an abundance of scones this morning. Did you have anything particular in mind?"

"Hmm... well, I suppose I hadn't really thought that far."

Katherine smiled and leaned a little closer, saying quietly,

"We do make a lovely Cornish pasty here, which I'm told some have been known to eat for breakfast. Would that do?"

Mr. Patten smiled back a little sheepishly. "Yes, I think that will be just the thing. Thank you."

At the kitchen door, Katherine stopped and took a quick glance around. What a jumble of secrets and emotions were seated in that room!

* * * *

Just before the noon rush, Miss Harriet popped into the kitchen. Putting on her apron, she asked, "Well, how are you getting on back here? Everything going well?"

Katherine looked searchingly at her friend. "I could ask you the same question."

"Oh, things are going quite well indeed. I know I won't have time to do it all justice at the moment, so you'll just have to be content to know that everything is... is as it *should* be, and I'm quite delighted with it all!"

"Now, if that isn't a teaser, I don't know what is! But I'm glad it's all right. Is Mr. James still out there?"

"Yes, he had some work he needed to get done."

"Aha... Perhaps I'll just go see if he needs anything."

"Now Katherine, don't you go pumping him for information. I'll tell you all about it after we close. Let the poor man work."

"All right... but if I *happen* to pass his table and he *happens* to divulge a few of the details you're so skillfully withholding, I'll be forced to stop and listen, just to be polite, of course."

"Oh, go on with you!" said Miss Harriet, throwing a tea

towel at Katherine in mock frustration. Katherine ducked and picked up a tray, giving Miss Harriet one last teasing grin before heading out of the kitchen.

* * * *

As soon as the shop door closed on the last customer of the day, Katherine rushed over and turned the lock. Whirling around again, she asked,

"Well?"

"Let's have some tea." Miss Harriet replied with a grin as she headed towards the kitchen.

Soon they were sitting at one of the tables, each warming their hands around a steaming, fragrant cup of tea.

"So what was it he wanted to ask you about?"

"He wanted to ask if I would like to know what he almost said the other night."

"And did you?" Katherine said, holding her breath for the answer.

"I told him yes, so long as *he* wanted me to know."

"And?" Katherine set her teacup down on its saucer and leaned forward.

"He did." Miss Harriet said simply, smiling as she took a sip of her tea.

"Oh, good!" Katherine exclaimed.

"You act like you knew what he was going to say all along."

"Well, it *was* rather obvious..."

"And there I was, thinking I must have imagined it was anything out of the ordinary."

The two giggled, then lapsed into a happy silence for a few

moments, sipping their tea and smiling at each other. Then Miss Harriet said,

"I suppose you'll be wanting to know that Mr. James and I are, well, let's just say we're cautiously getting to know one another better in the hopes of being something more than 'just friends.'"

"And what does that look like?"

"Much as it has done, only without the awkward hiding of interest and dancing around issues. We have the freedom now to talk about anything we feel is necessary, and I think it should be a much more comfortable friendship moving forward."

"But... that sounds exactly like what it *has* looked like, awkwardness aside. Shouldn't there be something... more, now that the plan is to be more than friends?"

"Not necessarily. You see, we both feel that a healthy marriage is best built upon a healthy friendship. We have the friendship already, but it needs to grow, to deepen, before we can be sure it's meant to be more."

Katherine leaned back in her chair and sat silent, pondering this new idea of relationship. After a while, she sat up, drained her teacup and said with a mischievous grin,

"Well, now that you two have things settled, I'd better go finish putting away all that food you baked this morning!"

25

Becalmed

A few days later, Katherine was sitting on the floor of the Harborside, dusting the jars and tea bowls on the lowest shelf. Captain Braddock had come in to tend the fire in the old wood stove and had sat down in the old chair to enjoy its warmth. He was apparently in no hurry to get up again, and Katherine felt glad for the company. Miss Harriet had been spending more time with Mr. James, and although Katherine felt genuinely happy for her friend, she was beginning to miss having her all to herself.

"Captain," she said over her shoulder as she lifted one last jar and wiped down the shelf underneath it.

"Yes'm?" the old man answered, surfacing from a reverie of his own.

"When did you decide to go to sea?"

Captain Braddock leaned back in the chair and looked up

at the ceiling. His brow furrowed as he worked to recall the memory he wanted.

"I don't know as I could fix the exact moment. I always wanted to, ever since I was a little mite, listening to Great-Grandpa Braddock's tales of the Anne and her grand old seafaring adventures. I suppose it was them that made me want to go."

Crossing the room, Katherine set her rag behind the counter and curled up on the floor opposite Captain Braddock by the stove. "But... how did you know it was time—that it was what you were actually meant to *do*?" she asked with a little frown.

Captain Braddock sat up straight and looked at Katherine with raised eyebrows.

"Why? You fixin' to go away to sea?"

"No, it's just..." Katherine gave an impatient little sigh, "When I was little, the world seemed so wide and full of possibilities, and I had ever so many dreams. One day, I would dream of being a doctor; the next, I would be *sure* I wanted to be an artist; and the next, a ballerina or a librarian. It was as if I could change the direction of my life anytime I chose. Now that I'm grown up and on my own, I feel sort of... I don't know..." Her voice trailed off and she stared absently at the toes of her boots which peeked out from under her warm full skirt as she sat, hugging her knees.

Captain Braddock watched her for a moment, then spoke up.

"Becalmed. That's what you are." He said, leaning forwards in his chair.

"Becalmed?" Katherine looked up, puzzled.

"Yes. It was one of the most dreaded things for a sailor in the days before motors and engines. You see, when a ship would make a voyage, its progress was largely dependent upon the winds. A good, stiff wind from the right direction could bring you into port well before schedule, but a wind from the wrong direction or no wind at all would stop a ship dead in its tracks until the wind changed.

"Captains were careful, you see, to travel during the right times and seasons, so that the winds would be favorable, but every now and then a ship would get stuck out in the ocean because the winds weren't right.

"Sometimes it was because the wind was against them, from the wrong direction, see. With an unfavorable wind like that, at least there was something you could feel you were fighting against, and there was hope that the wind might change direction and blow the right way again.

"The worst was when there was no wind. Sailors called that being *becalmed*. Day after day, sometimes week after week, the ship would sit there, resting on a calm sea with sails limp as seaweed and completely still. There was nothing to do but wait and keep the ship ready for the moment the wind picked up –if it ever did.

"The danger to a shipful of sailors who found themselves becalmed was grave: food and water supplies could run out before they could get anywhere and restock. That was bad enough, but to my mind, the real danger was that the crew might get impatient and give up hope. Once that happened, desperation would set in, and men can do some pretty awful things when they're desperate.

"The Anne was becalmed on several occasions, and Captain

Jeremiah used to say that the only thing to do when you're becalmed is to keep your eyes on the sails, pray, and expect them to fill."

Captain Braddock reached down and put his hand on Katherine's shoulder. "You'll dream again, Missy. I'm sure of it—and this time the dreams will be real and alive, not far-off mists in the distance. Then your sails will swell and you'll be on your way again. Just wait, pray, and stay hopeful."

Katherine laid her hand on top of the captain's and tried to smile, though her eyes were glistening with tears. "Thank you," was all she could manage to say.

The old captain gave her hand a squeeze and then stood and went back to the paperwork he had left unfinished in the next room. Katherine stayed there by the fire for a while, then got up, straightened her canvas apron, picked up a new rag and began dusting the counter.

* * * *

That night, when she let herself in at the front door of Miss Harriet's, Katherine noticed her employer's voice coming from the kitchen. She listened for a moment, expecting to hear Mr. James as well, but hearing only Miss Harriet, finally decided that she must be on the phone.

Katherine ran up the stairs to put her hat and coat away, and then came back down to see if the Miss Harriet needed any help. As she neared the kitchen door, Miss Harriet rushed out. The two almost ran into each other, and Katherine started to laugh, but then she caught a glimpse of her friend's face.

"Miss Harriet, whatever is the matter?" Katherine led her

friend to a chair and made her sit down. She was white and trembling, and tears were brimming in her eyes. Katherine pulled another chair close and sat down.

"I've just had a call from my brother in England. Mother is unwell, and he thinks—" Miss Harriet broke off abruptly, and Katherine reached over to squeeze her hand. After a few moments, she continued. "He thinks she may not have long left and says I should come right away."

Katherine's eyes grew wide as the full weight of the situation sank in. "You must go, of course," she said, a bit breathlessly. "I can try to hold down the fort here. I'll...I'll ask the captain if he can spare me while you're away. I'm sure when he knows why you're gone, he'll be willing to work something out."

Miss Harriet, calmer now that she had spoken the dreadful words, took both Katherine's hands in hers and looked her in the eye. "Yes, Dearie. I know I must go, but I'm so sorry for the load you will have to shoulder to keep this place running. If there were another way... but I want you to know that there's no one on earth I would rather have look after things here. No doubt it will be a stretch for you to do everything all on your own, especially with such short notice, but I know you will come through it just fine."

Katherine's heart swelled in spite of the nervousness and concern which had begun to tie knots in her stomach. For Miss Harriet to trust her with the shop meant more than anything she could think of –but it also meant carrying a terrifyingly great responsibility.

Miss Harriet wiped her eyes on a tissue fished from the pocket of her cardigan, squared her shoulders, and began telling Katherine the particulars of her plan, as if determined not to give way to her emotions until all was arranged.

"I've called Harold already and asked him to be at your beck and call, as much as possible, just in case. I also reassured him that you really *do* know how to make a decent cheddar scone." She gave Katherine a watery smile, then continued. "I have a flight booked for midnight. At the moment, my return flight is scheduled for Saturday, but it all depends…"

A tear slipped out, and Miss Harriet had to stop to apply her tissue again before going on. "If you'll come with me to the kitchen, I'll run through the baking schedule with you and make sure you have everything you need."

Katherine followed Miss Harriet into the kitchen, amazed at her friend's strength and wondering how she would ever begin to fill Miss Harriet's place while she was away.

26

Captaining the Shop

"Hello!" shouted Mr. James the next morning as the bell over the shop door announced his arrival. Katherine rushed out from the kitchen, hands covered with flour, and asked breathlessly, "Did Miss Harriet get off all right?"

"Yes. I got her there in plenty of time, although when I picked her up at her house, I thought it might be a close-run thing. She was ready, but I can't imagine how she will manage in the airports with all the luggage she had packed."

Katherine smiled, remembering what Miss Harriet had told her about overpacking to come to America. "That sounds about right. And how was she?"

"About as well as can be expected. I've never met such a strong, brave woman."

"I know what you mean."

"It's a good thing she did handle it all so well," Mr. James said earnestly, "or else I would have bought a ticket right then and there and gone with her. I don't think I could have stopped myself. It was hard enough seeing her go off on such an emotionally difficult trip, all by herself."

"She'll be all right." Katherine said reassuringly, "If she were here, she would remind us that a child of God is never alone, and that she'll be well enough taken care of."

Just then, there was a loud *ding* from the kitchen, and Katherine laughingly said, "And she would probably also tell me to go take your scones out of the oven before they burn."

Coming back from the kitchen, she set a tray down on Mr. James' table.

"I've brought out extra scones and another plate and cup because I'm going to join you for a bit. I hope you don't mind."

"Not at all." Mr. James moved the flower arrangement aside and put away his laptop.

Katherine poured them each a cup of tea, then looked frankly at the reporter as she said,

"Miss Harriet told me a little about your conversation the other day, but I wanted to hear the story from your perspective: how do things stand between you now?"

He smiled broadly, "Is this the 'what are your intentions towards my friend' conversation?" They both laughed, and he continued, "Well, I can tell you they're as honorable as can be. I think Harriet told you that we're proceeding 'cautiously,' taking time to intentionally build and strengthen our existing friendship?"

Katherine nodded.

"Then, to put it bluntly, the way things stand is that I hope with all my heart to marry Harriet in due time, and I know she feels the same. We want to make sure it's done right, though, and decided it was wise to take things slowly at first, giving us each time to pray and seek God's will about each step forward."

"I'm glad to hear that you're both on the same page. I can't imagine two people more perfect for each other!"

"I take that as the highest of compliments. From what I've gathered, you probably know Harriet better than anyone else."

Katherine grinned. "That sure won't last long!" she said, teasingly.

"Yes... well, that is one thing I've been wanting to talk to you about, Katherine. Harriet values your friendship deeply, as do I, and I want you to know that I'm not looking for that to change as she and I grow closer. You will always have a place in her life, and I never want to discourage or hinder that."

Katherine smiled. "Thank you. I know it's only natural that things should be a little different now, but it would be terrible to lose such a dear friend altogether. She's become just like family to me."

Mr. James nodded, then said with a twinkle in his eye, "Look at it this way, Katherine, you're not losing a family member, you're gaining one!"

Katherine chuckled, and replied, "I think that's the very *best* way to see it."

The kitchen timer sounded again, and Katherine jumped up, loading her dishes onto the tray quickly as she said, "Well, I'd better take that second batch of scones out of the oven and get Mrs. Penelope's tea started. Thank you for the chat."

"Anytime, Katherine." Mr. James said sincerely as she hurried away towards the kitchen.

* * * *

The day flew by in a flurry of taking orders, waiting tables, handling money, and cleaning. Mr. James stayed at his table much of the day, which Katherine knew was probably a result of Miss Harriet's request that he be available in case she needed anything. Still, she was thankful to have someone there just in case, and it was nice to feel someone was watching over her as she faced the frightening responsibility of running things on her own.

By the end of the day, she felt more exhausted than she remembered ever feeling before, and as she closed the door after the last customer, she turned around and looked over the shop with a sigh. How Miss Harriet had done all this six days a week, and without any help, astounded her.

As she pulled the cart out of the kitchen and cleared the last few tables, there was a knock on the door. Pulling aside the curtain, her tired face lit up with a smile as she recognized Captain Braddock standing outside, holding an old-fashioned picnic hamper.

"Captain Braddock!" she exclaimed as she opened the door. "Whatever are you doing here?"

"I came to see how my favorite employee had done captaining her own ship all day." He looked down at the hamper in his hands, and said a little shyly as he held it out, "I also figured you mightn't have eaten supper, and you shouldn't have to cook yerself dinner on yer first day."

Katherine's heart swelled till she thought it might burst.

Reaching for the hamper, she said, "Will you come in? I know it's Miss Harriet's and all, but coming in just once won't hurt."

The old man shifted uncomfortably from one foot to the other, then looking up into Katherine's face, said, "Well, I suppose... just this once." As he walked through the doorway, he said with some of his old gruffness, "I packed you some real tea, so you won't be stuck with the awful bagged kind that woman serves here."

Katherine smiled as she unpacked the hamper onto a clean table. "This was so kind of you. I needed to take a break anyway. The tidying up can wait, and to tell you the truth, I was just beginning to notice how very quiet it is around here after hours without Miss Harriet to laugh with."

"And how is she?" the captain asked, taking the top off a thermos and pouring the tea out into two cups Katherine had quickly fetched from the kitchen.

"Mr. James heard from her this evening, and she had made it safely there. It took her nearly twelve hours to get from here to her brother's house. I can't imagine how exhausted she must be."

"Yes. And her mother? Is she as poorly as they said last night?"

"I believe so. It sounds like it's good thing Miss Harriet left when she did."

"So she'll likely be gone for a while, then?"

"I'm afraid so."

"Well, when you're settled into things here, if you can find the time and energy to come to the Harborside for a couple hours each week for however long she's gone, I sure would find it a help." Katherine took a deep breath and nodded.

"I'm hoping to. Miss Harriet did say I could close the shop early a couple days a week if you needed my help."

"That's mighty kind of her. I wouldn't want to interfere with yer regular customers... I know this place is a pretty important part of people's lives in this town."

"So is the Harborside," Katherine said decidedly. "At least, it's an important part of *my* life, so I will do everything I can to come by and get at least a little of my normal work done."

Captain Braddock smiled at her, then frowned and said sternly, "I won't have you exhausting yerself, though. So if you find it too much, you just tell me."

"I will," she promised.

* * * *

The next evening, Katherine arrived at the Harborside after closing. She felt weary from the day's work, but happy to be back in the Harborside. It had been strange being away from it all day.

"Hello, the shop!" she cried as the bell over the door rang out its musical welcome. A shuffling sound came from the captain's office, and as Katherine neared the doorway, she saw Captain Braddock hurriedly sweeping a number of papers into a file folder. The floorboard creaked under her weight, and the old man looked up suddenly, as if she had surprised him.

"Hello, Katherine," he said, a bit distractedly, as he set a large ledger book on top of the folder. "How did yer second day go?"

"About as well as the first: tiring but no major upsets."

"That's good. Means yer gettin' yer sea legs under you."

"Shall I get a rag and start on the jars?" she asked, moving towards the counter where the rags were kept. Captain Braddock stood stiffly and started to limp after her.

"Yes, I think we might both work on the jars tonight. I'm in need of a break, and I want to enjoy your company while I have it." He gave Katherine a weary smile as he picked up a rag from the pile on the shelf. "You start with the *Anne*. I know that's yer favorite."

"How did you know that? I'm sure I never mentioned it."

Captain Braddock dropped his weariness for a moment and said with a twinkle in his eye, "A Braddock knows about these things, you see... Besides, she's my favorite, too."

Katherine smiled as she took the dainty model ship down off its stand.

"Who made this model?" she asked, as she lightly brushed the rag over the delicate rigging.

"I think it was Captain Jeremiah's youngest son, William. He made it when his father and the *Anne* both had to be retired. It happened all at once, you see. Captain Jeremiah nearly died of a fever on their last voyage. When he returned home, the doctor said his heart was damaged, and he couldn't sail any more. The *Anne* was so dilapidated from all the sea voyages and storms, it was decided that she should be retired as well. They had two other ships by then, you see, and Captain Jeremiah's two older sons had taken charge of those."

"It must have broken his heart to give her up." Katherine said, with tears brimming in her eyes.

"Yes, I think it nearly did. He was sick for some time— bedridden, you see. William, who ran the shop, spent his evenings with his father, talking to him and listening to his stories while carving pieces for this ship, never saying a word to his father about what he was making.

"Finally, when Captain Jeremiah was strong again and able to come to the shop, they had a bit of a party in his honor. The two older boys were back from their voyages, and the whole family gathered together. William gave a speech, saying how much he loved his father, how hard Captain Jeremiah had worked to make the Harborside what it was, and how he knew his father would miss the sea and his beloved ship, and presented him with this as a reminder that those days would always live on in his memories."

"Oh, that's beautiful!" Katherine exclaimed softly, slowly polishing the ship's hull.

"He was like that: always knew what to say and how best to say it."

Katherine set the model back on its stand and picked up a jar. "What did Captain Jeremiah do, once he couldn't go to sea anymore?"

"He just poured himself into the running of this place."

"Just like you." Katherine said brightly.

Captain Braddock gave a heavy sigh, and muttered a barely audible, "Much good that's doin'."

Katherine studied the captain as he bent over the jar he was dusting. He looked so sad and old tonight, and she wondered if she should ask him what was wrong. He looked up and caught her gaze for a moment, then straightened and set his jar on the shelf. He glanced at the clock and said hurriedly,

"Now, it's time for you to be gettin' back. Don't want to

wear you out. You've got a long haul ahead of you." Katherine set her rag on the counter and reached for her jacket.

Captain Braddock's eyes widened suddenly and he exclaimed, "I nearly forgot. I've an order for you to drop in the mail on yer way back, if you don't mind." He hurried off and Katherine heard the storeroom door open.

While she waited for his return, she wandered into the office. Catching a glimpse of the folder the captain had so hurriedly put away, she wondered if that might be what had made him so sad. Walking softly to his desk, she looked over at the open door. She could hear him rummaging still, and knew she had enough time just for a peek. Hovering near the table, she fought with herself. It was really none of her business...but oh, how she wanted to know what was in that folder!

Finally, she gave in. Lifting the ledger and the top flap of the file folder, she just had time to catch a glimpse of the paper on top of the stack before she heard the captain's heavy tread on the stairs. It was enough. With heart pounding, she closed the folder and slipped the ledger back on top. Reeling from what she had just seen, she tried to smile cheerfully at the captain as if nothing were wrong.

He gave her an odd look as he handed her the package. "Yer sure you don't mind? I could probably drop it by in the morning before I open, if it's any help to you."

Katherine took the package with a hurried, "Oh, no. I don't mind at all. I'm heading right by there anyway. Goodnight, Captain!"

She rushed away, leaving a bewildered Captain Braddock to wonder what had gotten into the girl.

Katherine stopped just outside the door to collect her thoughts before going home. As she walked past the large shop window, she peeked in and saw the captain sit down at the desk and open the folder again, looking older and sadder than she had ever seen.

Oh, poor Captain Braddock! she thought, then hurried on to drop the order by the post office and get home to finish the last of the washing up before bed.

27

The Harborside
in Danger

Katherine woke the next morning with her mind all awhirl. She rushed through her preparations for the day, trying not to let her thoughts run away with her.

"Why, Katherine, what's the matter?" asked Mr. James as she opened the door to let him in.

"I'm not sure... that is, I'm not sure if I can tell you—that is, if it would be *right* to tell you. I don't even know what it means yet."

Mr. James pulled out a chair for her and took a seat opposite. "Just tell me whatever you think appropriate that will help relieve your mind—off the record, of course."

"Of course." Katherine said, taking a moment to collect the thoughts that had run circles around her mind since the night before.

"It's about the captain." She began, then stopped. "You see, I came across...no, that's not exactly true. I *saw* something—a paper—on the captain's desk. He had hidden it away quickly when I came in, but he looked so sad and grave afterwards, that I wanted to know what was wrong." She blushed, then took a breath, forcing herself to make a full confession. "So sneaked a look at the papers on his desk while he was out of the room."

Her voice dropped away into silence, and she hung her head while she said these last words. Her "nosing around" seemed so much worse when stated out loud.

Mr. James leaned forward. "And you think from what you saw that there is some reason for concern?"

"Yes." Katherine said, simply, struggling to know how to describe her fear without betraying the captain's trust even further by repeating details she had no right to know. "I'm not exactly sure what the paper means, but if it means anything like it seems to, I fear that the captain—that the Harborside itself—is in great danger, and I..." tears brimmed in Katherine's eyes. "I just don't know what to do to help."

"That is a dilemma." Said Mr. James soberly, reaching across the table to offer Katherine his napkin as two big tears escaped from her sorrowful blue eyes. "I won't try to pry. I agree with you that it would not be right to tell others what you saw on a paper the captain didn't want you to see, but I feel I should make certain: No one is in physical danger?"

"No."

"And there's nothing criminal involved?"

"Of course not." Katherine looked up in indignation.

"Well then," the reporter leaned back in his chair and

studied her tearful face. "The only other question I have is, have you prayed and asked God what *He* wants you to do about it?"

Katherine's look softened and she managed a weak sort of smile. "That's just what Miss Harriet would say."

Mr. James grinned and said with a wink, "Where do you think I got it from?"

Katherine laughed in spite of herself, then sobered again, saying, "I did pray... but I'm still not sure what God wants me to do. All the other times I've asked God about decisions, there has been something specific I was asking about, and I'm not sure how to tell how He's leading when there aren't clear options to choose between."

"Yes, that can seem more difficult. But wait. God will make it clear in due time what you should do. You keep praying, and I'll pray too."

"Thank you." Katherine said, and stood, wiping her eyes one last time on the napkin before wadding it up in her hand. "I do feel a little better just having talked it out."

"I'm happy to have been of service."

Katherine turned to walk away, but Mr. James called her back.

"It occurs to me—and I 'm not fishing for you to tell me what the trouble is—but if it were to happen to be financial, I believe Mr. Patten handles the Harborside's accounts at the bank. He probably wouldn't be authorized to tell you any-thing specific about the Harborside's financial situation, but he may be able to explain what the paper meant, if you can think how to ask in a general sort of way."

A light dawned in Katherine's eyes as he spoke. "That's it!"

she said, then caught herself and said, "At least, if the problem *happened* to be financial."

"And there is another person you could talk to, one who knows all about it already."

"Who is that?"

"Captain Braddock."

Katherine sighed deeply. "I know. I'm planning to talk to him, but not just yet. I will, though... once I have a better idea of what's really going on."

The truth was, Katherine dreaded having to confess to the captain what she had done. She couldn't bear the thought of damaging the bond they had formed, and yet, the damage had already been done—he just didn't know about it yet.

* * * *

When Mr. Patten came in later that morning, Katherine found herself struggling to keep her questions in until the right moment. She tried to be calm as she took his order and tried equally hard not to be irritated with the young couple who came in at just the moment Katherine was going to speak. She greeted them cheerily and showed them to a table.

As she prepared Mr. Patten's tea and pasty, she heard the bell over the door again, and wondered if she would ever get a chance to talk with the elderly banker.

Oh, Lord, she silently prayed before leaving the kitchen again. *If You want me to talk to Mr. Patten, please make a way.* She took a deep breath, picked up the tray, and walked through the curtained doorway.

The young couple were deep in conversation, and Mr.

Patten had just put down the newspaper he had been reading as Katherine walked up. She set the tray down, and before she could speak, Mr. Patten said,

"Thank you, Katherine. Now, there's something I want to speak with you about. I know that you are very busy, but would you mind joining me for just a few minutes as soon as it's convenient?"

Katherine could hardly believe her ears! She nodded and hurried around to all the tables, taking orders and bringing checks. Finally, when everyone in the shop had been served, she went to Mr. Patten's table and sat down with a breathless, "I think everyone's set, but you'll have to excuse me if we get interrupted."

Mr. Patten nodded. "Of course."

"What was it you wanted to talk about?" Katherine asked.

"It regards Captain Braddock. I gather you have enjoyed working at his shop?"

Katherine nodded, her heart fluttering with suspense. "Very much."

"And do I understand correctly that the Captain considers you his friend?"

"I think so."

"Then I feel justified in telling you something that I really ought not discuss. The truth is, Captain Braddock has been asking for information about a course of action which I feel would be very much to his hurt. I am bound by the confidentiality of my position, so I cannot give you specifics. I can only say that the step he is considering would be very unadvisable." He paused, and Katherine asked timidly,

"Would it help if I asked you to explain, generally, what

it would mean to a person's financial state if he—or she—signed over their retirement savings to a business that was losing money?"

Mr. Patten's eyes grew wide. "He has told you, then?"

"No." Katherine said, her face growing hot. "But I have...gathered, you might say."

"Then I can tell you—generally, as you say—that if a person's income were limited to his or her retirement savings account, he or she would be very unwise to sign that account over to anyone or anything, for it is their only means of support. Even if the individual expected some return on their investment, the loss of personal income long term would nevertheless be catastrophic."

"And, can you tell me if a business like the Harborside, for example, could survive very long with the addition of such an amount of savings as its only income?"

Mr. Patten considered before answering, as if weighing the information he wanted to give with the limits of what was appropriate to share. "I can tell you that a business such as the Harborside could only survive for a short time on such a sum. Even with so large an investment, a business with so few customers cannot last very long at all. I have seen several such businesses destroyed, and their owners along with them, by similar conditions."

Katherine's heart sank. "What can I do to help?"

"Nothing. That is, nothing short of convincing the owner to branch out, perhaps advertise... the main thing is to generate more sales."

"I understand." Katherine said. "Thank you for telling me. I will see what I can do."

Mr. Patten stood and reached out to shake Katherine's hand.

"I am sorry to give you such a bleak account, but I thought you should know."

"Thank you." Katherine said, and with an amount of composure worthy of Miss Harriet herself, she walked calmly into the kitchen, pulled the curtain carefully shut, and began to sob.

28

Confessions and Sorrows

Katherine stood with her hand on the doorhandle, trying to gather courage to open the door. She knew she had to confess to the Captain, and it needed to be sooner rather than later. Closing her eyes, she willed herself to open the door, but to no avail.

It took all the strength she could muster at that moment to accomplish the monumental effort of standing still when all she wanted to do was turn and flee back to the safety of solitude at Miss Harriet's. No, she would stay. But, oh! Where would she find the words to say? And how would she be able to bear his response?

Lord, help me! Her heart cried, as she leaned her head against the doorframe, eyes squeezed tight against the tears that threatened to spill out. *Help me do what I know is right. Help me to be brave and not run away!*

She straightened up, smoothed her hair back from her face, and turned the door handle.

"Hello, Katherine." Captain Braddock came in from his office with a smile, wiping his hands on a dust rag. "Ready to unpack the week's shipments?"

"Yes, I mean, no...that is... I have to tell you something first."

The old man's eyebrows knit together as he surveyed Katherine's troubled face. "Oh? Well, then. Go ahead."

He was remarkably quiet and calm as Katherine spilled out her confession. The words tumbled out one after the other, completely different from the way she had planned to say them. And yet, calm as he remained, the captain's face bore an expression of deepening sorrow which tied a sickening knot in Katherine's stomach.

She had hurt him, and what was worse, she had no just excuse for her behavior. And now! Her rapid stream of words finally came to a halt and Katherine stood still, waiting for the unleashing of the captain's wrath.

But he just stood there, looking down, silently. Finally, after what seemed to Katherine a miserable eternity, he spoke. His words came slow and grave, seeming to Katherine even slower for their contrast to the rushing flood she had just unleashed.

"If it were anyone else, I'da fired you on the spot for what you've done. And perhaps I should anyway, but I know yer curiosity, and I hired you supposin' something like this would happen eventually. But I'm disappointed in you for *how* it happened. This place has plenty of secrets of its own,

I know, but I never would have thought you'd a gone nosing into mine."

Katherine hung her head as the Captain continued, a little more gruffly,

"I know you meant well, Katherine, and that lessens the sting of it, but it's a serious thing you've done."

A wave of sorrow such as Katherine had never felt before swept over her as he spoke.

"I understand." she said meekly, looking up with pleading eyes. "It *was* wrong of me. I do want you to know that I only did it because I wanted to help. I should have just asked you what was wrong, but..." She paused, then plunged recklessly ahead. "Oh, isn't there anything else you can do? Must you take such a drastic step?"

Now the Captain's face clouded over, and his voice took on the harshness that came whenever his temper flared.

"I'll take whatever step seems best to me, and I say now just what I would've said if you'd asked me then: that it's none of yer business, so I won't have none of yer help."

Tears sprang to Katherine's eyes at this, and Captain Braddock looked away, saying gruffly, "I think you'd better be goin' now." He limped over to the stove and stooped to stir up the fire. Katherine slowly turned to leave, head bowed and heart aching. As she reached for the door handle, the captain straightened and said in a softer tone, "I'll bring yer order by tomorrow, like we planned."

* * * *

Tears trickled down Katherine's face all the way home.

leaving warm tracks down her icy cheeks, chilled by the cold January wind. The sun had set behind thick grey clouds while she was at the Harborside, and now the growing dusk seemed to sympathize with the gloom inside her heart as she walked.

She had broken the captain's trust, and she didn't know how to begin to earn it again. And on top of that, he had rejected her feeble offer of help, keeping her outside of the situation, at arm's length. Somehow, she still felt strongly that he needed help of some kind. But what could she do? Her mind raced as she neared Miss Harriet's and walked through the door. She locked it behind her and wound her way between the tables to the kitchen.

Turning the tap to fill the sink, she dropped her coat and bag on the floor moved a tray of dishes to the counter. She began the washing up almost mechanically, her mind still busy reliving the sorrowful conversation with the captain and turning the problem of the Harborside over and over in her mind.

At least Miss Harriet will be back soon, she thought wearily as she dried the last dish and turned out the kitchen light. *Maybe she can help me straighten all this out.*

* * * *

The night of Miss Harriet's return, Katherine tried to speed through the closing-time cleanup, but she was careful to be more thorough than even Miss Harriet had been when the two had cleaned up together. When Miss Harriet walked through the door, Katherine was determined that she should find the place sparkling from floor to ceiling.

Katherine longed to see her, even more than she had expected to. Miss Harriet's absence made her realize just how much she had come to lean on her employer as both friend and confidant. She had so many things stored up to discuss with her, she could scarcely contain her anticipation as the expected time for her arrival drew nearer.

As she got out the furniture polish and began to set to work on the long counter, Katherine noticed that there was also a great amount of nervousness to her excitement. She had been in charge of the shop for over a week now, and she was anxious lest she had forgotten some important task or missed some crucial detail.

How desperately she wanted to prove herself! Not, of course, because she felt she must; she knew Miss Harriet would not have left the shop in her care unless she had been completely certain of Katherine's ability. Nevertheless, she wanted to show that Miss Harriet's trust had not been mis-placed. She also felt that she wanted to prove to herself that she was capable of handling such a great responsibility.

Her arm ached as she worked the polish into the counter, but she was determined it would shine like never before. Her thoughts began to race along at the pace of her polishing. She thought of the Captain, who had been grave and quiet when he brought the tea order the previous day, and hadn't stayed around to chat like he had the few times he'd been by the shop before. Maybe Miss Harriet would be able to help her figure out how to repair their broken friendship.

* * * *

The hours crept by slowly, but at last Katherine heard the familiar sound of the key in the lock of the shop door. In stepped Miss Harriet, looking rather weary, but glad to be home. In her excitement, Katherine began talking a mile a minute as soon as her friend opened the door.

"Oh, Miss Harriet, I'm so glad you're back! There's just so much to tell you about. The customers asked about you every day, and as much as they missed you, I do believe I've missed you more, especially when I was washing all those dishes by myself." Miss Harriet laughed gently, then grew strangely wistful and sober.

"Why, what is it?" asked Katherine, with growing concern, "Is your mother still unwell?"

"No." Miss Harriet said with quiet calm. "She died Wednesday."

"Oh, I am so sorry!" Katherine's eyes filled with tears, and she gently led Miss Harriet over to a table so she could sit down while they talked. Miss Harriet smiled softly as she saw the tea tray Katherine had already placed on the table.

"I figured you might need some tea after your trip." Katherine said shyly.

"That's *exactly* what I need—that, and the company of my dear friend."

Katherine poured a cup of tea and handed it to Miss Harriet. "Do you..." she said hesitatingly, "Will it help to talk about it? Your mother, I mean."

"It's all right." Miss Harriet gave a sad, but reassuring smile. "I was with her at the last. We had known it would be but a matter of time until she went. My brother sat up with her all night and had just gone to rest while I stayed with her. The crisis was sudden, but quick—mercifully so. There was no time even to call for my brother to come. And then, she was gone. I wish I could paint a prettier picture of her last moments or give you some romanticized view of her with hands and face upraised with rapturous smile, but I cannot. To be sure, there's no poetry in death."

"And you were all alone? Oh, how did you bear it?"

"Well, Dearie, the end came so quickly, and unmistakably. I wanted my brother to get some rest while he could. There was no use in disturbing him just to say she was gone, so I just went out into the back garden, where Mother used to sit and look out at the hills we had all loved to roam together.

"The sun was just coming up, and I walked over to the garden fence, as far from the house as I could get. Then--I'll not lie to you—I wept. Hard. Perhaps harder than I've ever wept before. I leaned on the fence rail and gave in to the flood of loss that swept over me afresh with every new thought of Mother.

"But then, a little robin came soaring by with hope in his beak and joy in his wings. He perched on the fencepost and let out the happiest, soaringest trickle of notes I've ever heard. His song seemed to bubble up out of his heart in exuberance over the new day. His song struck joy to my own heart as well, for, you see, Mother wasn't the only one who could pray.

"While I was in the midst of that first overwhelming ocean of grief, I poured it all out to God. I poured out all my sorrow to Him. It seemed as if there was a yawning chasm that just appeared and life seemed ever so bleak, but I poured that out to God as well. When that robin sang, it was as if it startled me out of the bleakness. It reminded me that there was still hope and beauty in life. Of course, it didn't erase the sorrow; it simply reminded me that joy was still there."

Miss Harriet leaned forward in her chair as Katherine listened, wide-eyed. "I'll see her again, Katherine. I'm as sure of it as I am of anything. For you know, the same Savior that welcomed her into heaven just a few days ago has promised to let me in, too. It's only a matter of time. Remembering that truth brought me the greatest comfort."

Looking frankly into her friend's tear-brimmed eyes, she admitted, "I do still have moments where the loss sweeps in, but I cry it out to God, and He brings me through all right."

Miss Harriet took a deep breath, squeezed Katherine's hand and said brightly, "Now, let's have some more tea, shall we? I want to hear all about how things were for you while I was away."

* * * *

The next morning, Katherine woke in the darkness to the smell of fresh scones. She sighed happily and reset her alarm. She had been unable to convince Miss Harriet to stay home a day and rest, though she had tried her best.

"I'll be just fine, Dearie. The best way to get back into American time is to get back into my normal schedule," Miss Harriet had said confidently as she left late the night before. As much as Katherine doubted the soundness of that plan, she still felt glad not to have to rush to get the baking in. She reset her alarm and basked in the luxury of letting her mind drift drowsily.

Miss Harriet had listened sympathetically the night before

as Katherine related her tale of woe. But even the wise Miss Harriet had been unable to suggest a way to fix the rift between Katherine and the captain.

"Begin again." Miss Harriet had said, "Just be as trustworthy as you know to be from now on. Do your duties well, but remember, Katherine, a broken trust doesn't heal overnight. It will take time, and it will also take a willingness in Captain Braddock, both to forgive, and to choose to trust again. It is possible that things may never be the same again." Here, she had put her arm around Katherine and smiled encouragingly. "But don't give up. Do what God wants you to, and it will all come out right in the end."

Katherine hoped Miss Harriet was right, and she knew that God said He would work all things together for good for those who are His, and yet... it was so hard to believe that anything so badly broken could be fixed, especially when it had been so fragile in the first place. For the first time since she came to Harborhaven, she dreaded Tuesday.

29

Tuesday

When Tuesday came, Katherine woke with a sinking sort of nervousness. As she hurriedly dressed, her mind raced, imagining out what she should say, how she would act. Oh, how she wished she had never looked at those papers!

Sitting down on the window seat, Katherine opened her Bible. She had been reading through the book of Psalms, and as she read through chapter 27, her eyes filled with tears. It seemed to her as if the words had been written just for her that morning. She stopped at the last verse and read it again slowly, letting the words soak into her soul.

"Wait on the Lord: be of good courage, and He shall strengthen thine heart: wait, I say, on the Lord."

Bowing her head, Katherine prayed.

I'll wait, Lord. I'll wait for you to make it all right with the captain. Just please, strengthen my heart to bear it all till then."

* * * *

When she arrived at the Harborside, Katherine found the captain sitting at his desk. He looked up when he heard her come in and gave a tight little smile.

"Jars first, I think." He said, then turned back to the ledger he had been writing in. Katherine meekly picked up a dust rag and walked over to the shelves. She dusted each jar thoroughly, thankful to have something to do. After a while, Captain Braddock came in. He grabbed a rag from behind the counter and silently joined Katherine at the shelves.

They stood side by side for a while, until Katherine could bear it no longer.

"Captain?" She began.

"Yes?"

"Thank you—I mean, for letting me stay on. I really am so very sorry."

"I'll have none of that," interrupted Captain Braddock gruffly. Then with just a little more softness to his tone he added, "I said I forgave you, and that's the end of it."

They continued on in silence, but a cautious wave of joy thrilled through Katherine's heart, for she knew now that, however slowly it might progress, things had at least begun to mend.

* * * *

The weeks passed, and January blustered icily into February. Katherine and the captain began to interact a little more normally, but there was still a disconcerting reservedness on the captain's part. It wasn't as if he ever said anything—it was just little things, a look, an almost unconscious attentiveness to where she was and what she was doing. Katherine was sure it had not been purposeful. He now even left the bank papers on his desk out in the open, instead of trying to hide them when she came in or when he left the room, but even that felt to her like a silent rebuke.

Katherine slid the navy apron over her head and reached for a rag. The dusting had become her favorite task in the past few weeks. It gave her hands something to do while her heart and mind were busy.

Things had been a little better lately between her and the captain, and she had been quite hopeful that they were returning to something like their old camaraderie, until the fuss he had made about the mail yesterday.

Katherine shook her head and reached for another jar, remembering how the captain had come in from an errand and asked whether any packages had arrived. He seemed quite anxious about it until she told him that none had come.

"Well," he had said with a greater sternness than usual, "Yer not to open any packages this week or inventory them until I've looked through the lot first. In fact, just have the delivery man leave them over there behind the counter till I can see what's come in."

Katherine nodded, astonished and puzzled by this sudden departure from normal shop procedure.

Captain Braddock began to limp back to his office, but stopped near the doorway and said coolly, "This time, I'm tellin' you: *don't go snoopin'*."

"Yes, sir." Katherine bent her head over the jar she was

filling to hid the tears that had started to her eyes. *I deserved that*, she thought. Somehow, the fact that the captain had *reason* to tell her not to snoop hurt more than the gruff tone he had used. Katherine sighed. Despite the progress made recently, she had not yet regained the captain's trust. It had been a miserable afternoon for Katherine.

She sighed again as she mulled over the previous day's events, turning each detail over in her mind as she deftly turned each jar in her hands. Suddenly, the bell over the door rang. Turning around, Katherine saw a man in a stiff-looking uniform standing in the doorway.

"Harborside Tea Shop?" he asked nervously, glancing at his clipboard.

"That's us." She said. *Must be his first day*, she thought.

He turned and wheeled in a stack of boxes on a dolly. "Sign here, please." He said, holding out a clipboard and a pen. "Where do you want these boxes?"

Katherine pointed where the captain had shown her. "Over here, please." She said, trying very hard to keep down the curiosity that threatened to rise at the sight of the tall stack.

"Have a nice day." The man said, already out the door.

She watched him jump nimbly into his truck and drive down the street. Then she eyed the stack of boxes. Picking up her rag from the counter, she deliberately turned and walked across the room. She took down the model *Anne* and began carefully to dust every last intricate piece, focusing her full attention on the task, determined not to give in to her curiosity this time.

* * * *

She had a hard fight, and long, too, for it was nearly an hour before the captain arrived. Katherine breathed a sigh of relief when she finally heard him enter through the back door and drop his keys on the desk.

He didn't seem in a hurry to ask about the delivery; so Katherine, who was by then full to bursting with curiosity, called over her shoulder in a tone she hoped would sound nonchalant, "The mail's arrived."

She heard a creak, then a rustle, and the sound of a drawer being opened and closed again. Then, Captain Braddock entered the room, and with a glance at Katherine, whose back was still turned toward him, he slowly and deliberately walked over to the pile of packages by the front door.

Katherine finally gave in to her curiosity enough to watch the captain over her shoulder as he searched carefully through the boxes until, with a grunt, he picked up what Katherine assumed must be the one he had been looking for.

Katherine whirled around as the captain straightened up, almost in time to evade his quick glance in her direction. In that brief moment she noticed something clutched in one hand, and the box tucked under his arm.

She expected to hear his footsteps receding into his office, but instead, he was crossing the shop towards the shelves, where she was vigorously dusting the remaining few jars. She looked over at the captain, who, to her surprise, had his foot on the first step of the spiral staircase.

Her eyes lit up with a fresh curiosity, but the Captain only gave her a look in return which plainly said, *Be about yer business, and nevermind mine.* She had heard him say this often enough, with precisely that look, so she was well versed in its meaning.

As she turned to the jars again, she slyly watched the captain out of the corner of her eye. The thing she had seen in his hand was now revealed to be a key; heavy, old, and made of what looked like iron. With a thrill, she realized that the door at the top of the stairs was surely about to be unlocked and opened!

She turned a little, under the pretense of reaching one of the ships on an upper shelf, and looked up just as the Captain opened the door and passed quickly through, closing it heavily behind him. She caught a glimpse of rough beams on the ceiling, and a faint fragrance reached her, even at the bottom of the stairs—a familiar fragrance, but one Katherine couldn't quite place.

There had been light in the room as the door was opened, so Katherine had surmised that there must be a window of some kind. She began on the last few jars, dusting as slowly as she could, prolonging her task in order to have a reason to remain in her place until the captain came out again.

There was a tantalizing squeak of floorboards above, then she thought she discerned the quick swipe of a box cutter through packing tape, muffled, to be sure, but faintly discernable. She heard the captain's characteristic grunt, then a scrape and creak. *There must be a chair up there... and maybe a desk?* Katherine thought to herself. She held as still as possible, straining to catch even the smallest clue to what was happening there.

After a minute or two, there was another grunt, and then a long, moaning creak, as of hinges unused to motion, and the slightest rustle that might have been something like stiff paper, then another moan from the unseen hinges. Katherine could hear the captain nearing the door again, and she looked back at the jar she was dusting, knowing that she dared not be caught watching when he came out.

She heard the door open and sneaked a glance upwards as it closed behind the captain. His broad shoulders blocked her view this time, however, and she turned around again, hoping he hadn't noticed her curiosity.

"Anything interesting in the mail today?" she asked over her shoulder, trying to sound careless and disinterested. The captain grunted and replied,

"Only this, but it'll keep till Thursday with the rest." Katherine turned and stared at the box, which was again tucked beneath the captain's arm. It had been opened, but the flaps had been folded closed again, and the shipping label had been removed. The captain set it gently on the counter, then returned to his office. Katherine heard the drawer again, and decided he was probably replacing the old key in a drawer of his desk.

"You can take the boxes down to the storeroom now" came the captain's voice from the other room, now returned to its normal tone.

Katherine set down the last jar, which had by that time been dusted four or five times, and gladly walked over to the counter. She eyed the mysterious box, but seeing no clues to its contents or sender, took it to the storeroom along with the rest of the stack. She saved it for last, however, the captain's gentle treatment of it inspiring the same in her, and set it almost reverentially on the top of the others. *A day and a half,* she thought, *and I will be opening that box... I wonder what could be inside?*

When she left that afternoon, she walked around to the back of the building, gazing up through the gloomy dusk to see if she could spy the window which she knew must exist to let light into the room at the top of the staircase.

Standing as far back as she could, she craned her neck, but all she could see was the brick wall, a roofline, and then more brickwork behind. She stood right at the middle of the building where she knew the staircase to be and stood on tip-toe. But there was no window to be seen in that part of the building, not even in the higher section of the brick wall. So, she turned and walked slowly home, puzzled and impatient.

30

The Mysterious Package

Katherine walked down the empty street, too full of anticipation to savor the morning stillness of the downtown blocks. She was earlier than her usual time but had been too excited to wait out the last ten minutes before it was time for her to leave.

Even this had not allayed her impatience, though, and her pace quickened with every step that carried her nearer to the Harborside. Her heartbeat quickened as well, and the closer she came to the shop, the more intense her desire became to sprint the last few steps and arrive at last.

Katherine always enjoyed Thursdays at the Harborside, but today was to be no ordinary Thursday. Today, the Captain was going to open the mysterious package.

The sun had just begun to light up the grey clouds over the harbor and all the world seemed still, but Katherine's mind was spinning with speculations and wonderings. The first birds were singing by the time Katherine got to the front door, and the sky was painted with vivid shades of pink and orange, but all she could think of was getting to that box.

As usual, she stopped just inside the door to don her plain canvas apron while calling out a greeting so the captain would know she was there. She quickly stepped behind the counter and pulled out the drawer where the box cutter was kept. Then she flew to the side door of the shop which led to the storeroom, taking a clipboard from its nail on the wall as she opened the door.

Captain Braddock, who had been looking over a ledger at his desk, looked up in surprise and arrested Katherine's flight by saying in an astonished tone,

"Well, good mornin' to you. Why the hurry, there, young miss? It's ten minutes before starting time, and you're already here, apron on, and bolting out the door. What's there to rush off to in the storeroom?"

Katherine blushed and turned to meet the captain's gaze. Hesitating for a moment, she decided to be completely honest.

"It's just that... well, I've been so curious about that extra package. You were so mysterious about it, and I've been wondering what it could be."

Katherine's honesty brought a smile to the old man's face and melted the gruffness out of his voice as he replied, "Well, then, why don't we go see what's in those boxes?"

He led the way into the storeroom and handed Katherine the box. She sat down on the floor with the clipboard beside her as she usually did while unboxing and slowly lifted the tightly-folded flaps.

Inside the box, she found a loose mass of packing paper, which she lifted, exposing a black wooden box, intricately carved and tied shut with a silky red ribbon. She looked up at the captain in wonder.

"What is it?" she asked, lifting the box carefully out of its nest of paper.

The captain smiled as he reached for the box, then looked it over thoughtfully, turning it over in his hands. Finally, he spoke. "I suppose I could have told you about it Tuesday; I didn't know it would hold you in such suspense. It's tea, but *special* tea. Finish the unpacking, and I'll tell you all about it."

Katherine took no time that day to spin daydreams of the far-off places from which the boxes had been sent, as she usually did. She unpacked each box quickly, marking its contents on the inventory sheet attached to the clipboard. When she was finished, she walked back into the captain's office, hanging the clipboard up by the door as always. She was about to go back down for a box so she could empty its contents into jars when the captain stopped her.

"Come take a break for a bit, Katherine. We've an hour yet till we open, and I want to tell you about this tea so you can talk it up with the customers." There was a twinkle in his eye which told Katherine that this was only part of his reason. He led the way over to a narrow curtained doorway between two bookshelves which Katherine had never noticed before. He twitched back the heavy green curtain and led the way into a small sliver of a room with a sink and a cooktop.

"I never knew this was here." Katherine said, wondering how the curtained doorway could have escaped her notice for so long. The captain gave a grunt.

"There's a lot you don't know about the old girl" he said, laying a hand reverently on the wall, as he might have done to an old ship. "She's got her share of secrets, for sure."

He filled a brass kettle and set it on the stove, then pulled a teapot and two sturdy white teacups down from a shelf. He went out into the office and returned, holding the black box. Katherine watched as the captain untied the heavy satin ribbon and handed it to her. Then the lid, which had been fitted with some sort of gasket to keep the air out, was ceremoniously lifted.

A fragrance filled the air. Katherine recognized it as an aroma of tea, but it was fresher and more delicate than the varieties she was used to. She edged closer to the captain to get a better view of the contents of the box.

"It smells like tea, but these leaves look so different from the leaves in the jars."

Katherine had learned to recognize the different teas the Harborside carried by sight, but she had never seen anything quite like these leaves. They were a silvery grey and fuzzy, and, if it weren't for their fragrance, she might have thought they were some strange variety of pine needle.

"It's called silver needle white tea, and it's the rarest tea you'll ever set your eyes upon. It's the first flush, you see." The captain took the singing kettle off the burner and put some of the hot water into the pot.

Katherine watched him, looking puzzled. "I heard you and a customer discussing first flush teas the other day, but I don't know what the term means."

"You don't?" The captain was surprised. "The first flush is

the first harvest of the season, and with most any type of tea, the first is considered the very best. With white tea it's even more special, you see, because it's picked so early in the season. It's just the buds of the leaves, picked while they're young and tender. That's what gives them such a different color and texture.

"This tea grows high in the mountains in the Fujian Province, and is picked very early in the spring, just before dawn. It's important, you see, that the dew still be on the buds when they're picked. They're rolled, but only gently, you see, and dried in the sun. It's all done by hand, and they're very careful which buds they use—only the best are chosen. They also won't harvest if it's raining."

"And all that really makes a difference?" Katherine sounded a bit skeptical. The captain smiled as he poured the water out of the teapot and reached for the box of tea.

"You're about to find out for yourself, there, Missy." Katherine's eyes grew wide.

"Really? You mean we get to try it?" she asked excitedly.

"Of course." He replied with a chuckle, picking up the kettle and saying, "Now, here's the trick to this tea. It's gotta be brewed just right, or it will ruin the flavor."

Katherine nodded solemnly, taking mental notes.

"First, you saw me warm the pot. That will make sure the water doesn't cool too much when it's poured in. Then, the water has to be the right temperature. Did you notice I've let the kettle set a bit after it whistled? Well, the water should be ready just about now."

As Captain Braddock slowly poured the water over the

leaves, the fragrance filled the small kitchen, now stronger and with a hint of floral sweetness. Katherine took a deep breath.

"It certainly smells like it should be rare and precious!" she exclaimed. The captain, nodding, set the lid on the pot and continued.

"Now, it's important not to leave the leaves to steep too long. Otherwise it will be bitter and the flavor will be lost. He took out a pocket watch and steadily gazed at its face. A minute and a half... yes, I think that will do."

He cautiously poured a little into a cup. "Yes, it's ready now. See that pale color? If it were any darker, it would be over-brewed." He poured out the rest into the two cups and handed one to Katherine. "Let's go have a seat, and I'll tell you a story."

The two walked into the office, and the captain pulled a folding chair from behind a tall bookcase and set it near his desk for Katherine. Settling into his chair, he began.

"This tea was picked just two weeks ago. It was dried, rolled and shipped express to the Harborside. This is the freshest tea you could get, without going there yourself. My sister used to say—" Just then the big old clock in the corner chimed eight o'clock, interrupting the captain's reverie.

"Oh, it's opening time. I suppose I'd better get that door opened." He rose abruptly and walked into the shop.

Katherine, astonished and disappointed, was more curious than ever. Captain Braddock so rarely mentioned Serena, and now, just when he had been about to say something about her, he stopped mid-sentence and walked away. It was almost too much. Katherine sipped the last of her tea thoughtfully, trying to piece together a connection between this valuable tea, the long-lost sister, and the forbidden room at the top of the staircase.

31

Advertising

Once Captain Braddock had unlocked the front door and flipped the old pasteboard sign to "Open," he wandered back into the office, resumed his seat, and picked up his cup of tea. To Katherine's delight and surprise, he revived their previous conversation with a bright, "Now, then, where was I?"

Katherine, not thinking it prudent to begin with the half-finished sentence about his sister, replied, "You were telling me about the tea being so fresh."

The Captain leaned forward in his chair. "Ah, and so I was. You see, I always get the first flush white tea from this particular plantation, because... well..." he fumbled for a moment, then charged ahead with a hurried, "never you mind about that. The fact is, it's the best of the best. Not only is it the finest cup of tea I have from one spring to the next, it'll make the Harborside three times the profit of any other tea. We just have to wait for the right customer to discover it."

The two silently sipped their tea for a moment before Katherine asked thoughtfully, "Captain Braddock, if the tea is so valuable, why don't you advertise it? I'm sure Mr. James would be glad to help you put something in the Gazette about it."

The old man's brows knit together in a heavy frown and drew himself up tall and straight in his chair to declare solemnly, "The Harborside never advertises. Never! If we do our jobs right, our customers come back, and tell their friends, too. Word of mouth, they call it. That's how we've operated for over a hundred years, and it's never failed us yet."

The captain sat back in his chair and continued to sip his tea. After a moment, a smile slowly spread over the captain's face. "Mind you," he began with a chuckle, "there was a time, generations ago, when a Braddock uncle placed an ad in the paper. It put the whole Braddock clan in uproar, and he was nearly disowned on account of it."

Katherine leaned forward, eyes sparkling and face alight with anticipation of a story.

The captain recognized her look and chuckled again as he continued, "You see, it wasn't as if he had just advertised in the *Harborhaven* newspaper. No indeed! He had advertised in the paper of a town further up along the coastline, and that was really what threw them all out of sorts. They said, it was bad enough that he'd even done such a *vulgar* thing as advertise, but to degrade the Harborside in the eyes of *strangers* was just too much." He paused and took another sip of tea before continuing.

Katherine sat, wide-eyed, enthralled by the story, imagining the ire of the offended Braddock elders.

"Yes, the reigning Braddocks of that generation were furious, and wouldn't be appealed to. He was sent off to sea, so he was. And the Harborside, which he had been meant to inherit, was given to my great-grandfather instead."

"And the Harborside Braddocks never advertised again?" asked Katherine.

"Nope. It's one of our cardinal rules here."

Katherine silently wondered if keeping secrets about sisters and rooms at the top of stairs were cardinal rules of the Harborside as well, then dismissed the thought as ungracious and attended to the matter at hand. She looked over at the captain, comfortably sipping his tea, and suddenly remembered Mr. Patten's advice: *branch out... advertise.* Gathering up a little courage, she said,

"But... such a fine and rare tea as this one seems like something the Harborside should be proud to have in stock—and when you're proud of something, you tell everyone about it."

The captain stared at her in blank surprise.

"Don't you think notifying the town, not necessarily with a newspaper ad, but with something else... like a sign in the window, for instance...however you chose to do it, don't you think telling people that such a treasure can be found here would bring honor, rather than degradation to the Harborside?" With a sly grin, she added, "After all, aren't you *proud* of the quality of the teas sold here?"

Captain Braddock stood abruptly, stacked the now empty cups and headed towards the tiny kitchen, gruffly tossing the words over his shoulder as he went, "It's about time to get those jars filled, now. Best be about it."

Katherine, knowing she had pressed her point as far as

she dared, took a tray of empty jars from the built-in cabinet under the counter and went back into the storeroom to do her work.

When she came back in to place the filled jars on the shelves, she noticed the beautiful black box had been placed prominently on the counter, with a small sign next to it in the Captain's own handwriting:

"Silver Needle White Tea: Freshest. Rarest. Best."

Katherine smiled to herself. *Well, it's a start, anyway.*

* * * *

Katherine hardly saw the captain at all the rest of that day. She expected this, because she had come to know his moods well over the winter, and she knew that the concession he had made in the writing and placing of the little sign had cost his pride much. But when, just before closing, he had gone out without a word, leaving her to lock up, she began to be worried. He had never done that before.

"He'll be all right in a day or so, you'll see." Miss Harriet had said soothingly that evening. Katherine had told her of the tea, and the conversation about advertising, but hadn't mentioned the reference to his sister. She felt that anything the captain said on that topic would be entrusted to her confidentially, and she meant to prove her trustworthiness by keeping the secrets of both Captain Braddock and the Harborside with all her might.

* * * *

The next day, Katherine walked to the Harborside to pick up Miss Harriet's order, unsure of how she would be received. To her surprise, Captain Braddock opened the door as she approached, saying with enthusiasm Katherine hadn't seen in a while.

"I am glad to see you today, Katherine. I know I left abruptly yesterday, and I know you probably thought I was cross with you—now don't try to shake yer head, I can see it in yer eyes I'm right."

Katherine smiled sheepishly and nodded.

"I'm sorry, but I'm an old coot, and new ideas make me squirm, even if they're good ones. I want you to know that I did listen to what you said, and... well, I'm considerin' on it."

Shocked at this surprising change in the Captain's heretofore stubborn nature, Katherine could only smile and stammer out, "Thank you."

He walked over to the large old sea chest in which he kept the stock of bagged teas hidden away out of sight. He opened the lid and bent over it, handing boxes to Katherine as she read from the list. After the last few items had been read, Katherine began timidly,

"Captain, I'm afraid I've done something you might not like." The old man looked up sharply from the sea chest with concern in his face.

"What is it?" Captain Braddock's eyebrows were knit together in uncertainty.

"I, that is... I" she stopped short, then with a sudden burst of courage, said all at once, "I told Miss Harriet about the white tea, and she said that she wants me to have you add some to her order this week, so she can try it, too."

The old man's face relaxed into a mischievous grin. "Well, I suppose it's about time that woman had a taste of the real thing." he said, and promptly grabbed a small plastic bag. Opening the lid of the box, he asked, "How much does she want?"

Much relieved, Katherine grinned. Well aware of the fury she was about to unleash, she answered innocently,

"Miss Harriet was very specific. She said she wants *four teabags' worth*." Captain Braddock's face turned red as he spluttered,

"Bags! Bags! How can she go on about teabags all the time? Why, do you know what they put in those bags she loves so dearly? Floor sweepings, that's what. *Bags...*" He continued his rant while agitatedly measuring out the precious tea. "To speak of this tea in the same sentence as that rot. Ha!"

He tied the little sack of tea and held it up. "Do you know what the difference is between this tea and the shoddy powder they put those bags? These leaves are carefully, painstakingly, gently processed by hand, the best leaves searched for and chosen. And do you know what they call the process they use to process the teabag leaves? CTC. That means 'crush, tear, and curl'. Imagine! They completely destroy the leaves, so that there's hardly any remnant of flavor left. About four teabags' worth...Ha!"

Then, having measured out the desired amount, he handed Katherine the bag and said, "Here, she can have her 'four teabags' worth'. You just make sure she brews it correctly, now. I won't have her ruining the flavor by brewing it like one of her tea bags. And no milk, you hear? *No milk!*"

Promising quite solemnly to make sure Miss Harriet knew

the proper method of brewing and enjoying the valuable tea, Katherine finished packing the order and started off for Miss Harriet's.

* * * *

That night, after Katherine and Miss Harriet had enjoyed a hearty laugh over the scene caused by her purposefully provoking request, they put the kettle on. Katherine, with no small degree of nervousness, endeavored to repeat the brewing process Captain Braddock had shown her the day before.

All was carefully and precisely done, and soon the floral kitchen timer was ringing. Katherine carefully placed a silver tea strainer over Miss Harriet's favorite cup and poured the tea from the floral chintz teapot.

"It smells lovely!" Miss Harriet exclaimed as the aroma filled the air. "I've never smelled the like. And you say it's just the buds?" Katherine nodded her reply. "... How interesting!" Miss Harriet murmured as she held face over the cup, savoring the delicate floral steam that gracefully curled as it rose from the pale liquid.

"Taste it!" urged Katherine eagerly. Miss Harriet raised the cup to her lips, took a cautious sip, and thought for a moment, before a bright smile spread over her face.

"Well, now, the captain was right. It *is* the best tea I've tasted all year—not that I would for a moment have him think I'm converted. I'm no tea snob, and I still love my 'floor sweepings' well enough. But this really is remarkable. I can see why it's so expensive. It's well worth the price, and perhaps even worth enduring the captain's gruffness."

Katherine could tell Miss Harriet was half joking, but she was reminded of the Luncheon Club's description of the "feud" between the two shops.

"Miss Harriet," She asked gently, pouring herself a cup of tea. "Why haven't you and the captain gotten along better all these years? I know it can't be just the teabags."

Miss Harriet, suddenly pensive, took another sip of tea and thought for a while before replying. "I suppose, my dear, to begin with, it's partly because we're so very different. And then, when he first arrived..." She paused, sighed, and began again.

"I was a good friend of his sister Serena's, you know, or at least, I thought I was... but when she left without a word, and then he wouldn't say where she had gone or why—it's very hard to form a cordial friendship with someone who is purposefully keeping something from you."

Katherine nodded sympathetically, thinking of the room at the top of the spiral staircase.

"I know I should have tried harder, but he can be so disagreeable at times. He's really just an old grouch, and I knew from the first I ought not to let him get to me. But by the time I finally decided I wouldn't, it was too late. He viewed me as the enemy, and the enemy I have remained. Though I think, thanks to you, that is not so much the case anymore."

Katherine sighed. "I can't deny that he's secretive. It's one of his most aggravating traits. But I think he's less of a grouch than he used to be." She brightened suddenly. "He might even be losing his stubbornness. He actually *listened* to a suggestion I made yesterday, and said he was considering it. And when

I got to the shop today, he even apologized for leaving so abruptly yesterday without speaking to me!"

"That *is* unusual! My dear Katherine, keep it up, and you might *actually* succeed in making him into a civil human being!"

The two giggled, and deep in her heart, Katherine was delighted to think that perhaps there was hope for her two employers to truly become friends.

32

Searching for Serena

The next morning, Miss Harriet was in the middle of mixing up her last batch of scones when the bell over the door rang.

"That will be Harold," Miss Harriet said, frowning at the sticky dough she was kneading currents into.

"I'll go out," Katherine volunteered, picking up the reporter's tray of tea and scones and hurrying through the curtain before Miss Harriet could reply.

The tall reporter had already settled in at his table by the window. He smiled at Katherine as she approached.

"Well, good morning, Katherine!" he said cheerfully, then nodded towards the kitchen. "Is Harriet hard at work back there?"

"Yes. She's just finishing up the last of today's baking."

"I see," he said, still smiling.

"Mr. James, can I ask you something?"

"Go ahead," he said, moving the flower arrangement over and motioning to a chair. "Have a seat if you like."

Katherine set the tray in front of Mr. James and sat down. "What did you want to ask me?"

"Well, I was talking with Miss Harriet yesterday about Captain Braddock, and the more I hear about Captain Braddock's interactions with people, it seems like everything always comes back to Serena."

Mr. James nodded. "I suppose that's a fair assessment."

"So I was wondering. Have you ever looked into what happened to her? No one seems to know where Serena went or why, except possibly the captain, but even he just gets angry or sad when her name comes up in conversation."

"Well, Katherine, the *Gazette* doesn't make a habit of running a story on a person just because he or she leaves Harborhaven."

"But couldn't you try to find out? Isn't there some database you could search somewhere to find out where she is? I know she isn't dead or anything, because of the way Captain Braddock talks about her."

"I'm a reporter, not a detective. There are very few ways to get that kind of information, and I'm not sure I could if I tried."

Katherine's heart sank. "But couldn't you please try? I just *know* if we found her, she would help save the Harborside."

Mr. James leaned back in his chair and raised his eyebrows as he surveyed her pleading face. "Didn't Captain Braddock tell you he didn't want your help with 'saving the Harborside'? Why do you feel so strongly about this?" he asked.

Katherine frowned. She hadn't stopped to think about why

the old shop meant so much to her. After a few moments, she said, "Ever since I left Harborhaven for college, I have longed for a place, for people I felt I *belonged* to. I've found that, to some extent, here at the shop with Miss Harriet, but... this may sound silly to you, but when I went to the Harborside the very first time, I felt instantly that I belonged there. I felt the Harborside was home, and Captain Braddock was family. I don't know how or why, but the moment I stepped through the doors, I knew I had found that place of belonging I had been searching for."

Mr. James nodded. "That's almost exactly how Harriet describes her feelings towards this place."

"I know. We talked about it once. But don't you see? If the Harborside closes, the shop, the captain, the history of the place –all of it will be gone. I've only just found where I belong, and I feel I can't lose it now!"

Tears trickled down Katherine's cheeks. Until this moment, she hadn't let herself think about what life would be like if the Harborside really closed. Miss Harriet laid a hand gently on her shoulder.

"I came out of the kitchen while you were talking, but didn't want to interrupt." She said apologetically. "I couldn't help but hear." Looking across at Mr. James, she asked. "Isn't there anything you can do, darling?"

Mr. James shook his head. "I can check to see if a missing persons report was filed with the police station, but we would have heard about that at the time, I'm sure." He reached across the table and squeezed Katherine's hand. "I want to help –more than I can say, but I just don't think I can."

Katherine nodded dejectedly. "I understand." She stood up

to go back to the kitchen, and Miss Harriet enveloped her in a motherly hug. "I'm sorry, Dearie. It was worth a try, though." She said, stroking Katherine's hair.

Mr. James settled back in his chair, staring out the window, deep in thought. As Katherine turned to walk away, Mr. James suddenly sat up, bumping the table and sloshing tea into his saucer as he exclaimed, "That's it!"

The two women turned back towards him in astonishment.

"What is it?" Miss Harriet asked, as he stood and began hurriedly packing things back into his briefcase.

"Keep my tea and scones warm for me, Harriet, I'll be back in a bit." He squeezed Miss Harriet's hand, grinned at Katherine, and was out the door before they could say another word.

"Well, Dearie," Miss Harriet said as the door slammed shut behind him. "I suppose that must mean you're not to give up hope yet. When Harold has an idea like that, it's always a good one!"

* * * *

The morning had dragged by, despite the fact that the shop had been very busy. In a brief lull after the lunch rush, Katherine and Miss Harriet went back to the kitchen to quickly wash up a few of the morning's dishes before more customers arrived.

As they worked, Katherine looked up at Miss Harriet. "Do you think Mr. James will be able to find Serena?" she asked.

"I don't know." Miss Harriet said frankly. "As much as I'm inclined to tell you that Harold can do anything he sets his mind to, I simply don't know if it's possible, especially since we're not family. In the eyes of the officials who could access such things, we're all just curious bystanders."

"Would you be happy? —If we found her, I mean."

Miss Harriet smiled. "Of course I would. One doesn't just erase a friendship because the friend is gone."

"But I thought..."

"That I was angry at Serena for leaving without telling me? I was, at first. But then, I stumbled upon another of the old paths. I was reading in Matthew, in the Lord's Prayer, and Jesus' words fairly jumped off the page and into my heart. He said when we pray, we should ask God to 'forgive us our debts, as we forgive our debtors.' I realized how wrong it was for me to come to God asking forgiveness for my own sins, while holding on to bitterness over what I perceived to be Serena's abandonment of our friendship. So, I decided to forgive."

"And if she came back?"

"I think I would be thoroughly glad to see her again. Perhaps she didn't mean to leave like that. As Harold would say, we can't make an assessment of someone else's actions until we have all the facts."

Just then, the bell over the door rang furiously and Mr. James burst into the kitchen.

"Hello ladies! Have you saved me anything to eat?"

Miss Harriet held up a plate of scones "Yes, but we'll only surrender them if you tell us why you darted off this morning."

"Ah, you drive a hard bargain, but how can I resist?" he said jokingly. "Katherine's comment about everything coming back to Serena gave me an idea."

"We know that already," Katherine said impatiently.

"Let him tell it like a newspaper story, it's what he's used to." Miss Harriet interjected with a wink.

Mr. James stood up straighter and struck a noble pose as he continued in his best imitation of a radio announcer's voice. "The intrepid reporter left his breakfast steaming on the table and went off to chase his lead, only allowing himself one brief, longing look at the meal he left behind as he bolted off to save the day."

"And? Where did you bolt off to?" Katherine asked, even more impatiently.

"To City Hall."

"Why did you go there?" Miss Harriet asked, still holding the plate of scones.

"Because that's were the city's business records are kept."

"Business records?" Katherine asked. "What could the business records tell you about Serena?"

"You wanted to save the Harborside, right?" Mr. James asked.

Katherine nodded.

"Well, then, you might like to know that Captain Braddock doesn't own the Harborside outright. He shares it with Serena, fifty-fifty."

"How does that help?"

"I wrote a story once about a small general store whose joint owners disagreed on whether to keep the store or sell it. One owner decided to quietly sell it without telling the other, which was sad, really, because they were cousins, very close as children. They never spoke again after the incident with the store."

"And?"

"Well, as I wrote the story, I had to look into what the law had to say about joint-owners. I learned that in an equal partnership, each has to have the consent of the other in order to make any major financial decision pertaining to the business."

"But I don't think the captain's decision is exactly a business one. It's more of a decision about his own assets, not the business."

"That's why I went to the bank next, to have a hypothetical chat with Mr. Patten. He said that the bank's policy requires the signature of both owners before unlocking funds from investments above a certain amount. He hinted that this had thus far prevented the captain from turning in the paperwork you saw that day."

"That means that he can't sell the Harborside *or* take the drastic step he was considering without Serena's approval." Katherine took the plate of scones out of Miss Harriet's hands and handed them to Mr. James. "Thank you! You're the best reporter I know!"

Mr. James beamed, looked down at his scones, and said brightly. "Do you have any tea to go with these?"

33

The Braddock Gift

Katherine stood at the counter, gazing at Mrs. Penelope, deep in thought. She had gotten to know the old lady quite well in her time at Miss Harriet's, and had observed that Mrs. Penelope was decidedly a creature of habit.

All the dailies were, of course, but Mrs. Penelope had proved to be the most resistant to change. When presented with a change, she became hesitant, almost stubborn. And though the quiet, unassuming old woman enjoyed her tea and scones each day, Katherine wished she could get her to try something different. She felt *sure* the demure old lady would enjoy something more flavorful than the English Breakfast tea Miss Harriet had served her ever since the first day when Miss Penelope had ordered "plain black tea."

In the months Katherine had spent at the Harborside, she had picked up a fairly thorough understanding of the flavors and nuances of the different varieties and blends of teas and had begun to notice that certain types of people tended to like certain types of tea. She wondered if this was something like the "gift" everyone spoke of when referring to Serena's ability to pair people with just the right tea. She also wondered if she would ever be able to do that.

Looking at the sweet, but slightly frail woman in her brown tweed skirt and blazer, with a little brown hat perched on her head, she decided to act. *I'll never know if I never try,* she thought, as she crossed the room to speak to Mrs. Penelope.

"Good morning, Katherine."

"Good morning, Mrs. Penelope. I wondered if you might like to try a cup of Earl Grey this morning?"

Mrs. Penelope frowned. "Well, I'm not sure... you see, I'm *used* to my plain black tea."

"I think you'll like Earl Grey even better." Katherine said.

"Well, I don't know..."

Just then, Mr. Patten walked in, giving Katherine an idea. "Would you be willing just to try a cup? Mr. Patten orders it every day, and highly recommends it."

"Mr. Patten? Well..." Mrs. Penelope shyly looked across the room to where Mr. Patten was seated. "Perhaps, I could try just a *little*, then." she said quietly.

"Good. I just *know* you'll like it. I'll be right back." Katherine walked to the kitchen and began triumphantly preparing Mr. Patten's order on a tray.

"Why did you put two cups and saucers there? Does Mr. Patten have a guest?" Miss Harriet asked as Katherine headed to the doorway with the tray.

"You'll see." Katherine replied archly, sweeping away with the tray balanced on one hand.

When Katherine came to Mr. Patten's table, she set the tray down and said in her politest manner,

"Good morning, Mr. Patten. I was just speaking to Mrs. Penelope, and she would like to taste some Earl Grey to see if she likes it, but is a little hesitant to commit to something new. I wondered if you would allow me to ask her to come and share your pot of Earl Grey with you?"

A smile spread across Mr. Patten's face. "Certainly. What a good idea! In fact," he said, standing up from his chair and leaning in conspiratorially, "I think I might just go invite her myself."

"Now *that's* a good idea!" Katherine said, beaming. "I'll leave you to it."

* * * *

"How ever did you accomplish that?" Mr. James asked, as Katherine brought him a fresh pot of tea. "They've been talking and smiling and having a fine old time for two hours now."

"It will probably sound silly if I tell you."

"What is it? I promise not to laugh at you."

"Well, I had noticed that Mrs. Penelope is just the type of person who usually enjoys Earl Grey. I felt certain she would like it so much better than the English Breakfast she usually has, and as I was trying to convince her to try it, Mr. Patten walked in. I thought that she might be less nervous about trying something new if it was *his* pot of tea she was sharing."

"I see. Well, it apparently worked." The reporter said, nodding towards the table. "Hold on, they're getting up to leave."

Katherine walked over to where the two were standing by their table, still deep in conversation.

"How was your tea, Mrs. Penelope?" Katherine asked, her stomach full of what felt like very lively grasshoppers. Mrs. Penelope paused, head cocked to one side like a little bird. *Oh, no!* Katherine thought. *She must not have liked it.*

"I have to be honest, my dear..."

Katherine's heart thudded wildly as the old lady paused to find the right words.

"That was the most *delightful* cup of tea I have ever tasted! How did you know I would like it so well?"

Relief swept over Katherine. "Oh, just observation, that's all. You seem like the kind of person who would like Earl Grey." She shrugged, grinning shyly.

"Well, I'm certainly glad you suggested it." The elderly lady said, looking at Mr. Patten as she continued, "And thank you for inviting me to share your tea this morning."

"You're very welcome." Mr. Patten said, his eyes sparkling in his otherwise dignified face. "May I walk you out?" he asked, offering his arm politely.

The genteel couple strolled away down the street, still arm in arm, as Katherine returned to the table where Mr. James sat, gazing after them in pleased surprise.

"Well done, Katherine!" He said at last, grinning up at her. "Now, tell me: do you think you could do that again? Tell just the kind of tea someone would like, I mean."

"Maybe." Katherine said thoughtfully. "I have been trying to notice which types of people like which types of tea, but I don't know how accurate my observations are."

"I'd say you were pretty accurate this morning." Mr. James

leaned back in his chair and surveyed her narrowly. "Now, how about me? What kind of tea do you think I would like?"

Katherine thought a moment before answering decidedly, "I think you would like Assam. We don't stock the exact variety I think you'd like best here, but the Harborside has it. The closest we have here is Irish Breakfast tea. Have you ever tried it?"

Mr. James raised his eyebrows, "No, I haven't. What makes you think I would like it?"

"Because unlike the English Breakfast tea you usually order, our Irish Breakfast is one hundred percent Assam tea, though not the best quality."

Mr. James chuckled and said teasingly. "I see you've picked up the captain's obsession for subtle nuances and high quality. When it comes to tea, only the best will do!"

Katherine laughingly nodded. "Perhaps I have. It really does make a difference, though."

"Then pick up some of the 'best' Assam when you go over to the Harborside tomorrow, and I'll try it. Since this little experiment was my idea, I'll gladly pay for the tea."

* * * *

"I have a tea order to fill today!" Katherine said, bursting through the door of the Harborside.

"Really? Does Miss Harriet want hers early?" Captain Braddock leaned back in his desk chair to peer at Katherine through the doorway.

"No. It's for Mr. James. He wants some second flush Assam."

"That sounds about right." Captain Braddock nodded.

"The Orange Pekoe will be right for him, I think. Not so light as the Flowery Orange Pekoe, but not as earthy as the ordinary Pekoe."

Katherine's eyes widened and her face lit up. That was exactly what she had planned to bring to Mr. James!

Perhaps I've got the Braddock gift, after all, she thought to herself as Captain Braddock went back to the ledger he was poring over, leaving Katherine to the happy task of measuring out the dark, twisted leaves with the golden tips which gave the tea the nickname "tippy tea."

When she finished, she set the little bundle of tea on top of her purse and rang up the sale, putting Mr. James' money into the ancient cash register with a satisfied little smirk.

"Captain," she asked, standing in the doorway. "I've never been able to figure out why Orange Pekoe teas have 'orange' in their name. They don't taste or smell at all like orange."

"That used to baffle me as well." Captain Braddock said, shaking his head as he jotted down one more number in the ledger and closed it with a sigh.

Looking up at Katherine, he leaned back in his chair again and explained, "You know that the various pekoes are classifications of Assam teas."

Katherine nodded and recited, "Flowery Orange Pekoe is the small leaf next to the bud, Orange Pekoe is the second leaf, Pekoe is the third leaf and Souchong is the fourth leaf."

Captain Braddock smiled broadly. "You *have* been paying attention! And since you've been paying attention, you can probably tell me when and by whom the Assam tea plants were first discovered?"

"Was it... 1823?" the captain nodded and Katherine

continued. "a man named Robert Bruce noticed the plants and asked for samples to send back to England. But he died soon after, so his brother Charles is really the one who got Assam tea classified as a variety of *Camellia Sinensis*."

"Good! Now, as to the word *orange*, I have heard some say that it is because of the golden tips on the leaves or because of the Chinese practice of mixing orange blossoms with the tea leaves. Others have argued that it is because of the color of the tea when it's brewed, and still others say that it is because of the Dutch East India Company."

"Why that?"

"Because of the House of Orange, the reigning dynasty of the Netherlands. It's thought that the Dutch East India Company might have stuck *orange* in the name to honor their royal family."

Katherine thought for a moment. "I suppose any of those could explain it. What's your opinion?

"Don't know. We'll probably never really know for sure."

* * * *

The next morning, Katherine offered to prepare Mr. James' order so he and Miss Harriet could enjoy a nice long chat before the first customers came in. When she brought out the tea, Mr. James put on a serious face.

"Is this it?" he said with an air of mystery.

Katherine adopted his same manner and silently nodded in reply.

"Is this what?" asked Miss Harriet, gazing inquisitively from one to the other.

"It's an experiment, Dearest." Mr. James replied. Turning to Katherine, he declared imperiously, "Pour the tea!"

Katherine poured a cup for each of them, then drew a chair up to the table and sat down. She watched, hands clenched, shoulders tense, as Mr. James made a show of carefully swirling the tea in his cup, smelling the steam which rose from the dark liquid, and blowing across the surface of the cup to cool the tea. Finally, he took a sip.

"Well?" said Katherine, holding her breath.

"It's good."

"How good?"

"*Very* good. In fact, I think I might have to talk Harriet into carrying it so I can order this in the mornings." Katherine tried to contain her excitement as Mr. James turned towards Miss Harriet. "What did you think of it?"

"I must say, it is quite nice." A teasing grin spread over her face as she took another sip. "I *suppose* we could make an addition to our weekly order... for such a faithful and distinguished customer as yourself, Darling."

34

The Envelope

Katherine woke with a start, her heart racing, her breath coming in quick, short gasps. Sitting up in bed, she brushed beads of sweat from her forehead. She had been running... no, swimming... wait—it was the Captain. *The Captain* was swimming...no, drowning! The horror of her nightmare swept over her again as she struggled to separate dream from reality.

It had all been so real. She had seen Captain Braddock fall into the harbor at the end of the pier and had run down it, trying to get to him. She shuddered as she remembered how he had come up, arms flailing, out of the water, spluttering as he gulped desperately for air before disappearing again beneath the stormy harbor.

She had run, but in that awful suspension of reality peculiar to dreams, the pier had grown longer and longer, the boards firm and hollow sounding beneath her feet, stretching out in front of her. She couldn't reach him, and just as he came up for one last breath of air, she heard him gasp out a desperate cry:

"*Serena!*"

That was when Katherine had jolted awake, the captain's voice still ringing through her mind. She had fallen asleep the night before thinking about the Harborside and Captain Braddock and could trace those thoughts through the awful dream.

There must be a way to save them, she thought.

Flinging back the blankets, she swung her feet out onto the hardwood floor, cold with the early chill of a frosty February morning. She walked to the window seat and nestled herself into the pile of cushions. Pulling a blanket out of the basket next to the window, she wrapped herself up against the cold which radiated from the frost-edged window and leaned her head against the glass pane.

She thought about the captain's last cry in her dream. *Serena,* she thought, *it all just comes down to Serena. But where is she? And how can I find her?*

With a deep sigh, she pulled the blanket tighter and looked out at the faint blue light of early dawn. *Lord, please show me what to do.*

* * * *

Later that day, Katherine walked by Miss Harriet with a tray of dishes as the older woman stood behind the counter, refilling the glass-domed pastry displays. Stopping suddenly next to her, Katherine asked,

"What did this shop used to be before you came?"

Surprised, Miss Harriet stopped polishing and turned to look at her. "I don't quite remember... I think it was a haberdasher's shop, or something like it. Why do you ask?"

"I just noticed all those tiny drawers in the back of the counter. It's like the counter at the Harborside, but with more drawers, and smaller."

"Yes, I've been hard put to find a good use for those drawers, I'm afraid. They're quite small, and there are so many of them."

"I can see how they would be good for a haberdashery, though. All those little bobbins and buttons and bits of trim. It would have been perfect."

"Yes, I see what you mean."

Miss Harriet went back to polishing, and Katherine carried her tray into the kitchen. An idea had begun to form in her mind.

* * * *

"Mr. James, I need your help," Katherine said the next morning, sliding into the chair opposite the startled reporter.

"Of course, Katherine. What is it?"

"I have an idea, but I'm not quite ready to tell Miss Harriet about it yet. I need to iron out some details, and wondered if I could talk it over with you?"

"Of course. But you know I don't like keeping anything secret from Harriet."

"It won't be for long. Just until I can get the details worked out."

"All right, then. Tell me all about it."

* * * *

"Well, don't you two look conspiratorial," said Miss Harriet as she walked over to their table a little while later.

"Ah, well..." Mr. James began.

"I've been asking Mr. James for some advice." Katherine said, interrupting his search for just the right words.

"All right. I won't pry. But Katherine, you'll be late for the Harborside if you don't leave in the next minute or two."

"Oh, my! I lost track of the time. Thank you!" Katherine said, jumping out of her chair and throwing on her jacket. As she rushed out the door and hurried down the street towards the Harborside, she couldn't help but smile as a faint bit of hope began to take root in her heart. *It just might work,* she thought.

She stopped for a moment at the end of the pier she had run down in her dream. She could still close her eyes and see the horrific scene of the captain struggling in the water. A sudden pang of doubt pierced her.

It may work, but will it be enough?

* * * *

"What are you doing there?" Captain Braddock asked, limping up to the counter where Katherine had been poring over the ledger in which they recorded each sale.

"Just looking over our sales. That white tea really did bring in more than the others, just like you said it would."

"Yes," said the captain thoughtfully. "It's too bad it's nearly gone. But the rarity of it is what makes it so profitable for us."

He shrugged, then plunked a handful of envelopes onto the counter. "I'm off to run some errands. Would you mind handing me a rubber band? I don't want any of these getting lost before I get there, and I've a couple stops on the way.

"Of course." Katherine said, reaching over and tugging at one of the drawers. "It's stuck." She said, giving the drawer another sharp tug.

"Perhaps something fell out of another drawer and got jammed. I remember that happening once in a while when I was young." Captain Braddock said, coming around the counter to see for himself.

Katherine, without a thought of "snooping" this time, opened the drawer above—the very drawer she had been so curious about. She drew it out now and set it on the floor without even noticing its contents. She peered into the dark hole left where the drawer had been. "I think I see something."

"What is it?"

"Something white." Katherine reached back and tried to find an edge of the object that had jammed the drawer below. "It's an envelope," she said, as she tugged at it.

"Can you get it out?"

"Maybe... Yes! There it is." She brought the envelope out, turned it over, and froze, stunned into silence.

"What is it, Katherine?"

"It's...it's just... look at who it's addressed to." She held the sealed envelope up for the captain to see.

"Well, I'll be. Where did that come from, I wonder?"

Katherine gazed at the envelope, full of questions. Across the front, in beautiful flowing script, were written two words: *Miss Harriet.*

35

Serena

Captain Braddock's face grew somber as he held the rumpled envelope in his hands.

"What are you going to do with it?" Katherine asked, trying not to sound as anxious as she felt.

"Deliver it, of course. It's long overdue."

Katherine let out a sigh of relief. "Would you like me to take it for you?" she asked.

The captain shook his head. "No. I reckon this is somethin' I have to do myself."

Katherine nodded. She pulled out the drawer that had been stuck. "Here's the rubber band you wanted."

The old man took it absent-mindedly. "Thanks. I suppose I'll be off, then."

"All right. See you later."

Katherine watched the captain limp out the front door. He looked older, somehow, than he had a few minutes before.

I wonder if that letter is from Serena, Katherine wondered silently.

She knelt on the floor and peered into the empty space where the drawer had been. It looked clear now, so she reached for the drawer, meaning to put it back. Just as she fit it back onto the narrow runners, she noticed something sparkle under a crumpled bit of tissue paper. Lifting the paper, she saw a beautiful cut glass candy jar, just like Miss Harriet had described when she told her about Serena giving candy to the children.

Katherine pieced it all together in her mind like a jigsaw puzzle. The captain must have put away everything Serena had on the counter, and the letter must have gotten mixed in. It got shoved to the back of the drawer, and something must have shifted it—perhaps one of them had closed a drawer too hard, making the envelope fall back behind to jam the next drawer down. *If only we had found it sooner.*

* * * *

Katherine slipped through the door of the tea shop just after closing and found Miss Harriet sitting at a table with a cup of tea.

"Hello, Dearie. Have a good day?"

"Yes, though not without its surprises."

"Ah, so you'll already know I had a visit from Captain Braddock."

Katherine nodded.

"And you know what it was about?"

"I know he brought you an envelope we found with your name on it."

"So he did." She reached across the table and poured a cup of tea for Katherine. "I've just been sitting and thinking the whole thing over. It's quite astonishing."

"Is it?" Katherine asked, with an attempt to sound casual.

"I have to say, the captain was quite apologetic. He told me the letter had been lost, and you only just found it today."

"Yes. It had fallen down behind a drawer in the counter."

"Ah. Well, he handed me the letter, said what he came to say, and then left again."

"And what was in the letter?" Katherine asked, leaning forward in her chair. "Was it from Serena?"

A soft smile spread across Miss Harriet's face. "Yes, it was." She reached into her apron pocket and pulled out the letter. "You can read it if you want. I don't think she would mind, since you've become so involved at the Harborside."

Katherine took the folded papers and held them with something bordering on reverence as she read:

My Dear Friend,

You will be surprised at my news, but it's not so sudden as it appears. I am leaving tonight for China. My brother, Jeremiah, whom you won't have met, will be taking over the shop for me. I'm sure he won't mind. He was set to retire this month and come back to the Harborside anyway.

It sounds ridiculously like something in a novel, but I am going away to get married! You remember the tea plantation I told you about, that I visited just before you came to town? Well, the owner and I, (his name is Li Jun, by the way. Isn't it a lovely name?) well, we've been corresponding ever since, mostly about tea orders and my attempts to research growing conditions for tea plants.

Recently, I asked him for a cutting from one of his tea plants. He said he would gladly give me a cutting from the very best of his plants, but that it would have to be planted in the right kind of soil. When I asked what kind of soil the cutting would need, he replied, "Chinese soil" and asked me to come to China to be his wife. I was astonished, but so happy, and agreed to come. He sent me a ticket, and I'm flying out tonight. I'll send you my new address as soon as I'm settled.

I'm not going to tell everyone about this, because it seems too precious a thing to be turned into one of Rosie's gossipy tales. Please just tell everyone who asks that I am well and happy. And please keep an eye on my brother. He may need help getting used to running the shop on his own.

In fondest friendship,
Serena Braddock

"So *that's* why she left," Katherine said, laying the letter down on the table.

"I feel I owe the captain an apology. She likely asked him not to tell where she had gone or why, just as she did me. He wouldn't have known I was meant to be in on the secret, unless she had mentioned it to him, and I'm certain he didn't keep this letter from me purposefully."

Miss Harriet took a sip of tea and sat deep in thought for a moment. "Come to think of it, it isn't at all unlike Serena to go off to China. I remember how she used to talk about her trip there, how beautiful it was, and how kind the planter had been. I just never realized she had kept in contact with him."

"Too bad she didn't ever send you her address," Katherine said, slumping down in her chair.

"Oh, she did."

"What?" Katherine sat up again.

"Just because I never received it, doesn't mean it was never sent," Miss Harriet said. "Serena was always responsible and trustworthy. If she said she would send her address, I know she did. It's just a pity it never arrived."

"I had hoped that envelope would hold the key to contacting Serena and telling her what trouble the Harborside is in."

"I know, Dearie. But we'll just have to keep praying and watching for what God will do. He *is* the only One who can truly help, you know. Even if we found Serena, it wouldn't solve everything."

Katherine sighed. "I know. But if anyone could convince Captain Braddock not to take a foolish step, I feel sure Serena could."

* * * *

"Hello!" Katherine called as little bell above the door announced her arrival at the Harborside. "I've come for Miss Harriet's order."

Captain Braddock came into the shop, limping more heavily than usual. "Hello Katherine." His shoulders drooped and his voice sounded flat.

"What's the matter?" she asked, laying a hand on the captain's arm. "Won't you please tell me?"

The old man gazed at her for a long while, as if deciding

how much to say. Finally, he turned and led the way to his desk. He motioned for her to pull up the folding chair he kept tucked behind a bookcase, then sank wearily into his own chair.

"It's like this," he began. "I've tried to keep the Harborside going, but... I don't know how my sister did it. We haven't had enough sales to keep up with our expenses, and even with the profits from the white tea, well..." he shrugged defeatedly and let his words trail off.

"How much time is there to turn things around?" Katherine asked breathlessly.

"Not much."

"And..." Katherine hesitated, "And the bank?"

Captain Braddock shook his head. "Stuck in red tape, sadly enough."

At least there's one good thing. Katherine thought.

"I know you don't think I can help," began Katherine, but the captain interrupted before she could finish.

"You've helped already, more than you know, and I know you love this place like I do. Just wish I could do something to keep it afloat." The two sat in silence for a while, each with a heart too full for words. Finally, Captain Braddock looked over at her with an expression of sudden decision.

"I'm going to show you something," he said, opening a drawer in the desk.

Katherine drew in a sharp breath. He was pulling out the heavy, old key that unlocked the door at the top of the stairs!

"I've been pretty cautious, keepin' secrets from you and all, but I had to be sure I could trust you." The Captain stood and led the way to the stairs. Katherine's heart beat rapidly with anticipation. Halfway up, Captain Braddock stopped and turned towards her.

"Miss Harriet told you about her letter?"

Katherine nodded, and the captain gave a low grunt in reply before proceeding up the stairs. The lock gave a rasping groan before popping open with a click. Katherine held her breath in suspense as the door swung open.

Suddenly, Katherine found herself surrounded by light pouring in from windows in every direction. She blinked, trying to adjust her eyes, which had grown accustomed to the cozy dimness of the shop below. As her vision cleared, she gazed around her in wonder. They were standing in an octagonal turret, with a domed roof. There were large round windows all around, surprisingly clean and free from the cloud of grime that typically accumulated on windows facing the harbor.

Below each window was a heavy wooden sea chest, like the kind Katherine had always imagined pirate's treasure would be buried in. Captain Braddock watched her face intently, a smile playing around the edges of his mouth. He seemed to be enjoying Katherine's first glimpse of the Harborside's most closely guarded secret.

Katherine looked at the captain, wide eyed. "But, how... I went outside one day to try to see..."

Captain Braddock laughed. "That's the real mystery, now, isn't it? Come on, I'll show you." He turned and walked over to the round window that faced away from the harbor. Katherine saw that it looked out onto the brick façade that had been built on to the building in Victorian times. To her surprise, the captain turned a latch on the window and stepped through.

Katherine followed, feeling this to be the greatest adventure she had ever had.

"See?" the captain said, once they were outside. "This is another piece of Helen's legacy."

"Helen. The one who picked out the lamps? Who didn't want the Harborside to be rebuilt in brick?"

"That's the one. The tower was her favorite part of the Harborside, and before she died, she made Edward promise to leave it intact, with a view of the harbor. That was important, you see, because the tower was where the Harborside wives and children would watch for the ships to appear on the harbor when they were expected home."

"Like a widow's walk?"

"Exactly. Helen loved hearing about the old days, and the excitement when the *Anne* would be spotted on the horizon, and she somehow convinced her husband it was worth preserving."

"Oh, good for her!" Katherine said, gazing at the tower.

"Only Edward didn't want to be seen as a fool, with this old wooden tower rising out of his 'modern' Victorian brick, so he hid it on the front by making the façade so tall. The side facing the harbor presented more of a challenge, though, because he had promised to preserve the view. So, he made this terrace around the tower, and took care that it had enough space in front of it so that the tower wasn't visible from the wharf. Of course, you can see it from away out in the harbor, but no one bothers to look that closely at these hulks of brick."

Katherine walked to the edge of the terrace and looked down over the edge of the brick parapet. "It's such a lovely place. Why do you keep it a secret?" she asked, turning to face the captain.

"Well, at the first, Edward insisted on keeping it secret because he was embarrassed to have given in when he wanted to modernize the whole thing. He always told people that the staircase led to more storage areas, which I suppose is technically true, since we do store a few things in the tower. After that, I think it just became one more Harborside tradition, and besides," he said with a mischievous wink, "it's kinda fun to have a mysterious secret right there in the middle of the shop."

Katherine laughed. "I see what you mean."

Just then, they heard the bell ring faintly over the door below. Captain Braddock began to limp back to the round door, but Katherine quickly passed him.

"I'll go," she said. "You just take your time."

Katherine opened the door slightly and carefully slipped through, closing it quickly behind her. As she turned to descend the staircase, she saw a tall lady, somewhat older than Miss Harriet, with dark hair finely streaked with silver, and dark eyes gazing up at her in surprise.

"You must be Katherine," she said.

"Yes, I am. Have we met?"

"No," said the lady, watching Katherine come down the staircase. "But I've heard of you."

"Oh." Katherine wasn't sure what to say. "What brings you to the Harborside today? Are you here to order some tea?"

Then, looking the woman over briefly, she suggested, "We have some lovely *Pu-erh Sheng.*"

"I see you've been learning," the woman said with an approving smile. "My name's—"

"Serena!" Captain Braddock said from the top of the staircase, "Wherever did you come from?"

36

Saving the Harborside

Katherine stared at the woman in front of her. Could this really be Serena?

"Hello, Jeremiah. It's so good to see you. I've missed you." She looked around with a loving smile. "And I've missed the Harborside as well. There's nowhere else like it." She turned back to Katherine.

"I see my brother has let you in on the Harborside's best-kept secret. We'll have to go up there together while I'm here. I'm just dying for a good rummage through those trunks. There's one for each generation of Harborside Braddocks, you know, and I'm sure you've noticed there are a few more in the basement."

Katherine's eyes widened. "Really? That sounds fascinating."

"But, Serena, *why* are you here?" asked the captain, limping unevenly down the last few steps of the staircase.

"The bank contacted me about some paperwork you wanted to file." She looked her brother solidly in the eye and said, "We need to talk."

* * * *

"Miss Harriet, you'll never guess who I brought to see you. Not in a million years!"

Miss Harriet came out of the kitchen with a puzzled, "What's all this fuss about?" Then, as she looked past Katherine to the tall, dark-eyed woman behind her, she gave a little shout of delight and ran towards her, wrapping her in a sisterly embrace.

"Serena!"

"Harriet, oh, it's *too* good to see you again. You're not mad at me?"

"How could I be? I did get your letter eventually, though it was delayed."

"Jeremiah told me. I should have written again. I did send you my address, but never thought it mightn't reach you. I just thought you never cared to write back."

"And I thought you must not have cared to tell me where you had gone!" The two friends shook their heads and hugged once more.

"See?" Miss Harriet said, turning towards Katherine, "I just knew it would all get straightened out eventually."

"Yes, but there's still the Harborside to straighten out," Katherine said.

"Yes," Serena echoed. "And that's where I need your help, Harriet."

* * * *

When the shop closed that afternoon, Miss Harriet, Serena, and Katherine got to work right away. Katherine and Serena cleared the tables, while Miss Harriet buzzed efficiently around the kitchen. By six o'clock, all was ready.

"I hope they're not late," said Katherine, watching the clock and the doorway intermittently. The old anxiety she had felt when she first stepped into Miss Harriet's had returned, and she rubbed her hands together nervously, feeling that the next few hours would spell out life or death for the Harborside.

"I'm sure Harold will get him here on time." Miss Harriet said. "You've got five minutes left, Dearie." Then, squeezing Katherine's shoulders she said gently, "Don't fret. Pray instead, that will calm you."

Katherine smiled weakly. "You're right. I'll do that."

"Harold?" asked Serena, walking over from the table where she had been putting the final touches to a floral arrangement. "Would that be Harold James, that dashing reporter for the *Harborhaven Gazette*?"

Miss Harriet blushed and nodded happily.

"Well! I *am* glad for you. How long?"

"Just a few months."

"You mean it took him that long? It was plain he was head over heels for you even before I left!"

Katherine laughed in spite of her nerves. "It took a little shove to get them off." She said playfully.

Just then the door opened and Mr. James walked in with Captain Braddock. Miss Harriet went forward to greet them.

"Welcome, Captain Braddock. Thank you for coming." She smiled and shook Captain Braddock's hand. Katherine thought he looked decidedly uncomfortable. They all sat down at the table, and Miss Harriet brought out tea and several trays of snacks.

"Tea, Captain?" she asked, teapot in hand. "There's not a teabag in sight tonight, I promise you. It's all Harborside tea."

"Well, perhaps just a cup." The captain said, somewhat grudgingly.

When everyone had been served, Katherine stood. With a quick silent prayer for help, she began to speak, her voice trembling slightly.

"Captain, we're all here tonight because we love and value the Harborside. Ever since I first found out that it was in danger, I have been trying to find a way to help. Serena arrived at just the right time and has helped me think through the details of a plan I've been working on. Mr. James has also been a help, and you'll see in a bit why he's here."

Katherine took a breath as Serena reached across to squeeze her hand encouragingly.

"Jeremiah, I don't know if you noticed, but Katherine has soaked in the Harborside like a sponge. Before you came in yesterday, she inadvertently gave me a little demonstration of the "Braddock gift," as Great-Grandma called it. She recommended just the tea you did for me, when you were first coming into your own at the shop. In talking to the others, here, I've discovered that she's matched several other people with their perfect tea as well."

Captain Braddock nodded. "Yes, I've been wondering if she would pick that up."

"That's how I plan to help the Harborside. But it will take some cooperation between the Harborside and Miss Harriet's." Katherine looked from one to the other of the shop owners uncertainly.

"I'm open to it if you are." Miss Harriet said to the captain. "Please, tell us what you have planned, Katherine."

"Well, people are so different, and the right tea for any given set of people will differ widely. That's why the Harborside keeps so many different types of tea in stock. Now, Miss Harriet, what I propose is this: I would like to go on helping the customers here at Miss Harriet's to find their perfect tea, but that will mean ordering a wide variety from the Harborside. Not great quantities of each, especially at first, but enough for a couple pots of tea at a time. We could store them in those little drawers behind the counter. They're just the right size for a little sack of tea each."

"Ah, so *that's* why you asked about the drawers. I've been wondering what you were thinking of."

"And as I introduce people to the different types of tea, I could send them to the Harborside to order some for themselves. That way, the Harborside would not just have more orders from Miss Harriet's; it would gain new long-term customers as well. And they would tell their friends and family about it, and the Harborside's customer base would grow by word of mouth, just as it always has. It just needs a little boost to get it going again."

"And that's where I come in," began Mr. James, looking the Captain straight in the eye. "Katherine has told me that you prefer not to advertise, and that's fine, but I have a suggestion to make. Word of mouth works, and it does work better than advertising—except when public opinion is against you. Now, for a variety of reasons, the Harborside has lost most of its local customers. You'll only save the Harborside by winning back the community that once supported it."

Captain Braddock grunted. "What do you have in mind?" he asked, frowning.

"A series of articles on the history of the Harborside and the Braddock family's impact on Harborhaven over the years. You see, sir, people don't shop at the Harborside anymore because they have lost that sense of connection with it. No one knows better than you and Serena just how steeped in history the Harborside is. Believe it or not, that is your greatest asset."

Captain Braddock sat silent, brows knit, deep in thought. Everyone was still, and silent as they waited for his reaction. Katherine held her breath. Finally, Serena spoke.

"Jeremiah, we're not here to bully you into doing what we think you ought to do. But as part owner, and one of the last remaining members of the Braddock family, I must say, I heartily approve of Katherine's plan. As Mr. James has said, the history of the Harborside is what draws people to it. Isn't it what makes the shop so precious to you and me? Surely it's only right to share that heritage with others."

The captain took a deep breath. "Well... Katherine, Mr. James, you've thought through this well. But do you think it will be enough? We're in quite a bit over our heads. Do you expect this will really bring in enough more customers?"

Katherine nodded. "I looked over our current sales ledger, and I think with Miss Harriet's initial order setting her up with a wide enough variety, and with the publicity of the articles and our personal recommendations, it should go a long way towards doubling or even tripling our sales in the next few months."

"I looked over her calculations, Jeremiah, and I agree." Serena added, "There's a good chance this will work."

"So," Katherine asked, looking at the Captain and Miss Harriet. "Are you willing to work together to save the Harborside?"

Captain Braddock rose from his seat and looked gravely at Miss Harriet. Then, he picked up his teacup and held it towards her. "I'm willing if you are."

Miss Harriet nodded and raised her cup as well. "Here's to saving the Harborside!"

37

The New Beginning

The sunlight streamed through the tall windows of Miss Harriet's as Katherine bustled between the tables. Passing a table by the lace-enshrouded side window, she paused. A soft smile spread over her face as she realized that it had only been a year since she first stumbled upon Miss Harriet's. She remembered the loneliness, the pain, the gnawing heartache —how different she felt now!

She turned and looked around the room. Rosie and her faithful group of followers sat in the middle of the room where several tables had been pushed together. Their noisy voices were dominated by Rosie's boisterous exclamations as they discussed the latest gossip.

The little girl whom Katherine had seen having tea with her mother a year before sat a little way from the Luncheon Society. The girl had put off the costume jewelry in favor of a simple pendant, a little silver heart. She had matured much since that first day.

You and me both, thought Katherine, as she watched the mother and daughter giggle together and sip their tea.

Mr. James sat by the window, typing rapidly as always, pausing now and then to sip his Harborside Assam. He looked up as Miss Harriet passed him, and the two smiled as only a newly-engaged couple can smile.

Katherine's heart swelled with happiness for them, and she couldn't help but cast a glance towards the elderly couple by the window, conversing so politely, yet wholly engrossed in each other. Mr. Patten and Mrs. Penelope looked just about as happy as Miss Harriet and Mr. James as they quietly sipped their Earl Grey and shared their scones and Cornish pasties.

She wished Serena could have stayed to see this. The little drawers in the back of the counter were filled with a variety of teas, and Katherine had begun to teach Miss Harriet some of what she had learned about matching people with their perfect tea. Mr. James had written three articles, and each had caused quite a buzz around town and brought in customers to both Miss Harriet's and the Harborside.

Serena's visit had laid to rest the specter of unknown horror and broken down the last remaining wall of mistrust between the Captain and Miss Harriet. *What a mess that lost letter caused!* Katherine sighed, and picked up a tray of dishes to take to the kitchen.

She thought of Captain Braddock and the weighty sacrifice he had been willing to make, just to keep the Harborside going. She sighed happily as she remembered the joy on his face as he tallied up last week's sales.

"I think," he had said as a grin slowly spread across his weather-beaten face, "we might just be afloat again!"

* * * *

That evening, as Katherine flipped the sign to closed and turned the lock on the Harborside's green door, she turned and said thoughtfully, "Captain,"

"Yes, Missie?" he had answered, hobbling in from the office.

"Do you remember that day when you said I was just *becalmed*, and that my sails would swell again?"

"Yes, I remember."

Katherine gave a happy grin. "Well, tonight, I feel like they finally have."

"How do you mean?"

"Well, I came to Harborhaven looking for a new beginning, hoping to begin my old life again, without the hurt. But I was like the Harborside. I didn't need a fresh start down the same path I'd been on. I needed God to help me find *His* paths, the paths that would lead me to the crossroads where my real new beginning was already waiting for me."

She looked up into the eyes of the man who had become like a grandfather to her. "I belong here at the Harborside now, and I feel like *its* new beginning is also mine."

Captain Braddock's eyes shone as he threw his arm around Katherine. "It's a new beginning for all of us, my girl, and I'm ever so glad you followed those 'old paths' home!"

Other Books by This Author

The Hymns for the Heart Series:
Tune My Heart
Jesus, I Come
Hark
Risen
We Gather Together

Devotional Commentaries:
Contentment: Truths from Proverbs 30:7-9
Beatitudes: A Study of the Beatitudes

Visit www.learningladyhood.com for information on new releases and to read the Learning Ladyhood devotional blog.

CPSIA information can be obtained
at www.ICGtesting.com
Printed in the USA
LVHW081707160822
726007LV00013B/568

9 781736 601116